A REBEL YELL

"Good with a gun—are you, Reb?" he said. "Let's see how you do against a butcher knife!"

He bolted forward, and James thrust his own blade up just in time to deflect the Union lieutenant's ten-inch blade from his own naked belly. The man, snarling and cursing like an outraged mountain lion, drove forward. The move caught James off guard, and he felt himself thrust up against the bridge's downstream side, the rails pressing against the backs of his legs. . . .

James felt the bridge rails gouging into his ankles, bending his knees. He was leaning too far back, and a quick glance to one side showed him the dully gleaming creek twenty feet below, opening like a dark glove.

He was going over!

Loosing a raucous Rebel yell that seemed to cut the night wide open, he gave one powerful thrust with his knife, ramming half the blade into the Union officer's upper left chest. Then he and the blue-belly were tumbling over the rails, grunting and snarling as they continued to struggle in midair before the water came up to slap them both like a giant fist.

continued . . .

THE BELLS OF EL DIABLO

Frank Leslie

A SIGNET BOOK

SIGNET
Published by New American Library, a division of
Penguin Group (USA) Inc., 375 Hudson Street,
New York, New York 10014, USA
Penguin Group (Canada), 90 Eglinton Avenue East, Suite 700, Toronto,
Ontario M4P 2Y3, Canada (a division of Pearson Penguin Canada Inc.)
Penguin Books Ltd., 80 Strand, London WC2R 0RL, England
Penguin Ireland, 25 St. Stephen's Green, Dublin 2,
Ireland (a division of Penguin Books Ltd.)
Penguin Group (Australia), 250 Camberwell Road, Camberwell, Victoria 3124,
Australia (a division of Pearson Australia Group Pty. Ltd.)
Penguin Books India Pvt. Ltd., 11 Community Centre, Panchsheel Park,
New Delhi - 110 017, India
Penguin Group (NZ), 67 Apollo Drive, Rosedale, Auckland 0632,
New Zealand (a division of Pearson New Zealand Ltd.)
Penguin Books (South Africa) (Pty.) Ltd., 24 Sturdee Avenue,
Rosebank, Johannesburg 2196, South Africa

Penguin Books Ltd., Registered Offices:
80 Strand, London WC2R 0RL, England

First published by Signet, an imprint of New American Library,
a division of Penguin Group (USA) Inc.

First Printing, July 2012
10 9 8 7 6 5 4 3 2 1

PUBLISHER'S NOTE
This is a work of fiction. Names, characters, places, and incidents either are the
product of the author's imagination or are used fictitiously, and any resemblance to
actual persons, living or dead, business establishments, events, or locales is entirely
coincidental.

The publisher does not have any control over and does not assume any re-
sponsibility for author or third-party Web sites or their content.

ALWAYS LEARNING   PEARSON

To Wayne Dundee—
good friend, terrific writer

Chapter 1

He'd fashioned the bayonet himself back at his family's Seven Oaks Plantation—ten inches of double-edged steel cut from a plow blade—and it slipped so smoothly through the Union soldier's dark blue tunic and into his belly that for a second Lieutenant James Allen Dunn thought he'd missed his mark in the misty darkness.

But then there was a crunch of bone as he lowered the Enfield's rear stock and drove the bayonet up beneath the federal soldier's sternum and into the hot, thudding fist of his heart.

The Union corporal gasped.

There was a snick of steel against bone as James pulled the blade out of the soldier's belly.

Another gasp. A strangled sigh.

James stepped out away from the tree he'd been crouched behind. He closed his broad left hand over the corporal's nose and mouth, and the soldier dropped his Sharps carbine as James drove him back and down, until he was on his back on the spongy ground. The corporal kicked and quivered and flailed his arms, blinking horrifically up at James, who snarled savagely as he applied more pressure to the dying man's mouth, forcing back a possible scream that would alert his Union ilk skulking about these wooded north Georgia hills and eerie hollows on this hot, chillingly quiet late-summer eve.

James pressed a knee against the man's expanding and contracting belly. His knee was bare, as was the rest of him, clad in nothing more than sticky, dark river clay, and he could feel the hot wetness of the man's blood oozing out of the wound through the torn wool tunic, just above his cartridge belt.

The soldier heaved a few more times and then gradually fell still.

James straightened, glanced toward the bridge that crossed Snake Creek Gap before him. The stream was tar black as it slid down the fold between two high hills, glistening like oil under a gauzy dark sky. The bridge crossed to James's left—a long stretch of oak timbers standing about twenty feet above the creek, the near end thrusting out from the pine-clad mountainside over James's left shoulder and disappearing into the pines of the ridge on the gap's other side. Not an oft-used road or bridge, anymore, but one that, according to General Nathan Bedford Forrest's spies working behind the Union lines in Tennessee, would be used soon by a covert Union cavalry detail shipping guns and ammo to Sherman's forces now moving on Atlanta.

James Dunn's guerilla platoon was known as "Forrest's Raiders," prized by the general himself and nearly all the Confederate leaders for its proficiency at covert operations in dangerous terrain—stealthy employments that included ambush and assassination, tying knots in supply lines, blowing up Union rails and ammunition depots, and setting fire to bridges. Leading such exploits had lofted James to legendary status amongst the Confederate troops, and earned him the complimentary monicker of "Forrest's Rapscallion." Over the last two bloody years, the raiders had accounted for the deaths of an uncountable number of Union officers and soldiers and had helped invaluably to complicate Lincoln's efforts at whipping the South into final submission.

Northern forces were now being led by General Sherman on his brutal march toward Atlanta in a desperate attempt to put the finishing touches on the War of Aggression that the Union had all but won. The young lieutenant knew this to be true but would not, could not admit it to anyone, least of all to himself.

The South could not be subjugated by the tyrannical rule of Washington. The consequences of such a tragedy were unthinkable—James's beloved home state of Tennessee and all the Confederacy conquered by a government no less corrupt than that which they'd originally won their freedom from! Sometimes, as he did now, James felt as though he were the last man standing between the Yankees and victory.

If that were true, he would not appear at first glance as a formidable last foe. He was of average height, flat-bellied, and slender, with a clean-lined, strong-jawed, dimple-chinned face that many a young Southern lady had found dashing. Not intimidating in the least. Cobalt blue eyes gazed serenely out from deep, hard-mantled sockets framed by straight, dark brown hair that hung now to his shoulders. His voice was as soft and subtly lilting as a spring rain in the heart of Dixie.

No, James Dunn did not stand out as the cool, efficient killing machine he'd proved himself to be on many a Southern battlefield since marching off to war barely before the first shots at Fort Sumter had ceased echoing. But amongst the Union forces that he'd bedeviled in the long months since, he'd earned the reputation of a wily, tough-nut guerilla, and those eerily serene eyes must have confounded many a Yankee soldier staring into them from only inches away as his guts slithered out his gaping belly.

It was the crafty young Rebel lieutenant's mission now to blow up the bridge crossing Snake Creek Gap. Not his alone, thank God. Not yet. But that of his and his few loyal, hickory-hard, mostly mountain-bred Confederates who'd been handpicked by General Forrest himself. Seven men were all that remained of James's platoon, which had been so badly decimated at Chattanooga and again a few weeks ago at Kennesaw Mountain, when they'd tried to stem the howling Yankee hordes' plundering of Georgia.

James was glad to see that the information of Bedford's spies had proven reliable, as it so often had not been, and that this stretch of road and the bridge would, indeed, likely see a Union supply detail soon. Any chance to further complicate the efforts of the federal troops, and to draw more Union blood, quickened the young Confederate officer's wild heart. The best indications of the supply train's approach were the picket James had just gutted and the other soldiers prowling atop the bridge itself.

The young Confederate, long hair tucked behind his ears and dangling to his mud-smeared shoulders, could see the silhouettes of three men milling around atop the bridge, hear the low, desultory mutter of their voices above the creek's watery chitter. The faint orange glow of a cigarette or cigar shone sporadically in the darkness around a silhouetted head. The peppery fragrance of Union tobacco reached James's nose, made his mouth water. He hadn't had a good smoke—or a good meal or a good drink—in months.

Or a woman—good or bad—in nearly a year, an inner voice silently reminded him.

Lieutenant Dunn had suspected the bridge might be guarded. That's why he'd left the rest of his seven-man contingent farther up the ridge behind him before he'd stolen down the slope with two others—Corporals Billy Krieg and Lawrence Coker—clad in nothing more than river mud to keep their pale skin from glistening in the hollow's steamy darkness.

The two men sidled up to their slender, rugged leader now—Coker a year older than James and a fellow Tennessean. Billy Krieg was all of seventeen, buck-toothed and golden-haired, but the heart of a barbarian beat in the south Georgian's chest. He hailed from Cairo, where his father was a wheelwright. Bowielike knives strapped to their naked waists, they, too, looked up at the bridge and then swung their heads slowly from right to left as they stared along the shore of the creek before them and along the creek's far side, looking for more pickets.

When James was reasonably sure they were alone here on this side of the bridge, he glanced at his two subordinates, then canted his head to indicate behind him. Krieg and Coker disappeared. When they stepped back up beside him a moment later, they carried a coffinlike rifle crate between them. The crate was covered with a strip of tarred burlap that kept the moisture away from the small bound bundles of dynamite nestling inside, on a bed of dry straw.

James nodded, then, holding his Enfield .50-caliber breechloader up high across his chest, stepped into the river that at first felt shockingly cold against his bare feet and ankles. The other men followed, moving soundlessly as stalking Seminoles, and set the rifle crate in the stream, each man holding a hide-handled end as they guided it along between them. The creek bottom was soft and muddy, and James felt the slime close over his ankles and lift tendrils of sodden weeds and roots up to tickle his calves.

The river climbed higher up his body until he was waist deep and moving into the center of the stream, which moved more quickly here, with slight riffles and eddies, for the rain had been falling in the north Georgia mountains for three long days, filling the creeks and streams and flooding the lowlands. The Snake Creek Gap canyon was deep, however, and the bridge still stood a good thirty feet above the tarry water.

James moved slowly, lifting each foot in turn from the slime, keeping the Enfield above the water. A single cartridge nestled in the chamber, nippled and capped. It was the only round James had, as he couldn't carry his cartridge pouch into the stream without fouling the ammunition. The other two men were armed only with knives. So between them they had three knives and a single, .50-caliber cartridge . . . against at least a dozen Union soldiers guarding the bridge and waiting for the supply wagons.

Hopefully, James and his men wouldn't need the bullet or the knives. If they did, their mission would likely have failed.

James looked at the top of the bridge that was a faint line against the gauzy sky. He could see the silhouettes of the guards moving this way and that, and he heard the mutter of occasional voices. He gritted his teeth nervously, not liking how exposed he and his men were. It couldn't be helped, however. This was their best means of approach, as both ends of the bridge were likely being closely watched by the federals. If any of the guards atop the bridge looked down, they'd likely think that James's party was merely flotsam churned by the unstable current.

The reassuring thought had no sooner passed over his brain before something flashed on the creek's far side. There was a loud, hollow *crack!* Billy Krieg grunted. His head snapped sharply to one side. Just as the kid began to lift his head, he slipped out of sight beneath the water.

"Shit!" cried Coker.

"Got us a pack of muskrats!" came the shout from the shore, from roughly the same place where the rifle had flashed and belched. "Three in the water, fellas! Can't you see 'em? *Who's awake up there?*"

There was another flash and a *crack*, and the bullet fired from the picket on the far shore slammed into the rifle crate with a loud *whump!* Coker cursed again as Billy Krieg's end of the coffin swung downstream, jerking Coker off his feet, and water splashed as he flailed his other arm, trying to keep his balance.

"Hold the box, Lawrence!" James ground his feet into the creek's muddy bottom and lifted the Enfield. He aimed quickly at the murky silhouette and fired, the single-shot carbine leaping and roaring.

The man on the far shore yelped, and there was the clatter of a rifle falling on rocks.

Rifles were precious amongst the Southern soldiers, and James hated to turn the Enfield over to the river, but after quickly releasing the bayonet sprocket at the end of the barrel and removing his homemade knife, he let the weapon sink out of sight in the murky stream. He took his knife in his teeth, and, hearing shouts from atop the bridge, helped Coker move the gun crate in amongst the stout log pylons, where they and the box would be out of sight from the top of the bridge.

"Gotta move fast, Lawrence!" he said as a rifle popped above him. He saw the flash nearly straight above his head, heard the bullet plop into the water with a hollow *zing* that echoed amongst the wooden piers and zigzagging braces that smelled like creek rot and wood tar.

"Graybacks under the bridge!" shouted one of the blue-bellies.

Running feet thundered on the bridge. Men cursed and quarreled. James heard brush snapping on the shore beyond the bridge's far side—another picket running toward the action. The picket's slender silhouette moved amongst the dark tufts of heather and laurel and the pale blue face of a stone slab jutting out from the slope toward the stream. The picket would soon be in prime position to pick the lieutenant and Coker off as easily as shooting ducks on a millpond.

"We ain't gonna make it, Jimmy!" Coker said, his teeth showing white beneath his dark mustache. He, too, was looking toward the picket running toward them along the rocky shore, on the opposite side of the bridge from the picket whom James had shot. "We're gonna have to let this one go!"

"Like hell, Lawrence!" James raked out almost incoherently around the knife in his teeth. "Them bluebellies get the guns and ammo that detail's carryin', Atlanta's finished!"

"Hell, it's probably finished anyway!"

A rifle barked. James saw the flash on the shore of the creek, about sixty yards away. The slug hammered the pylon that was now between him and Coker. The Union picket had found a position from which to shoot, and he'd be cutting loose now, most likely with one of the repeaters the Union had in its arsenal and which James would have given his eyeteeth for. Most of the Confederate soldiers were armed with badly outdated Enfield, Maynard, and Mississippi rifles, some still making do with Harper's Ferry rifled muskets that were no match for the sixteen-shot Henry repeaters many blue-bellies were now sporting.

James removed the savage, bone-handled, hide-wrapped blade from his teeth and clenched it in his right fist as he drew his end of the crate against the pylon between him and Coker. "Set 'em up, Lawrence. I'm goin' up top!"

"What the hell you gonna do up there?" Coker snapped, ripping off his end of the tarred burlap, exposing the three bundles of dynamite, four sticks each, nestling amongst the straw. Each had a small looking glass strapped to it, to make a target of reflected ambient light should the raiders have to detonate the bundles in the darkness with their rifles. That was only if for some reason their four-pounder field gun, which they'd stolen from a Union battery in the early days of the fight for Chattanooga, didn't fire. When the weather was damp, it often didn't.

The rifle barked again, another slug tearing into the pylon and scattering splinters in all directions.

"I'm gonna buy you some time, Lawrence," James said. "Stay behind this pylon and work fast. If you can't move around without getting a third eye drilled in that wooden head of yours, strap all the dynamite to this one here." He pounded the back of his fist against the stout oak post.

Coker drew a dynamite bundle and a long length of rope from the box. "What if blowing this one alone don't take the whole bridge?"

James winced as the rifle popped again. "Then I reckon we'll have to take out the supply train some other way."

"With six men?"

As the rifle barked twice more, one slug drilling another pylon and the other splashing water near James, the young lieutenant climbed up on one of the weblike braces angling between the pylons, supporting them. He grinned at his partner. "You got anything else to do this fine Southern evenin', Lawrence?"

"Ah, shit, Jimmy," Coker said.

Chapter 2

While Coker worked on the far side of the pylon from the soldier shooting regularly from shore, James climbed toward the bridge, zigzagging between the stout oak posts rising from the muddy creek bed. The soldiers on the bridge were shouting and running from one side of the bridge to the other, trying to get an angle on James and Coker.

A couple fired shots, but their slugs merely splashed into the oily water.

James had climbed trees and stony mountainsides as a boy, running wild through the Tennessee and north Georgia wilderness, so he made fast time of frogging up the bridge's girders. He hunkered just beneath the top of the bridge, a stout beam six inches above his head. Pausing to listen to the scrambling soldiers, who were all shouting and cajoling each other, he saw a couple of men from the bridge now running down the creek's opposite bank. James had figured they'd try to get around in front of him and Coker, and that's just what they were doing.

The Confederate felt his mouth and throat go dry.

Probably, he should have called off the mission just after Billy had died. Too late now. He and Lawrence would have to do the best they could. His other five men were lurking in the forest above where James, Krieg, and Coker had entered the stream, probably nervous as jackasses in a thunderstorm. But they'd hold their fire until James signaled them with his customary Rebel yell, so they didn't risk hitting their own boys or the dynamite and blow the bridge too soon.

The plan had been to blow the bridge just as the supply train was crossing it, but that was likely impossible now. Now, if they were lucky, they'd blow the bridge tonight and at least delay the train and the Confederates' convergence on Atlanta. Even that, under the circumstances, was a long shot.

James watched the three silhouettes run down to the water's edge, ambient light glinting off the rifles in their hands. There were now four men on the shore, the young lieutenant thought. How many did that leave on the bridge? From the thudding of the boots above him, he judged there were three or four up there now.

"Where are they, Lieutenant?" one of the silhouettes called to the man shooting at Coker from the bridge's opposite side.

The rifle blasted once more. Then the man on the far side of the bridge shouted, "I can't see 'em! Can't *you*?"

"Hell, no—it's dark as a well out there!"

"Well, just start shootin'. Eventually, you'll hit one o' them Rebel dogs!" James thought only in passing that the lieutenant's voice was hazily familiar—a remembered resonance from the murky, mostly forgotten time before the war.

James cast a worried glance down at Coker, who was a small dark spot against the silver-black stream. Something flashed, and James gritted his teeth. It was a looking glass attached to one of the bundles now armed with special detonation caps that made the dynamite especially sensitive and easy to ignite.

"There!" shouted one of the men on the shore, having noticed the reflection. "We got 'em now, Lieutenant!"

"Take 'em, then!" the lieutenant shouted, his voice quaking as though he was running.

"Take cover, Lawrence!" James shouted just before propelling himself up off his heels and around the side of the bridge.

He wasn't sure what he was leaping into, but he grabbed the bridge's lower side rail and hurled himself between that rail and the top one. As he gained his feet, he saw a dark-clad soldier to his left. The man had been facing James's side of the bridge, but now he was turning toward James and swinging a rifle in the lieutenant's direction. A cigar glowed between his teeth, dimly illuminating his large, craggy, gray-whiskered face and the pale smoke wafting around his head and leather-billed forage cap.

James squared his shoulders and flicked his double-edged knife behind his right shoulder. The knife spun with a menacing *swishing* sound end over end before the blade crunched into the middle of the federal soldier's chest. The Yankee groaned and, stumbling backward, triggered his rifle into the air—a burned-orange lap of flames stabbing at the murky sky. In the flash of light, James had seen the brass captain's bars on a shoulder of the officer's tunic.

"Hey-hey-hey!" a man shouted behind the dying captain, who lay flat on his back atop the bridge, kicking his muddy boots.

James saw the second man running toward him with a rifle. The Confederate ran over to the dying captain just as the man running toward him fired his rifle, flames stabbing from the barrel, the slug screeching past James's right ear.

James scooped up the captain's rifle, a Spencer repeater, and quickly worked the trigger guard cocking mechanism, seating a cartridge into the chamber beneath the hammer—oh, what he wouldn't give to have every Confederate soldier outfitted with a brass-cartridge-firing repeater!—and fired. The soldier running toward him jerked sharply to one side and fired his own rifle into the bridge rail to his left. James cocked and fired the Spencer again, aiming from his shoulder, and sent the second blue-belly spinning around and down, yowling.

Crouching and cocking the Spencer once more, James looked around quickly to see another man running toward him from the opposite direction of the other two soldiers—from the far end of the bridge. Now the men on the shore were shouting chaotically. The man running toward James shouted, "Hold it, you Rebel bastard!"

James threw himself to his left as the man cut loose with three quick shots, one after another, the slugs hammering the top of the bridge where James had been a half second before. James rolled and came up firing the Spencer, and the man, now twenty feet away from him, dropped to his left knee while clutching his other knee, which he held stiffly out to one side, his rifle clattering onto the bridge floor.

"Son of a bitch!" the man shrieked, lifting his bearded head, his hat tumbling off his shoulder.

James rose to a knee. The Spencer popped again, the slug driving the knee-shot blue-belly straight back onto the bridge, where he lay shaking his arms and legs and making weird gurgling sounds, like a huge, gasping carp.

James had noticed something odd about the man's rifle. Seeing no one else immediately around him, the lieutenant ran to the man now and reached for the rifle, raising it slowly, inspecting it carefully, heart quickening at the long, octagonal barrel and the sleek brass frame—smooth and solid beneath his left hand's gentle caress. Pale smoke slithered from the maw of the barrel, above the long loading tube.

"That damned Yankee rifle," as the saying went, "that they load on Sunday and shoot all week!"

A Henry. He'd heard about them but had never had the pleasure of seeing one before.

Boots thudded behind James. He swung around, straightening, to see several shadows running down off the pale road dropping out of the wooded mountainside and onto the bridge, dark blue capes buffeting like bat wings in the muddy darkness. The young Confederate lieutenant levered a round into the Henry's breech, vaguely appreciating the smooth, assured sound of the action, and fired the gun quickly from his right hip. He grinned devilishly as he levered and fired, levered and fired, until five brass cartridges had clinked to the wooden boards behind him.

The three soldiers who'd been running toward him lay howling and writhing while a fourth wheeled and ran back up the road a ways before darting into the woods on its right side.

James curled his upper lip in a mocking grin.

Something sliced across his left arm, and he realized the men on the shore were firing at him while a few were running back up toward the bridge behind him—scurrying shadows in the inky night. The rifles boomed and popped and the balls screeched around him, several hammering into the bridge rail before him. Another man was shooting from the bridge's far side, on the opposite shore of the creek from where James and his men had entered it.

James racked another shell—so easily!—into the Henry's chamber, and returned fire on the man shooting from the bridge's far end and whom the lieutenant figured was probably the man who'd first started throwing lead at him and Coker. He fired three shots in the rifleman's direction but couldn't tell if he'd hit anything except for the bridge rail, as the dark woods formed a stygian backdrop.

James then racked another shell, hoping he had a full tube of cartridges, and triggered round after round at the shore of the creek to his right, where most of the soldiers had gathered to throw lead in Coker's direction. The Confederate was mildly surprised they hadn't hit the dynamite and blown the bridge. Even a near shot would cause those sensitive caps to ignite.

Or had they killed Lawrence before he could place the bundles against the pylons?

As the cartridges clinked around his bare feet, he

heard men yelp and howl and curse, and several silhouettes dropped under his deadly aim. When he spied no more movement along the shore, he slid his attention to the south end of the bridge, saw the flash of two rifles, heard the slugs hammering the bridge rails on either side of him.

He watched with satisfaction as two more figures went down before the Henry's hammer pinged on an empty chamber. He gritted his teeth against a sharp, burning pain in his right side, and realized he'd been hit. When had that happened? He sloughed it off—far from the first of his many wounds since the beginning of the war. . . .

Dropping the Henry, he scrambled toward the first man he'd shot on the bridge and slid the man's Colt Navy .44 from the dead captain's holster.

Two rifles were still barking at him, spitting small javelins of flame. Balls sizzled around him, skidded off the wooden floor of the bridge, and pounded the rails. One clipped his ankle. He cocked the .44, hoping the charge hadn't been fouled by the drizzle, and dropped to a knee, raising the pistol straight out from his right shoulder. The first shot sputtered a hair but still threw the ball. The second time he pulled the trigger, there was only a *thwisht!* sound.

The damn cap was wet. . . .

James heard the thuds of running feet, saw a silhouetted figure running toward him. The federal triggered his own pistol, and James flinched as the bullet screeched off the bridge about one foot to his right. He heard a click as the approaching soldier triggered his pistol on an empty or fouled cylinder.

"Shit!" The man tossed the pistol away and came running, his cape buffeting about his torso.

James looked around for a weapon. He saw only his knife handle sticking up from the dead captain's chest, around a broad, dark stain on his tunic. James ran over, pulled the knife out of the dead flesh with a slight crunching, sucking sound, then turned to what appeared to be the last of the Union soldiers.

He was James's height, with long, gold-blond hair and an eye patch. Probably James's age or thereabouts. Not too many old men remained in either military. If the battles hadn't gotten them, disease likely had. James couldn't see many details of the man approaching him, except for the snarl on the broad mouth mantled by a mustache that appeared a slightly darker shade of blond than his hair.

He stopped about ten feet away, breathing hard, as was James. An eerie silence had descended in the wake of the battle. There were only the wet gurgling sounds of the water lapping against the pylons. A cool breeze had risen, shunting a drizzling rain.

It felt refreshing against James's naked body still partly clad in the sticky river mud.

The enemy soldier, his lieutenant's bars showing faintly on the shoulders of his dark blue tunic, cursed, curling his upper lip distastefully, and reached down to draw a bone-handled knife from the well of his right boot.

"Good with a gun—are you, Reb?" he said. "Let's see how you do against a butcher knife!"

He bolted forward, and James thrust his own blade up just in time to deflect the Union lieutenant's ten-inch blade from his own naked belly. The man, snarling and cursing like an outraged mountain lion, drove forward. The move caught James off guard, and he felt himself thrust up against the bridge's downstream side, the rails pressing against the backs of his legs. His right arm was straight up before him, knife gripped in his clenched fist, and hooked around the blue-belly's own knife arm. The man showed his teeth as he growled, turning his head and thrusting his black eye patch toward James as though it, too, were a weapon.

James felt the bridge rails gouging into his ankles, bending his knees. He was leaning too far back, and a quick glance to one side showed him the dully gleaming creek twenty feet below, opening like a dark glove.

He was going over!

Loosing a raucous Rebel yell that seemed to cut the night wide open, he gave one powerful thrust with his knife, ramming half the blade into the Union officer's upper left chest. Then he and the blue-belly were tumbling over the rails, grunting and snarling as they continued to struggle in midair before the water came up to slap them both like a giant fist.

James felt the cool liquid envelop him. Sideways, spinning slowly, he dropped into the mud at the creek's bottom, feeling the hairy tentacles of weeds wrapping their slimy fingers around his legs, torso, and neck. The acrid water slithered down his throat, and he heard himself convulse as he choked back a retch, keeping his mouth closed.

Plunging down hard with his left foot, he thrust himself up off the muddy bottom and, with his knife still clenched in his fist, flailed wildly for the surface.

He brushed against something yielding and clad in coarse, soaked cloth. When he opened his eyes, he saw the gritted teeth and the black eye patch of the snarling, fearless Union officer. The man swung his knife crossways, and James tilted his head back just in time so that his enemy's steel blade only made a thin, hot cut across his throat. Another inch closer, and his blood would be geysering from severed arteries in his neck.

James grunted savagely, feeling his lips stretch back from his teeth, and thrust up and forward with his own knife. At the same time that he buried his blade in the officer's chest, near where he'd stabbed him the first time, the blue-belly's lone eye thrust toward him— wide and blue and filled with a chilling golden light.

"*Oh, God!*" James heard himself shout. It fairly exploded from his chest.

The eye before him—the familiar orb he'd know anywhere, for it owned the familial blue of his mother's eyes . . . the blue of even his own eyes—dulled. It was like a lamp being turned down in the one lit window of a house he'd just recognized.

Quickly, he grabbed the handle of his knife and pulled. When it slid free of the young lieutenant's chest, he released it, letting the creek take it. The man before him groaned, winced, and bobbed toward James in the current that carried them both downstream. The Union soldier opened his mouth, gasping.

Only vaguely, James heard the rifle shots of his own men behind him. They were trying to ignite the dynamite. The pops and booms dwindled quickly as the current carried him farther away from the bridge. Just as vaguely, he was aware of the explosion of the dynamite, saw the orange radiance push back the darkness around him and reflect like rubies off the black water.

"Little brother," he wheezed, now pulling the Union officer toward him, kicking his legs to keep them both afloat as the man became nearly a deadweight in his arms. "Ah, shit, Willie." His voice rose shrilly, cracking as he started to maneuver toward the creek's left bank. "*Willie!*"

Chapter 3

James felt the creek bottom thrust itself against his kicking feet, and he set both feet down, finding himself in hip-deep water, ten yards from shore.

The young Union officer—who unbelievably appeared to be one and the same Willie Dunn, James's brother two years his junior, though with an unfamiliar patch over his left eye—slumped down on his knees in the shallow water, head hanging. His longish blond hair was pasted to his neck and cheeks and the black eye patch.

"Willie," James said, breathless. "Willie . . ."

James dragged his brother to shore, back-and-bellied him up onto the steep bank, and collapsed beside him. He vomited water, brushed his forehead against his arm, and then turned to the young man, who he was still hoping was not really his brother but only another soldier who merely looked like Willie Dunn.

After all, it had been three years since they'd last seen each other right before Willie had packed a satchel and ridden off on his Morgan-cross in the wake of their long, heated argument in their father's study back at Seven Oaks. . . .

"Willie!"

James pushed the lieutenant's left shoulder up. The man's blond head lolled back, and the single eye met James's. Even in the darkness, the dark blue orb betrayed a confused, puzzled expression. Then gradually, just as James himself realized, horrifically, that he really was in the presence of his brother—a man he'd most likely mortally wounded—young Willie's lips stretched in a wry smile of recognition. He blinked his lone eye, shook his head.

"Well, well—Forrest's Rapscallion." Willie chuckled raspily. "Fancy meetin' you here, James."

James pushed himself up on an elbow, thrust his brother's shoulder back farther until Willie reclined against the soggy, fern-cushioned ground on his back, wincing and grunting, flat belly expanding and contracting wildly as he tried to catch a breath. James looked at the blood pumping from the two wounds in his brother's chest. It was frothy, and it came in dark spurts, trickling down the soaked tunic toward the ground.

James's mind spun. The horror of what he'd done had a taut grip on his mind while the rational part of him tried to figure out what to do about it.

James had heard of such a nightmare happening before, and at times he'd imagined what it would be like to meet his younger, more idealistic brother on the field of battle. But those had been anxiety-inspired fantasies. Surely, it would never happen!

But it did, and James could not shake the feeling that it was all merely a nightmare. He could not maneuver through the shock and confusion that visited him now for the first time after three long years of bloody war, after three long years of cold, efficient killing.

His own brother, little Willie, lay before him dying from wounds that James himself had inflicted!

Willie was quivering. James pushed himself up higher on his elbow and looked into Willie's young face. No, he was not quivering. He was laughing, lips stretched back from his teeth, tears running down from his single blue eye. Then, suddenly, Willie Dunn pushed up on his own elbow and leaned forward, coughing raucously, dark blood spitting from his mouth and both nostrils.

James's blood ran cold. He'd punctured one of Willie's lungs.

"Damn near got the war won," Willie said, still laughing bizarrely, "and my dear old grayback brother goes and kills me!"

Someone called James's name. The shout sailed out over the creek and across the canyon, echoing. James had recognized the voice. "Crosseye, over here!"

"Crosseye?" Willie looked up at him, frowning. "You gotta be joshin'? He's with *you*?"

"What'd you think—he'd join the Union? Just like me—and *you*—he was born a Southerner."

"Oh, it doesn't surprise me ole Crosseye signed up with ole Jeff Davis. Just like you, he didn't want no Yankee tellin' him what he could or couldn't do—no, not even when it came to using men as *slaves*! I'm just surprised the old bastard's with *you—here* . . . not to mention still alive."

"Nothin' can kill that old bastard. You know that."

"Not bears, not Injuns . . ." Willie was talking memories now, memories he shared with his older brother while a fond look of reflection passed fleetingly across his otherwise pain-racked eye. "Not the whole Union army!"

James called for their mutual friend again.

"Jimmy?" came Crosseye's echoing shout, louder this time. "Where you at, boy?"

"Here!"

Panicking at the thought of his brother dying by his own hand, James pushed his brother down flat once more and closed his hands over the two ragged holes in Willie's upper chest. Willie screamed and kicked a low-heeled cavalry boot. "I'm finished, you bastard! You killed me!"

Two men came scrambling through the brush, stumbling down the bank and grabbing dogwood and oak branches to break their falls. The first man was stocky and bull-legged, and his battered, broad-brimmed hat hung down his back by a leather thong, exposing the thin, red-gray hair curling close against his domelike head. The second man was younger—Jackie Baker from Kentucky. Both men held long Enfield muskets in their hands, and their canvas haversacks flopped down their sides from leather lanyards. Their uniforms, like those of most of the Confederate soldiers, were nearly rags, and their wash-worn underwear shone through in scores of places.

Crosseye moved down the slope and stopped fifteen feet away from James and Willie, scowling down at the younger Dunn.

"Hold on there, Jimmy," Crosseye said, bringing his rifle up. "One left, eh? Well, not for long, no, sir!"

James snapped a look at Crosseye Reeves, who'd been a sharecropper back at the Dunns' Seven Oaks Plantation and a mentor in the art of woodsmanship to both James and Willie—against their mother's wishes, of course. Softly, James said, "Put it down, old man. It's Willie."

Crosseye lowered the Enfield from his craggy, patch-bearded cheek, narrowing the eye that did not wander. "Huh?"

"Gotta get him back up to the camp. Get him by a fire."

Crosseye moved slowly down the slope, followed by Jackie Baker. The two other surviving members of Dunn's Raiders were just now running down out of the forest. They were Cletus Moon and Moss Cline. Both men slowed when they saw James crouched over the fallen federal soldier, and came down cautiously, puzzled expressions on their gaunt, haggard faces, both men, like Jackie Baker, not yet twenty but having seen enough killing to last them twenty lifetimes.

James stood and crouched over his brother. "I'm gonna carry you up to our camp, Willie."

Willie's eye moved up and down his older brother, and he chuckled. "What's the matter—the Confederacy too poor to clothe its soldiers?"

James grabbed his brother's right hand, but Willie pulled it away. "Leave me, brother. I'm a goner."

"Ain't gonna leave you, Willie."

He pulled Willie up by one hand, but as he drew his younger brother up over his shoulder, Willie broke out in a coughing fit. James felt the warmth of his brother's blood dribble over his shoulder and down his back. He eased Willie back down to the ferns, then snaked his arms under the young lieutenant's arms and knees and lifted him and began to carry him up the slope through the pines.

Crosseye and the other soldiers followed at some distance, the others conferring quietly. Only once did James glance down at the bridge, the center of which had been blown out by the dynamite. It was a ragged hulk in the darkness. At least, James's men had accomplished that much.

James carried his brother up the steep slope a hundred yards before swinging left and walking along a deer path, moving upstream to the point where he and Coker and Krieg had first come down from their redoubt on the ridge.

Coker, like Krieg, was most certainly dead, as the bullets had come at him from both directions. The man James was now carrying back to their camp could very well be the man who'd killed poor Lawrence, who'd made it through so much only to die here, albeit in an effort to keep Sherman from getting his hands on any more guns. Maybe the Raiders had even delayed Sherman's receiving any more of those sixteen-shot Henry repeaters that hopelessly outmatched anything the Confederates were wielding.

"Made a fool out of you tonight, James." Willie's voice sounded like sandpaper as he stared up from his brother's arms, choking back coughs, breathing hard, his muscles tensing as he writhed.

"I reckon you did, Willie."

"Don't mean just this."

"What, then? That shipment of guns and ammo is gonna have to backtrack. Might not get to Sherman before he reaches Atlanta."

"Ah, shit, James," Willie said, mouth twisting in a weird grin between coughs. "Sherman's done already in Atlanta. Might be on his way east to the ocean by now."

James didn't say anything. He winced when his bare left foot came down on a sharp spur of rock pushing up out of the deep, aromatic forest duff. His brother was likely delirious from blood loss.

"Yessir, we was just hangin' back to clean up the little Confederate raidin' parties the main army done left behind."

James frowned down at his brother.

Willie said, "There wasn't no supply train, James. McClellan meant for that information to be intercepted by them dunderheaded Reb spies—so we could set up an ambush and clean you dogs out of the henhouse once and for all, so's you wouldn't be bedevilin' General Sherman all the way to the ocean. The general, you see, is the cantankerous sort, and he's just sick to shit of you yaller-bellies!"

James thought of his raiders and the several other packs of Confederate guerillas that were also on missions to blow up bridges or railroad lines this very evening. He was more concerned right now with his brother, whom he could feel growing cold in his arms, but the information was hard to swallow, for he'd built up so much hope for turning Sherman back from Atlanta. A faint hope, but a hope just the same.

Now, if Willie's Union word could be trusted, he not only hadn't accomplished that, but he'd murdered his brother in the bargain. He was strong, but he felt his arms and legs growing weak as he climbed the last stretch of the slope toward the rocks showing pale through the dark columns of the pines. They'd set up a redoubt there in the rocks capping the ridge, on the backside of the mountain from where the supply wagons had been supposed to pull through.

A horse nickered to James's left. He could see the Raiders' seven mounts tied to a picket line there, and the stolen cannon just below the ridge. Straight ahead of him, the rocks shone pale in the darkness. He found the hollow beyond which lay the black entrance of a cave, and stumbling painfully over obstacles in the darkness, he found his way into the cave and set Willie down, leaning him back gently against the cave's wall.

"I'll get a fire goin', Willie."

His brother said nothing. James lowered his head to his brother's, placed his hand on Willie's forehead. He couldn't hear him breathing. James's heart thumped fearfully.

He pressed his hand more tightly against his brother's cold, clammy forehead. "Willie?"

The young soldier rasped, convulsed, then drew a ragged breath. "James?"

"I'm gonna get a fire goin', Willie. Gonna get you warm."

"Don't blame yourself, James."

"Shut up, Willie."

James moved back out of the cave and found where his clothes were piled near where Billy Krieg's and Lawrence's were also piled, barely visible in the darkness. The four other Raiders were moving up the slope through the pines.

"One o' you fellas wanna get a fire goin'?" James said.

They all four stopped near him, and he could see their incredulous scowls even in the darkness. They thought he'd gone off his nut. Crosseye said, "With a supply train headed this way, Jimmy? You crazy?"

James shook his head as he pulled his long-handles up his legs, his body having dried, leaving uncomfortable, crusted patches of mud on his arms, chest, and thighs. It was caked between his toes. "No one's comin', Crosseye. It was an ambush."

"*What?*"

James's anger exploded like pent-up steam in an overheated locomotive. "One of you get a goddamn fire goin', goddamnit! Gather wood and build a big one!"

Three of the men jumped back with a start, wary of James's temper. Crosseye, somewhere in his forties though he'd never revealed his true age to anyone, even James, whom he'd practically raised back at Seven Oaks, studied the younger man dubiously. He scratched the back of his head under his broad-brimmed hat with its front brim pinned to the crown, then turned to the others. "You heard the lieutenant, ya damn junipers! Gather wood and start a fire!"

Chapter 4

When James had stomped into his worn boots, he shrugged into his Confederate-gray tunic—or what was left of it. It virtually hung in ribbons on him. Crosseye stood before him, head turned toward the black hole of the cave. "You sure that's him, Jimmy?"

"I'd know my own brother, wouldn't I?"

"Well, I'll be a sober shoat," Crosseye said, raking a thumbnail down his beard. "Never thought I'd see that boy again. Figured the Union had done swallowed him up. Why'd they spit him out here?"

"To kill us. It was a trap."

"Figure that!" Crosseye's slightly high-pitched raspy voice sounded sad. "I remember when that boy was no higher than a tit on a mama coon."

James walked into the cave, let his eyes adjust to the darkness once more, then walked over to his brother's vague image slouched against the wall. Willie was breathing softly, raspily. James quickly gathered stones littering the cave's floor and arranged them into a circle. When Moss and Cletus had each deposited armloads of relatively dry wood in the middle of the cave and coaxed a small fire to life in James's ring, the Confederate lieutenant fetched his haversack and canteen. The flames danced wan orange light and shadows across the cavern's uneven stone walls.

When he had shoved a relatively clean neckerchief into the largest of his brother's two wounds—the lesser one appeared to have stopped bleeding—James tried to get him to drink, but Willie only turned his head away, coughing. Sweat shone like beads of molten gold on his forehead and cheeks carpeted in a fine, blond beard. He squeezed his lone eye shut, groaning softly. His lips formed a white line beneath his untrimmed, red-blond mustache.

James lowered the canteen. He turned to see Moss and Cletus hunkered on their haunches on the far side of the fire, regarding James and the wounded Union lieutenant dubiously. Jackie Baker sat on a boulder just outside the cave, his Enfield across his knees, staring cautiously into the night.

Crosseye stood with his back to Baker, and crouched down, hands on his knees, regarding Willie with a haunted look in his deep-set eyes across which the light of the fledgling flames danced. His left eye had wandered since it had nearly been plucked out in a skirmish during the Mexican War. There was a short, faint, white scar above and below it. Crosseye claimed that the Mexican who had so assaulted him had paid for it with a bloody disemboweling, though Crosseye was given to exaggeration and idle boasting, so no one knew how true the story was. He was as tough as a hickory knot, though. And that was a fact few around Seven Oaks would try to contest.

James looked back at Moss and Cletus, both of whom regarded Willie as though he were a caged bobcat. "You two got somethin' you wanna say?" James asked them tightly.

They slid their moody eyes to him.

Moss said, "Shit, Lieutenant, that's a Union officer there. Whoever he may have been once, that's who he is now."

James straightened slowly, uncoiling like a rising panther. His mild expression framed by his long, wet dark brown hair belied the fury that burned behind his cobalt eyes. He no longer had his knife, and he was glad he didn't. He was making a conscious effort to not wrap his right hand around the grips of the Griswold & Gunnison brass-framed pistol wedged behind his cracked leather belt, just over his belly where it was easy to get to. The mud and weather had claimed his leather holster many months ago.

"Get the hell out of my sight, you son of a bitch." His voice was like low, distant thunder.

Moss, still on his haunches beside Cletus, stared up at him darkly. An exasperated sneer etched itself on Moss's long face framed in bushy muttonchop whiskers, and he gestured toward Willie. "Come on, Lieutenant—look at the uniform . . ."

"That's my brother in that uniform, you son of a bitch!" James's voice rocketed around inside the cave. "Get the hell out of my sight now, and stay there—you hear? Or so help me, I'll pop a ball through your ugly head, Moss!"

The threat was like a slap. Both Moss and Cletus stared up at their lieutenant, hang-jawed, wary as treed coons. They blinked. And then Cletus stumbled back a little as he rose, bracing himself on the cave's far wall. Then he cursed, wheeled, and stumbled on out of the cave. Cletus regarded the young lieutenant a moment longer, then glanced at Crosseye, who betrayed nothing on his haggard, cross-eyed face, then went the way of Moss.

"Can't blame them, Jimmy," Crosseye said. "Been a long fight. They didn't know Willie like we did."

James dropped back down on his knees beside his brother. "Just keep 'em away from me, Crosseye."

"I'll do that, Jimmy." Crosseye straightened, his eyes serious, doleful. "You need anything?"

James shrugged. "I don't know what to do for him."

"Probably nothin' you can do, Jimmy. Just sit with him." Crosseye gave a fateful chuff, then turned and ambled on out of the cave.

James regarded Willie for a long time, and then he turned and leaned his back against the wall beside him. He raised his elbow to his knee and stared into the fire, silently praying for Willie's recovery, hanging on his brother's every breath.

He sat there with Willie for a long time, mopping Willie's head frequently with a neckerchief that he wetted from his canteen, keeping the fire going. After maybe two hours of silence save for the flames' crackling and Willie's ragged, shallow breathing, the young Union officer said suddenly, with startling clarity, as though he'd been awake all along, "James? Do me a favor, will you, brother?"

James had been stirring the fire with a pine branch.

Now he laid the branch on the flames and scuttled back over to his brother. "What is it, Willie?"

The younger Dunn reached inside his bloody tunic and pulled out a gold-chased watch with a chain of linked gold Confederate coins. He held it in his open palm atop his thigh, occasional pain spasms causing the hand and the watch to twitch slightly.

"Find Vienna for me," Willie said.

James shook his head. "Willie, I got no idea what became of her or her family—"

"Denver City," Willie said. "Her daddy sent her there, to family, to keep her away from the war. I got a letter from her a couple years ago. I want you to give her this watch."

Vienna McAllister had been Willie's betrothed before the war had broken out. She'd been born into a wealthy plantation family four miles from Seven Oaks, and she and Willie had been sparking since nearly the day they'd both started walking.

Willie flipped open the gold-finished lid, extended the watch weakly toward his brother. James took it, read the inscription in flowery cursive writing on the inside of the lid. "To my son, Thomas, with love from his father—William Thomas Dunn, 1863."

James felt his jaw drop as he looked at his brother.

"Bought it in Richmond. Had it engraved special."

James shook his head uncomprehendingly. *"Son?"*

"Didn't tell no one back home, but that night when I rode out of Seven Oaks for the last time, after that argument with you and Pa about the war, I rode over to Rose Hill. Vienna snuck out of the house to meet me, and we had Preacher Lawton marry us." Willie stared at the watch before lifting his bleary gaze to his brother and adding, "Was only proper I marry the girl. Besides, hell, I loved her."

James thought that over for a time, then nodded in understanding. "How . . . do you know . . . ?"

"She had the baby in Denver City. Or she would have by now. I never did receive word. We'd chosen the name the same night we was married. The McAllisters' firstborn has always been boys. Ours is most likely a boy, too. Thomas. . . ."

James just stared at his brother, digesting it all. When he had done so, he felt as though his heart had been torn in two by a Union cavalry saber. He felt a great weight settle on his shoulders, and tears began to wash down his cheeks as though a spigot had been turned on. His gut churned, his lungs spasmed as he bawled until he dropped forward onto his hands, sobbing openly, his thick hair hanging down over his face.

"You're a helluva fighter, James," his brother said. "Always was. Despite our differences about the war, I'm proud of you."

James looked at Willie, felt a roiling rage rising up around his aching heart. "Really, Willie? You're proud of me?" Then the sobs turned to laughter—a wild, bizarre, half-mad laughter. "You're proud of me—are ye, little brother?" He continued to laugh and sob at the same time. Christ, he'd killed him, and Willie was proud of him!

How could he not have realized what a better man Willie was than he?

"Wish we'd had you on our side, James." Willie

grabbed his brother's arm and squeezed, wheezing, "Find Vienna and my boy, James. Give little Thomas my watch, so's he has something to know me by. And tell—"

His voice pinched off. James looked at him. Willie was gasping, leaning his head back against the cave wall. All the color had leached out of his face, and his cheeks were hollow. His lone eye was flat, as though an inner lid were closing down over it.

"Willie!" James took his brother's face in his hands, and squeezed. "Please don't, Willie!"

Willie placed his own hands on his brother's wrists. He gritted his teeth. "Don't blame yourself, brother. Just find my wife . . . my son . . . give 'im that watch. And all's forgiven."

A faint smile lifted Willie's mouth corners. The light left his eye. His fingers slackened on James's wrists, and then his hands fell down like rocks at his sides.

"*Willie!*" James screamed.

Willie gave one last rasping exhale, and then he sat unmoving against the cave wall, staring unseeingly out of his single eye at his brother.

James spent the night in the cave, holding Willie in his arms. He let the fire go out and merely stared into the black velvet of the far wall, neither asleep nor awake but existing in a no-man's-land between both worlds, shuddering from time to time when he remembered shoving his razor-edged plow-blade knife into his brother's chest.

He'd looked into that lone blue eye, the same blue as his own eyes, and realized what he'd done.

When the soft gray light of dawn shone beyond the cave opening, touching the sky above the dark pines, James eased his brother down to the cave floor. He felt oddly numb, but clear. Somewhere over the course of the long night, he'd decided that the war was over for him. He was going to follow Willie's bidding and deliver the watch to Vienna. He rose and walked out to where the other men were milling, eating a meager breakfast of dried chicken, some pecans they'd gleaned from an orchard, and hardtack washed down with water. They hadn't had any coffee for months.

Jackie, Cletus, and Moss all stopped talking when they saw James emerge from the cave's black mouth. James glanced at Moss. "Sorry about last night. I was out of line, Moss."

"You ain't got nothin' to be sorry about, Lieutenant. I was the one out of line. I am sorry about your brother."

Crosseye was down by the horses and the twelve-pounder field piece they'd acquired from a battlefield along which the dead had been stacked like cordwood, cleaning out a hoof with a stick. When he saw James walk out away from the other men, he released the horse's hoof and ambled over to him, flicking the stick across his thigh clad in torn gray wool. Around his neck he wore a fancy Lefaucheux pin-fire revolver that he'd taken off the body of a dead Union general, wearing the fancy piece for a trophy as well as a formidable weapon, though the ammo was hard to find in the South.

"You boys go on back to the outfit," James said. "I'm gonna be takin' Willie home."

Crosseye stared at him, blinked. The others muttered

amongst themselves. "That's desertion, Jimmy," Cross-eye whispered, unable to say the taboo word aloud.

James looked his old friend and mentor in the eye. "Willie deserves to be buried at Seven Oaks, and that's where I'm gonna take him."

"You comin' back, Lieutenant?" Jackie Baker asked from the rock he was sitting on, chewing a chunk of stale hardtack, crumbs dribbling into his sandy spade beard.

"No," James said. He'd made his decision. When he'd buried Willie at Seven Oaks, he was heading west to find Vienna, to give her Willie's watch.

Crosseye said, "I'll ride with you, Jimmy."

"No."

"You're gonna need hel—"

"Deserters are shot on sight, Crosseye." Any soldier found away from his company without furlough papers was considered a deserter.

"That's what I'm worried about, Jimmy."

"Don't worry about me. You worry about gettin' these boys back to General Forrest's company. He'll likely have a new assignment for you. If the war's still goin' on after I've buried Willie, I'll be back." He lied about that last; he was only trying to placate his old friend.

Crosseye cursed, doffed his hat, and slapped it against his thigh. "Ah, hell, Jimmy—it wasn't your fault!"

James walked down and picked up a saddle blanket piled with Coker's tack under an oiled tarpaulin, and carried it back into the cave. He wrapped Willie in the blanket and sat there for a time while the others rustled around outside, saddling their horses. They weren't saying anything, as though they were all too shocked for words at the news of James Dunn's intention to desert. If anyone had told him just yesterday that he'd soon join the ranks of the much-maligned deserters who had helped to decimate the Confederate army, he'd have shot the man.

"We'll be goin' now, Jimmy," Crosseye said, astraddle his gray mule just beyond the cave. A fine drizzle was falling out of a sky the color of dirty white curtains, ticking off his hat. The mule shook its head, rattling its bit in its teeth. Billy Krieg's horse stood behind him, its bridle reins in Crosseye's gloved left hand.

Crosseye waited as though for James to tell him he'd be joining them after all, but then he said, "I'm leavin' you a hoss for Willie, takin' Billy's." He touched stiff fingers to his hat, turned the mule, and rode off along with the others, Moss pulling the wheeled field piece by a lead line.

When they were gone, leaving James alone with his dead brother wrapped in the horse blanket, James left the cave and tramped down the slope to where his own horse stood with Lawrence Coker's copper-bottom bay. James's mount was a steeldust gelding that he'd taken off a Yankee farm several months ago, when his previous horse had been killed by a Vandenburgh volley gun in a skirmish in eastern Mississippi. He saddled the steeldust and Lawrence's bay and then led both up to the cave. He felt heavy and numb, barely aware of the stablike pain in his chest, only vaguely aware of the rain ticking down on his battered, low-crowned campaign kepi.

With rope from his saddlebags, he tied the blanket around Willie's body, which was already beginning to stiffen, and tied it so that his arms were close against his sides. A memory erupted in his brain, and he saw a laughing Willie, ten or eleven years old, as James and their now-deceased older brother, Frank, wrapped the youngest of the Dunn brothers up in a quilt and threw him into the pond behind Seven Oaks Manor, one warm spring afternoon, when the redbuds were in full bloom.

They were pretending that Willie was a worthless pup, and, like a worthless pup, would be wrapped up and drowned. But Willie swam like a toad. He got out of the quilt and came splashing back to shore, throwing mud balls until their mother and two Negro maids came running out of the house, down the long, brick-paved path to the pond. Each had been armed with a wooden spoon, and they gave James and Frank a tanning for ruining a perfectly good quilt and "nearly drowning your poor youngest brother."

Only, the maids had been laughing, especially the young, sparkly-eyed Eulia, whom James had once caught with her bloomers down around her ankles in the woodshed, with a bare-assed Frank pumping hard between her spread, chocolate-colored knees.

James pulled the blanket down from his brother's face.

"Willie," he whispered, running his fingers over the half-open lid, feeling the light caress of the young man's lashes across his war-calloused fingertips. "Damn it all, Willie."

But the eye would not stay closed. The lid was a papery light blue. His cheeks and forehead were the color of porcelain. Lips a thin, lilac line beneath his shaggy blond mustache that all but hid them. The patch looked barbaric on what appeared the face of a bearded boy-child.

James wondered what had happened to the other eye. Probably shrapnel or a bayonet wound. Maybe a knife. It did not surprise James that Willie might have been wounded in hand-to-hand combat. Doubtless, his opponent had fared worse. Willie had been the most artistic and sensitive of the Dunn brothers. He'd been given to poetry and the piano—Chopin had been his favorite composer—and romancing the young ladies of neighboring plantations. He'd also tried countless times to convince their father, Alexander Axelrod Dunn, considered a "benevolent" slave owner, to give his thirty-odd slaves their freedom. Willie had believed that no man, whatever color his skin might be, should ever be enslaved by another.

Despite his liberal political views and artistic turn of mind, Willie could be a fierce fighter when aroused, and James and Frank had both worn the wounds to prove it. It had taken a lot to get Willie's dander up, but once you did, as their father had often said—and as he'd remarked that bitter night that Willie had ridden off to join the Union forces in Washington—"all the saints in heaven couldn't appease that boy."

The elder Dunn, watching his youngest ride off down the wide lane through the mossy oaks while their mother had bawled her eyes out in the rose garden, had taken a sip of his bourbon and said just loudly enough for James to hear: "The damn Yankees are getting one hell of a fighter in that one, and before they let this thing go too far, I hope they realize there's more where he came from but fightin' on *our* side!"

"Willie," James whispered again, leaning down and pressing his lips to his brother's cold forehead.

Chapter 5

One month later, after he'd taken his brother home to bury him at what was left of Seven Oaks—which wasn't much except the manor house with a gaping hole from a cannonball in his father's library—James was headed west and thinking of the last time he'd seen the old man, when a young man in a ragged uniform stepped out from behind a tree and into the trail before James's horse.

"Ease down out of that saddle now, mister, and we won't blow you all to hell," said the young federal soldier, who held a cocked Starr .44 in his dirty, bare hand.

"But first," said another, older man, "kindly remove them pistols from them holsters and toss 'em down here. We'll take them, too. Griswolds, eh?"

James knew that his twin Confederate-made .36s, as well as his gray cavalry kepi, marked him as a Confederate. A Confederate too far north at this point in the war, as he was just now crossing northern Missouri.

He'd long since passed Chattanooga, from which

black smoke had curled unceasingly into the hot, damp air, as well as several other charred Southern cities. When he'd lit out from Seven Oaks, his father screaming at him and waving a sword from the second-story balustrade—the old man could abide James's killing his Union-turncoat brother, but not deserting the Confederacy—he'd followed mostly secondary wagon roads, including the one he was on now. At night he'd slept in abandoned barns or along lonely creeks, though a couple of nights he'd holed up in whorehouses, the pleasures of the flesh acting as a balm against his memories of death and destruction.

Nearly every day, it had rained. Now the rain had stopped but the road was muddy. There was a farm off to the left, the ground around it scorched, trees blown to black skeletons from canister shot. There was an old tavern and general store on the right. The low-slung, clapboard hovel had a hole in its roof, and a dead man in a tattered Confederate uniform hung from a charred tree to the right of the place, near a wheelless wagon and a dead mule. The man's neck was stretched to a grisly length, his body so bloated it was bursting through the seams of his clothes.

James looked at the two bearded men in dark blue Union rags before him. He studied them sadly—their tangled, tobacco-stained beards and wild, hungry eyes. The war had been nearly as cruel to the federal soldiers as it had been to the Confederates. James's horse nickered, and then he heard a slapping thud behind him and saw a third man in what was left of federal blues step out from behind a stock pen sheathed in half-burned shrubs and stop in the trail behind

James. The slapping had been made by the loose sole of his boot. Bare toes stuck out, white as snow.

Deserters, these men. James knew the look in their eyes. He probably had that look himself, though he was somewhat better attired in his navy blue linsey-woolsey shirt under a tanned buckskin vest, and black twill trousers. A red neckerchief was knotted around his neck. He wore a fresh pair of high-topped brown boots that he'd retrieved, like most of the rest of his gear, from Seven Oaks. He wore his two Griswold & Gunnison .36s in soft leather holsters positioned for the cross draw on each hip, and he had a Green River knife sheathed near the pistol on his right side.

He'd found his mount, only a colt when he'd left for the war, running free in the woods around Seven Oaks, somehow overlooked by both federal and Confederate soldiers. It was a chestnut stallion with the rare rabicano markings, as though the ends of the bristles of its chestnut hair were lightly brushed with cream.

James turned back to the two men facing him—a young man and an old man, equally haggard. The deserters were after his horse and his pistols, and he couldn't blame them. But without the horse, he'd have to find another, and he had damn little scrip and specie in his pockets—all of it Confederate and likely worthless out West.

James's voice was mild as he said, "You're pickin' the wrong carcass, old sons. This one ain't dead yet."

"What's that?" said the old man. He and the young one were each holding Springfields on him. The man behind him—a stringbean with buckteeth—was aiming a Sharps straight out from his shoulder, the hammer rocked back.

"He said he don't believe so," said the young, tangle-bearded boy beside him, speaking loudly, as though the older man were deaf—probably from a cannon blast.

"Oh, he don't believe so, does he?" The old man's pale, puffy face clouded up and got ready to rain as he stumbled forward. He stopped and took steady aim at James's head, narrowing one eye as he stared down the rusty Springfield's barrel.

He frowned uncertainly, lowered the rifle an inch.

"Say . . . ain't you . . . ain't you . . . ?" He paused, then added almost under his breath, "Forrest's Rapscallion?"

James stared at him.

The others shifted uncomfortably, sliding their gazes between James and the old man. They moved up nearer the old man and stood about ten feet off each of James's knees.

The stringbean with the buckteeth ran his tongue along his lower lip, sized James up carefully, both eyes twitching, and said, "Well . . . if it is him . . . he ain't nothin' so much. Hell, I'm bigger'n he is!"

"Is that who you are?" asked the other young one, blue eyes narrowed beneath an uneven shelf of dirty-blond bangs. "You Forrest's Rapscallion or is old Kelsey addlepated from all the mash he drunk in Kentucky?"

"He's got it right. Walk on."

The stringbean looked at James's sleek stallion—slightly hammerheaded but beefy through the barrel and tapering to sculpted hindquarters, with long, strong legs. "That sure is a fine horse. . . ."

His eyes returned to James. They turned glassy with nerves, and his lips twitched a wicked smile.

At the same time, the old man jerked the rifle back up. He was tightening his finger on its trigger but did not get the shot off before James had reached both hands across his flat belly and brought up the twin Griswolds. The old man's Springfield blasted toward the sky as James's .36-caliber ball punched through his right cheek just beneath that eye and slammed him violently back and down. James's other Griswold had punched a hole through the tangle-bearded younker's chest as the kid had gotten his own Springfield centered, but shot a misfire, which he appeared to realize as he flew back and slammed against the ground beside the jerking old man.

The kid's eyes were wide with fleeting shock and frustration.

Before the echo of his twin killing shots had died, James leaned back slightly in his saddle, snaked his right-hand Griswold across his chest, and fired from beneath his left arm.

The Griswold went *plam!*

The stringbean's own slug curled the air in front of James's nose before thudding into a fence post beyond him. James's .36 ball drilled through the stringbean's right side, shattering a rib before tearing through his heart and exiting his body from beneath his right arm, blowing his shirt seam out.

James's next slug plowed through the underside of the stringbean's chin as the lanky soldier, screaming shrilly, flew up and back toward the trail's opposite side. The slug tore through the man's skull, and exiting the crown of his head as he hit the ground, it streaked the trail beyond him with brains and blood.

The tangle-bearded kid lay jerking and gurgling.

James spied movement in the periphery of his vision, and curveted the chestnut rabicano, raising and aiming both smoking Griswolds straight out in front of him. A rifle boomed. James jerked, looking around quickly, half expecting the slug to tear him off the chestnut's back.

He heard a gasp and a soft grunt, saw a man in blue uniform pants, suspenders, threadbare undershirt, and dark blue kepi step out from behind a hickory about forty yards off the trail to James's left. He was short and scar-faced, eyes set close together. His lips were stretched back from his teeth, and he dropped the carbine in his hands as he fell to both knees.

Blood oozed from between his lips. It pumped from a hole in his chest.

He rasped, "Shit!" and fell forward on his face in the mud.

Keeping the Griswolds raised, James looked up the slight, muddy grade toward the farm, where he spied a potbellied, gray-clad figure in a gray sombrero rise to one knee. The man had a round, ruddy, patch-bearded face beneath the sombrero, the front brim of which was pinned to the crown. A big pistol hung by a cord around his neck. He held a Spencer rifle in his hands, cartridge bandoliers crisscrossed on his chest.

James shook his head as Sergeant Crosseye Reeves stood, brushed a fist across his nose, then turned away and sauntered back toward the farm. He walked in his bandy-legged gait around behind what remained of the barn, then came out a minute later, trotting his gray mule down the grade toward James. The banjo he'd always carried behind his cavalry saddle was still there, tied to his blanket roll.

Crosseye closed his crossed eye and looked from James to the dead oldster lying off the far side of the trail. "Damn Yankee, horse-thievin' sons o' bitches." He looked up at James. "How you, Jimmy?"

"What're you doin' here, you damn fool?"

"Someone's gotta back your play." Crosseye's face swelled and flushed. "You obviously can't do it your own self. If I hadn't trailed you from Seven Oaks, you'd be where he is 'bout now!"

James frowned, shocked and indignant. "You followed me all the way from home?"

"Hell, I followed you from the cave—you an' Willie! Didn't let on 'cause I know you'd make a fuss. But, shit, Jimmy—the war's over. And . . . after Willie . . . an' you headin' off . . . Bless me, Jimmy, my heart just ain't in it no more."

The big, bandy-legged oldster paused. Shouldering his rifle, he said, "I stopped by Seven Oaks just when you was ridin' out. Mordecai told me about the watch. You takin' it to Vienna McAllister out West."

Mordecai had been James's father's personal attendant for years, and James had been surprised to find the liveried black man still at Seven Oaks, tending the elder Dunn though he was no longer a slave.

James stared at Crosseye, unable to wrap his mind around the fact that the old hillbilly had followed him as far as he had. But then, hadn't it been Crosseye who'd taught him, James, everything he knew? Maybe the old mountain man still had more to teach him.

He said halfheartedly, "You best go on back to your farm, old man."

Crosseye looked off, scratching the back of his head. "Well, now, I was thinkin' I might just stay there. But you see, Jimmy, there's nothin' left. Nah, hell, them Yankees burned me out. All I could find of any use was a couple bottles of mash I'd hid in tree hollows, and this nice new Spencer fifty-six some federal soldier left lyin' atop his smelly carcass." He chuckled, cast his red-rimmed eyes at James. "I figure I'll try my luck out West. With you. Figured you'd try to turn me back, so I wasn't fixin' to show myself till you was across the Mississippi."

James stared at him. Then he looked at the dead man who'd been about to drill him with a Sharps carbine. James sighed, felt a burn of chagrin. "Well, it's good you showed yourself when you did. Damn, how'd I miss him?"

"I reckon you got your mind on other things."

"I reckon I do." James looked at Crosseye again. The old man was stout and puffy, and his clothes were dirty and torn. But James would be damned if those old blue eyes didn't exude the toughness and spirit that had once been his homeland. Despite Crosseye's having duped him, James was glad he was here.

James looked at the big, French-made pistol hanging down Crosseye's stout chest, over his cartridge bandoliers studded with .56-caliber cartridges. "You got ammo for that Lefaucheux?" It fired a pin-fire, twelve-millimeter cartridge that was hard to find.

"All I'll need less'n I live to a hundred," Crosseye said, hooking a thumb at the worn saddlebags draped over his mule's back. He ran a hand across the Leech & Rigdon revolver he wore for the cross draw on his left hip. "And I got this trusty ole iron for if the La-fa-choowey runs out. You figure we're gonna need a lot of ammo when we get West, do you?"

"I don't know. Injuns out there. If the stories are true, owl-hoots of every stripe run wild clear to the Pacific Ocean."

Crosseye's eyes brightened eagerly, and he nodded. "I heard tell." He poked a worn, mule-eared boot into his saddle stirrup and heaved himself with a grunt onto the mule's back. "I hear it's a prime place for a new start, Jimmy. You know my cousin Cooter once said the gold just screams to be plucked out of the creeks!" He swiped a gloved hand across his mouth and scratched his beard. "Maybe after you deliver that watch, we could fill us a couple o' croker sacks full . . . ?"

James smiled at his old friend. "Why not?"

They booted their mounts into spanking trots westward.

Chapter 6

As James traveled west across the Mississippi with his old friend and mentor, Crosseye, holing up nights in river or creek bottoms or on the open prairie, James's last parting view of his father's swollen, angry face as Alexander Dunn had waved the Confederate sword over the balustrade at him, threatening to eviscerate him with it, haunted his sole surviving son no end.

The vision didn't begin to recede until they had left Omaha, Nebraska, and the vast West opened before them like a giant's open palm stubbled with sage and wiry brown grass and yucca plants. Instantly, James felt lighter. This was a new and different world, one for the most part untouched by the War Between the States. Maybe Crosseye had been right, and this would indeed be a prime place to make a new start.

Construction of the First Transcontinental Railroad had been stymied by the war, so they traveled via horseback along the Platte River to Julesburg and then by way of a well-worn freight and stage road to Denver City, an old trading settlement and boomtown situated at the confluence of the South Platte River and Cherry

Creek, its mud-brick shacks and false-fronted business establishments scattered willy-nilly amongst the rolling sage coulees. The ragged-topped Front Range of the Rockies loomed about fifteen miles to the west, and both James and Crosseye had trouble taking their astonished gazes off such towering peaks, the highest of which, they learned from a liveryman, was called Mount Rosalie.

Denver City couldn't seem to make up its mind if it was a ranch-supply town or a prospectors' camp, as it was as rife with cowpunchers and the wafting odor of cow shit as it teemed with bearded, owl-eyed gents in canvas hats and the hobnailed boots of the miner, who pushed handcarts or rode in heavy-wheeled wagons pulled by braying mules. Whoever the treeless, dusty settlement belonged to, it was hopping, as there seemed to be a whorehouse or watering hole on every street, with more about a mile away in another mining camp called Auraria.

James and Crosseye were taken by the openness and the rollicking free-spiritedness of the region, not to mention the jaw-dropping majesty of the nearby mountains. But James was soon frustrated by his seeming inability to find out anything about the family of his brother's sweetheart, Vienna McAllister.

He spoke to bankers and business owners of every stripe as well as to several deputy town marshals, but no one claimed to have ever heard of Ichabod McAllister, the uncle whom Vienna had been sent to live with. There were several large, moneyed-looking houses up a side road off the town's east end, a neighborhood to which the McAllisters likely would have gravitated. James knocked on several doors only to be met with suspicious frowns and resolute head shakes. He wasn't sure what had evoked such an evil-eyed reception—his untrimmed beard, his smoke-stained vest and trousers, or all the dust that Denver's streets coated him with daily.

Probably, he decided, a combination of each.

So he paid an extra nickel for a bath—in used water—at the rat-infested hotel that he and Crosseye were flopping at, and headed out once more, Willie's gold watch in his pocket. He'd learn the whereabouts of Vienna McAllister if it was the last thing he did. He owed Willie that much. Maybe, once he delivered the watch, he could finally bury Willie for good.

Night had fallen on the third day of his and Crosseye's stay in Denver. The Front Range was a jagged-topped, black-velvety line against the western horizon. The sky was periwinkle blue over the mountains, velvety black directly over Denver. Piano and guitar music emanated from a half dozen saloons as James made his way to a little, cheap café, where he was to meet Crosseye. As he crossed an alley mouth, boots crunched in the darkness to his right.

James stopped, closed his hand over the wooden grips of the Confederate pistol holstered on his right hip, and turned to see a tall man with an eye patch step out of the alley. He was bearded, wearing a denim jacket and a blue neckerchief, his eyes set close. Working a stove match between his lips, he stopped in front of James and gave a half smile.

"A man'll be havin' a word, with you, mate," he said in a heavy English accent.

James frowned. "Who on God's green earth could . . . ?"

He let his voice trail off as he heard someone come up behind him. Just as he began to turn his head, something hard smacked into his skull just over his left ear. Both ears shrieked. His knees turned to hot water.

A warm black wave washed over him, and he was out before he hit the ground. His next sensory impression was that of someone hammering a chisel through his skull. Again and again they rapped the chisel with a hammer as though trying to work through the bone to his brain.

"Goddamnit," he heard himself groan. "Give it a break!"

He opened his eyes and lifted his head. He couldn't lift it far. His hands were tied behind him. He rolled to one side to ease the pressure on his shoulders.

Tobacco smoke wafted over him. Through the smoke he saw the one-eyed man sitting just beyond him. He looked around. No one was hammering a chisel into his head. He and the one-eyed man were in the back of a buckboard wagon. The banging had been the rough wooden floor of the wagon smacking against his head as they bounced along a rough, rutted trail.

"We'll stop when we get to where we're goin', mate," the man with the eye patch said, then took another pull off his loosely rolled cigarette. He sat with his back against the tailgate, one knee drawn up, the elbow of the arm he was smoking with resting atop the knee.

Another sharp pain seared James's head, and he lowered his chin, wincing. When the pain receded, he glanced behind him and up, where two men were sitting on the wagon's high seat, their backs to him. The man to the right of the driver was looking at James. It was too dark for James to see much about him except that he had a thick gray beard and a hawk nose, and he appeared to be smiling. He was holding a rifle, and a pistol was holstered on his left side, for the cross draw, the grips angling toward the hawk-nosed gent's right hand.

No easy reach for James even if his hands had been free. The hawk-nosed man must have been reading his mind, because his beard spread wider and a white line of teeth shone between his lips.

Propped on one arm, James turned to the man with the eye patch reclining against the tailgate. "What's this all about?"

"Shut up."

"Naturally, I'd be curious."

"Shut up," the man with the eye patch said again, with more menace.

James looked around the wagon. They were out in the country somewhere. The vast velvety line of the mountains loomed large ahead of the wagon, so they were somewhere between Denver City and the Front Range.

A few cabins with stock pens or corrals slouched in the sagebrush. It was rough country—rougher than it had appeared from Denver, where it looked as though a relatively level, dun-colored bench rose toward the base of the mountains. But the young Confederate saw now that it was more rugged than that, with low, rocky bluffs rising here and there. Just now they were descending a steep grade toward what appeared a brushy creek bottom.

James vaguely wondered if, when reaching the bottom of the creek bed, he could leap out of the wagon and into the brush before these gents could blow his lungs out.

This time it appeared to be the man with the eye patch who was reading his mind. "Don't do nothin' stupid, bucko."

James looked at him. He had a blank expression. The wagon turned, and the angling starlight glittered off a long barrel resting across the man with the eye patch's thigh. The rifle had a brass receiver and no fore-stock, a loading tube beneath the barrel. A sixteen-shot Henry like the one James had found on the bridge over Snake Creek Gap. Its oiled finish glistened.

Such a weapon would likely be useful out here in the rugged West. But the barrel of this one was aimed at his belly.

"Reckon you're not out to rob me or you'd have taken more than my guns." He felt his brother's watch in the left side pocket of his buckskin vest, and his few coins in a pocket of his pants.

He hadn't been carrying his Enfield carbine when they'd ambushed him, but his holsters and shell belt, with his twin Griswolds, were looped over the one-eyed man's left shoulder.

"Shut up," was the one-eyed man's only reply.

James decided he was probably a Yankee sympathizer. Only Yankees would pull such a cowardly stunt—smacking a man over the head with a pistol butt from behind, tossing him into a wagon unconscious, and tying him so he couldn't defend himself. Raw fury stoked a fire in James's chest; he pulled hard against the rope binding his wrists to no avail. The rope only cut into his skin.

The wagon rocked and jounced across the creek bottom and climbed the hill beyond it. After another fifteen minutes of pitching and swaying and bouncing over rocks, James saw lights slide up along both sides of the trail. The lights were lit cabin windows. The cabins appeared to be positioned along both sides of a creek that flashed darkly between them in the amazingly clear light of the stars.

The faint strains of a distant fiddle gave James his first pangs of homesickness. It passed quickly as the wagon pulled up to a long, low shack of adobe bricks.

The roof of the shack was shake-shingled. It had a broad front porch, and the porch roof was covered in brush. The place looked old and run-down, bricks crumbling, holes in the roof, a shutter hanging askew from a front window. Smoke unfurled from a broad brick chimney on the shack's near end.

A bull's horned skull had been nailed to a front post, and from around the long, massive horns—longhorn horns, James knew, as he'd seen the breed of cow corralled throughout Denver City—hung a sign that read in dry-dripped painted red letters—NO INJUNS OR HALF-BREEDS. NO SPITTIN, NO SHOOTIN, NO CUTTIN ON WHORES.

No sign said as much, but it must have been a saloon. Maybe also a stage relay station, as there were a big barn and several corrals on the far side of the yard. James had been a little surprised by how many such establishments west of the Mississippi didn't bother identifying themselves, as though their functions were obvious or widely enough known that painted signs would only be a waste of materials.

The wagon stopped. James heard the wooden brake shoes slide over the left front wheel. The man with the eye patch heaved himself to his feet, the Henry in his left hand generally aimed at James. The man stepped over the tailgate and leaped to the ground with a grunt and a thud of his boots in the well-churned dust of the yard.

When he lowered the tailgate, he said, "Climb on out of there, now. Don't try nothin' ill-behaved, all right, friend? Hate to kill a fellow Southern boy." He gave a half smile as he backed away from the tailgate. He loudly worked the Henry's cocking lever, ramming a live round in the chamber. "Forrest's Rapscallion, least of all."

James stared at him, puzzled. So, despite the English accent, he was from the South. And he knew him.

"Oh, I didn't recognize you," the man with the eye patch said. "But someone surely did. Someone, most like, who wore Yankee blue when you were all decked out in the Rebel gray, causin' all heaps of trouble for them federal boys. Come on out of there, now. A man like you shouldn't die out here, like this, no reason at all. What a pity that'd be."

James stared at him, apprehension raking cold fingers up and down his spine.

"Ain't gonna tell you again, though," said the man with the eye patch, as the driver and the hawk-nosed man cocked and aimed their own carbines, both maws centered on James. "Let's go in and see who knows you way out here in the West."

Chapter 7

James rolled onto his belly, got his knees beneath him, and climbed painfully to his feet. He leaped off the end of the wagon and into the yard. The man with the eye patch tossed his head at the cabin. The smoke unfurling from the brick chimney smelled of juniper and piñon. Warm, welcoming smells on a chill Colorado eve.

The cabin itself and the three men around James, holding guns on him, were less welcoming.

James winced again as pain hammered his tender head, then mounted the porch steps. A black cat meowed shrilly as it leaped from atop a barrel left of the batwing doors, hit the floor with a soft thump, and dashed off along the base of the saloon and around the far corner.

A black cat, to boot? Shit, James thought. Was this the end of the trail?

He pushed through the batwings and stopped, both doors propped against him. His feet felt like lead, not from any injury but because something told him that once he crossed the threshold, he'd likely only cross it again carried feet first. A rifle butt rammed his back, sent him stumbling forward and into the saloon, his boots thudding loudly.

In the periphery of his vision, he saw the hawk-nosed man moving to within a few feet of him, turning his rifle back around. Before he could get the barrel aimed directly at James again, James wheeled, lowered his head, bounded off his boot heels, and rammed his head and shoulders into the hawk-nosed man's chest. The man tripped his Spencer repeater's trigger, and the bullet sailed off across the room, evoking a shout from someone inside the main room.

The hawk-nosed man hit the floor with a *bang* on his back, cursing. James had no idea what he was trying to do; it was his instinct to fight honed after three years of bloody war. But the man with the eye patch and the man who'd driven the wagon—a beefy bulldog with a scrunched-up face beneath a green canvas hat—stood before him, the driver extending a Sharps carbine straight out from his right hip. The man with the eye patch had his cocked Henry aimed directly at James's right eye from two feet away. His own good eye smiled, the corner twitching faintly over the sleek rifle's cocked hammer.

"Now, what was the goddamn meaning of *that*?" asked a man somewhere behind James. He had a booming, slightly English-accented voice.

Breathing hard, the old fighting fury seething in him despite his previous resolve to live and let live, James turned back around to face the inside of the room. Three more men stood before him, about twenty feet away. Between the two on the right, James could see a fourth man sitting at a broad, round table with a bottle and a shot glass. One of the three, the one on the far left, near a long bar running down along that side of the room, was holding a gloved hand over his right ear. Blood oozed between his fingers. He scowled, gritting his teeth.

Apparently the spent bullet had found a target.

Two of the three were holding pistols on James. The one holding his ear aimed a sawed-off shotgun at him, straight out from his left shoulder. A leather lanyard hung free beneath the nasty-looking two-bore, both the rabbit-ear hammers of which were drawn back to full-cock.

"Melvin, put the blaster down," said the man sitting at the table. He canted his head to see through the trio before him. "I didn't have him brought out here so you could blow a wagon-sized hole in him." He rolled his gaze to James. "I ask you, Lieutenant—what good did that do you? My men are well trained, and they shoot to kill. Your hands are tied behind your back. How far do you think you could have gotten?" He shook his head in bemused disgust. "Isn't that just like the South, though? Determined to keep fighting against even the steepest odds."

James hardened his jaws. "Who the hell are you? How do you know me?"

The man jerked his head, beckoning. James glanced behind him. The hawk-nosed man stood, sneering, holding his Sharps up high across his chest, the other two flanking him, blocking the door. James looked ahead of him. The man with the burned ear had set his shotgun atop the bar and was now, while keeping an eye on

James, pouring whiskey from a bottle into one hand and then cupping that hand to his ear, sucking a sharp, painful breath, showing his teeth, tears shining in his eyes.

The other two stood holding their guns on James, who moved forward. The two stepped away from each other, opening a clear path to the table. The only sound in the room was the snapping of the fire in the broad hearth to James's right, and the thud of his boots on the worn, wooden floor. James kicked out a chair as he scowled down at the man sitting on the far side of it, who wore a gray Confederate greatcoat, with a gray kepi on the table before him, near the whiskey bottle and shot glass. The insignias of a captain adorned his shoulders. One was badly frayed. There was a tear in the side of his coat in the shape of a Minié ball.

He was a tall, gaunt, pale man. Hollow-cheeked, hollowed-eyed, the eyes themselves a washed-out blue. A sickly yellow waterfall mustache fell over his lips, nearly covering his mouth. Thin hair of the same faded-straw color hung straight down to his shoulders. The man's name floated up out of the battlefield smoke of James's past.

"Stenck."

The yellow-haired man who resembled nothing so much as a putrefying skeleton with eyes smiled, showing one gold eyetooth, dimpling his papery cheeks. His face managed to cling to a shadow of handsomeness. At one time, he'd probably been dashing.

Captain Richard Stenck looked at James with open admiration. "Forrest's Rapscallion."

"What the hell are you doing here? The war's still on."

"I might ask you the same thing."

The tips of James's ears warmed. He had no cause for self-righteousness, and that burned him further. Still, he couldn't help adding, "I didn't run from Napoleon's cannons and musket fire."

That was the story of why Stenck, who'd never been much of a leader in the first place, had deserted the Confederacy, just up and disappearing during some especially bloody fighting in Louisiana—him and ten men from his company, some of whom were likely standing around James now. James thought he might have recognized a couple of the faces, though not well enough to put names to—all, no doubt, Texans, as was Stenck, though the captain was from there by way of Scotland, where it was said he'd come from royalty and great wealth, though the bloodline had thinned considerably and the wealth had nearly run out. That's why he and several brothers had been sent to Texas to run a cattle ranch and freighting company before the start of the war.

One of the men behind James said, "Want me to pop him over the head for that, Captain?"

"No, no, no," Stenck said. "He was just getting a gibe in. What would you expect from one of Nate's Raiders?" Stenck smiled again with a combination of flattery and faint jeering, then changed the subject. "One of my compatriots and co-owner of the Overland Stage Company told me a gentleman with a Southern accent, likely a Tennessee hillbilly, had inquired about one Mr. Ichabod McAllister. Then I saw you myself in the Holy Smokes Saloon. We'd met, if you remember, in Richmond before the war."

"I remember." James and his father had been selling cotton to overseas buyers in Richmond when Stenck and one of his brothers had tried hawking interests in their freighting company to Alexander Dunn and several other businessmen from Virginia and Carolina. James's father, who had no interest in Western speculation, had summarily refused, later telling James he trusted no one who showed red eyes before noon.

"And I couldn't help wondering," Stenck continued, "why Forrest's Rapscallion was inquiring about Mc-Allister. Then I remembered that the McAllister plantation wasn't far from your own Seven Oaks, was it?" He arched a pewter brow. "Or . . . is it still there?"

"Far as I know."

"Why were you inquiring about McAllister?" Stenck asked without further ado, putting a businesslike crispness into his voice.

"I don't see how that's any of your affair."

Stenck laughed, showing his little teeth including the gold eyetooth. He leaned forward on the table, swabbing his piss yellow, waterfall mustache with two fingers, then wrapping his pale hands around his shot glass. He looked at James from beneath his brows, his eyes startlingly dead-looking. "You know I'll kill you if you don't tell me."

"Sure must be important."

"Oh, not really. I just don't like being insulted by the likes of a backwoods roarer. That's all you Dunns are, all you'll ever be, what's left of you after the war."

"Now you're insultin' me, Stenck." James hardened his eyes, damned if he'd tell the man what he wanted to know until he knew why Stenck was asking.

"I'm going to do more than insult you if you don't tell me why you were asking about McAllister."

James stared at him, sat back in his chair, and loosed a sigh of feigned resignation. He would have been happy to tell Stenck what he wanted to know, but he was leery of tipping his own hand. Something was very amiss, and it had him worried about Vienna.

"His brother had a message for him, that's all," he lied. "All's well back home. That's it. Now, if you could point me in his direction, I'll just go relay the message and find me another saloon. That tanglefoot looks mighty tasty, but it don't look like you're gonna offer me none." He clucked with false reproof. "Where're your Texas manners, Captain?"

"You're going to sit there and tell me you left the war, abandoned your beloved Confederacy, to tell McAllister that all is well back home?"

"Hell, yeah. For all intents and purposes, the War's really over, Stenck. Didn't you hear?"

Stenck stared at him in mute fury.

"What about McAllister's niece—know where she is, do ya?" asked the man with the bullet-grazed ear from the bar, his voice pitched with shrill impatience.

James jerked a look at him, but before he could respond, Stenck glared at him. "Shut up, Lieutenant!"

The lieutenant with the shredded ear turned away like a scolded dog. James turned back to Stenck, those cold fingers of apprehension beginning to rake him again, though not for himself this time, but for Vienna McAllister. What could that beautiful, black-haired, gray-eyed Southern belle and apple of his brother's eye have to do with these Texas vermin?

"Why, no," he said slowly, studying Stenck closely. "I wouldn't know anything about his niece." He cleared his throat, thinking fast. "Uh . . . what niece would that be?"

Stenck's face hardened. It looked like a death mask. Only his lips moved when he said tightly, "Take him out and shoot him. Haul him away and throw him in a deep ravine. Leave him to the coyotes."

Boots thudded behind James.

"All right, all right," he said, knowing he was at the edge of the proverbial cliff. "You called my bluff. I don't have a message for McAllister. The message is for his niece, Vienna, in the form of a watch." He glanced at the man with the eye patch behind him, now standing about ten feet away.

"Ah," Stenck said, nodding, sucking his upper lip. "I see. An innocent delivery of a watch."

"There you have it. Now, if you could tell me where she might be, I'll be runnin' along. As you know, I've inquired everywhere in Denver City, but no one even seems to know the McAllister name."

Stenck studied James closely for a time, tapping a finger on the rim of his shot glass. Finally, he picked the glass up delicately between thumb and index finger, and threw back half of it. He smacked his lips and set the glass down on the table.

He ran the back of his hand across his mustache, smacked his lips again, and looked once more at James from beneath his brows. "I don't believe you, Lieutenant. You're here for something more. You are Forrest's Rapscallion, after all. You're here to see McAllister on behalf of the Confederacy. And, since it has become clear I'm going to get nothing of any value out of you . . ."

He rolled his eyes up to the men now standing in a semicircle around James.

"Wait a goddamn minute!" James barked, frustration churning in him. "I just told you the truth. Where's the McAllister family, and where is Vienna? What the hell's goin' on here, Stenck?"

Stenck arched both brows, pursed his lips. "Let's just say, for the sake of argument, that I do believe your story, Lieutenant, as far-fetched as it is." He chuckled. "Forrest's Rapscallion leaving the war to deliver a watch!" He cackled.

James felt his nostrils flare at the captain's words and mocking laughter.

"If your story is true, Lieutenant, you haven't left the war as far behind as you thought."

Stenck glanced at the men behind James. "For the last time—take him out and shoot him!"

Two men each grabbed one of James's arms, hauled him to his feet, and half led and half dragged him toward the door. "Won't hurt a bit," said the man with the eye patch. "One bullet through the back of your head, and you'll be hearin' 'Dixie'!"

He and the others laughed.

Chapter 8

As Stenck's men led James through the batwings and onto the front stoop, James gathered himself for an imminent move. He was badly outnumbered, hands tied, so he'd most likely die, but he'd be damned if he wouldn't do some damage before he set sail for Glory. The man with the eye patch rammed his Henry's butt hard against James's back, and he stumbled down the steps and into the yard.

He was about to turn and lift a vicious kick to an unprotected groin, but stopped, staring straight ahead of him. The three men behind him must have seen it, too—the thin shadow of a man sitting a horse a little ways out from the parked wagon. All three froze, one giving an incredulous wheeze. There was another horse behind the rider's horse, and just as James recognized his chestnut rabicano in the silvery darkness, a familiar voice said, *"Down, Jimmy!"*

James dropped to his knees in the dirt, and ducked his head. A gun flashed and roared atop the lead horse before him. It roared two more times, the echoes of the blasts dwindling and falling beneath the groans of the riflemen now twisting and dropping behind James.

James recognized the shrill report of Crosseye's Lefaucheux, and grinned. "You crazy catamount!"

"Haul your skinny ass over here, ye shaver!" Crosseye's horse, a big Western-bred roan he'd traded his mule for, curveted.

James lifted his head and squared his shoulders, working against his tied hands as he heaved himself to his feet with a grunt. Hearing men yelling in the saloon behind him and the others continuing to groan and gurgle where they'd fallen, two on the stoop, the man with the eye patch on the steps, James ran over to Crosseye and swung around. The old frontiersman leaned down, and James felt the tugging of the knife blade sawing through the rope binding his wrists.

"Let's go!" the older man rasped when the cut rope dropped.

"I'm right behind you!" James bolted forward and grabbed his cartridge belt and holstered Griswolds off the steps, where the one-eyed man had dropped them. He also grabbed the sleek Henry repeater before sprinting over to his chestnut that pranced in place, reins dangling.

Crosseye swung his big roan around to face the direction from which he'd come, the lights of Denver winking dully across the black sloping plain, then stopped once more behind James's chestnut. His Lefaucheux roared, flames lapping from the barrel, the twelve-millimeter slugs plunking into the front of the saloon, one on either side of the batwings, sending another of Stenck's men wheeling back through the doors with a yelp.

"Let's go, Jimmy!" Crosseye screeched as James hurled himself into the saddle from the off-side.

The chestnut whinnied shrilly and buck-kicked as James swung it around, then ground his cavalry heels into the horse's flanks. With another whinny, the chestnut leaped off its rear hooves and flew off in the direction of Crosseye's jostling shadow, hooves thudding loudly on the hard-packed trail.

Beneath the rataplan James could hear Stenck's shrill voice shouting orders. The captain from Texas would not let him go without more of a fight, he knew. Stenck had brought him there to kill him, to keep him from continuing to ask around about the McAllisters, and he'd try his damnedest to accomplish the task. Stenck might have run from one war, but this one was just his size. James had to assume he had more gun hands than the small number he'd seen tonight.

James crouched low over his chestnut's buffeting mane as the horse galloped down a gradual grade, following the trail that was a curving pale line in the darkness. Crosseye was about thirty yards ahead, starlight glinting off his hat with its turned-up front brim, and off his saddlebags flapping like small wings. They dropped down into the brush-bottomed canyon, and Crosseye stopped his horse, curveting the blowing, prancing mount.

"How'd you find me?" James asked the old frontiersman.

"I saw the whole thing from the flophouse window, but by the time I got down to the street, they was rolling you off in that wagon. So I went and saddled our hosses and shadowed you." Crosseye spat, and chaw

splashed on a rock beside the trail. He wiped his fur-
covered chin with the heel of his hand. "Who were
them polecats, Jimmy?"

James glanced along their back trail, sensing more
trouble galloping toward them. "Later!" He booted the
chestnut on past Crosseye, clacking across the rocks of
the dry creek bed, then starting up the opposite slope.

He galloped about a quarter mile back the way he'd
come in the wagon, then turned the chestnut off the
trail's south side and into the sagebrush. A low, rocky
escarpment humped darkly ahead of him. When he
reached it, he swung down from the chestnut's back.

Crosseye galloped up behind him, then checked
down the roan, the horse's eyes flashing wildly as it
chomped its silver bit. "How bad's their tails twisted,
Jimmy?"

"You mean do I think they're comin'? Uh-huh!"
James left his cartridge belt and .36's hanging from his
saddle horn and raised the Henry, running an appre-
ciative hand down the long barrel. "Leastways, I'm
hopin' they are." He looked up at Crosseye as he
worked the Henry's cocking lever, racking a cartridge
into the chamber and absently enjoying the smooth,
solid sound of the sixteen-shooter's action. "And when
they do, I want one of 'em kept alive."

"Just one?"

"Yeah, one'll do."

James led the chestnut around to the far side of the
scarp, tied it to a piñon branch, then climbed the rocks,
moving quietly, carefully in the darkness. A cool breeze
blew, rasping amongst the brush growing out from
between the jutting rocks, and a coyote howled—an

eerie sound to a Southern man who'd only recently started hearing such forlorn cries.

James found a niche at the top of the scarp, from which he had a good view of the trail, and hunkered down, doffing his gray kepi. Wheezing, Crosseye climbed up behind him and settled down beside him. James could smell the familiar, reassuring fragrance of the older man's sweat, buckskin breeches, and chewing tobacco. Crosseye was breathing hard, but James knew the oldster could keep up with him in a long, hard climb, because he'd seen him do it at Kennesaw Mountain. His potbellied old carcass and broad, fleshy face with its scraggly beard sheathed the heart of a true Southern renegade.

Neither man said anything for over a minute. Then Crosseye, hearing the loudening thuds of oncoming riders, whispered, "Bushwhack 'em?"

"Hell, yes."

Crosseye gave him a skeptical look.

"I didn't ask for this fight," James bit out.

They waited. James stared up the trail curving down a grade to the west. Finally, three riders appeared strung out in a shaggy, single-file line dropping down the slope as they hunkered low in their saddles, wary of just what James and his partner were intending. James extended the Henry over the top of the rock and sighted down the barrel.

The lead rider jerked his horse hard left and angled into the brush up-trail from James and Crosseye's position, shouting, "Ambush!"

James cursed and eased the tension on his trigger finger. Starlight must have flashed off his rifle barrel. "These Texans are smarter than they look!"

The other two riders swerved into the desert, all three swinging wide of the scarp, trying to get around behind James and Crosseye. Lights flashed amidst their jouncing silhouettes as they cut loose with pistols. The bullets plunked into the rocks around James, who opened up with the Henry just as he had that night on the bridge, shooting and levering, shooting and levering, the beautiful piece leaping and roaring in his hands. He watched his targets tumble off their mounts, the horses whinnying and rearing and galloping straight west of the scarp— all three riderless and trailing their reins.

James glanced to his right at Crosseye. The oldster hadn't fired a shot. He shrugged and looked at the smoking Henry. "What the hell you need me for when you got that sixteener?"

"Play your cards right, maybe I'll steal you one someday."

"If you run into any extra jingle, you can buy me a woman." Crosseye raked in a breath and brushed a fist across his chin. "Ain't had me one now in weeks and my rocks is gettin' heavy!"

"Shut up, you old hound dog!"

Keeping his head down, James stared west of the escarpment, where the three riders had fallen. He couldn't see them amongst the widely scattered shrubs and rocks, but he could hear one groaning softly. "Looks like I mighta left one alive. Stay here and cover me."

"Hell, my old eyes can't see shit out there!"

"Give it a try!"

James dropped to the gravelly ground. Holding his new rifle straight out from his right hip, and keeping the darkness of the scarp behind him, he began walking out in the direction his quarry had fallen. He found the first man about forty yards out—the would-be killer's neck twisted awkwardly, obviously broken, glassy eyes staring at his bloody hand flung out beside him.

On one knee, James looked around. The groaning he'd heard from atop the scarp had fallen silent. He hoped the wounded man hadn't died. He wanted one alive to tell him what the hell was going on with Stenck and the McAllisters. Doubtless, Stenck wasn't one of the three out here. He was likely still tucked safely away in the saloon with his whiskey bottle. He'd leave the fighting to his inferiors.

Raking his tongue across dry lips, James continued forward, swinging his head from left to right and back again, scouring the dark ground with his eyes. There was a raspy sigh to his left. He swung his head that way, saw starlight glint on steel. He threw himself to his right. The pistol flashed. The bullet screeched through the air where James had been standing a moment before, and *spanged* off a rock, echoing. James rolled onto his elbows and fired the Henry three times quickly.

He heard two slugs kicking up gravel. A third made the telltale *whomping* sound. He'd found flesh.

Slowly, looking around for the third rider, James gained his feet.

Crosseye's voice cut the night: "Behind ya, Jimmy!"

James wheeled. A figure lurched out from the shadow of a giant boulder. James tried to get the barrel of the Henry up too late. A knife flashed starlight as it careened in a downward arc toward his throat.

Chapter 9

James dropped the Henry, then reached up to grab the wrist wielding the knife, stopping the blade eight inches from his neck. He glanced past the blade, saw the face of the man who'd gotten his ear burned in the roadhouse. James threw himself backward, hitting the ground hard, then, still holding the knife wrist, kicked his legs up.

The cutthroat flew over his head, ripping his knife hand out of James's own grasp.

Both men gained their feet instantly. The man with the knife lunged for James again. He was heavy and slow. Again, James grabbed his wrist, wheeled him around until the man's back was grinding into the side of the giant boulder he'd hidden behind. The knife was between them. James had hold of the man's wrist with both his hands. He stared into the man's dark eyes as, grunting, he got the knife turned. The upturned tip slid through the man's calico shirt.

The man's mouth widened. His eyes turned to brass in the darkness.

James gave another hard, grunting thrust and shoved

the blade into the man's chest, just beneath his breast-bone. Out of long-practiced habit, he lowered the blade and twisted. All the air seemed to leave the man's lungs at once as the blood washed out over James's hands—hot as tar. James stared into the man's dark eyes.

Willie stared back at him, gasping.

James stepped back with a start and turned quickly away from the dying man, burying his face in his fore-arm as though to rub the memory away. When he turned again to the cutthroat, the man's chin dropped to his chest, and his knees buckled. He groaned and dropped to the dirt like a fifty-pound sack of cracked corn.

The ground heaved around James. He stumbled off in the brush, his guts churning. He fell to his knees. His insides contracted, convulsed, and the contents of his stomach erupted into his throat and shot out of his mouth, hot and sour, splattering onto a sage shrub be-fore him.

Footsteps sounded from the direction of the scarp. He looked up and saw the bulky shadow of Crosseye moving toward him, holding his Spencer repeater across the bandoliers on his chest. The wily old fron-tiersman's big, gaudy pistol dangled from its rawhide cord around the man's bull neck.

James blinked to clear his vision of Willie gasping for life as James had pulled his knife out of his broth-er's chest. He ran a sleeve across his mouth, squeezed his eyes closed.

Crosseye stopped and looked around. "Thought you wanted one of 'em alive."

"I thought you couldn't see shit out here."

Crosseye dropped to a knee before James, put a hand on the younger man's shoulder. "All right?"

James gained his feet, hacked phlegm from his throat, and spat into the brush. His hands were trembling. Cold sweat covered his body beneath the linsey shirt, buckskin vest, and twill trousers. He glanced around at the dead men. Again, he saw Willie, and another wave of revulsion rushed over him, threatening to buckle his knees.

He fought it off.

He wiped the blood off his hands on the dead man's pants, then picked up the Henry, ran a hand down the still-warm barrel, removing the dirt and sand. It was a beautiful weapon, but he would have left it here if he thought he'd no longer need it, if he'd no longer be forced to use it. But it didn't look as if that was going to be true. He'd left one war only to be thrown into another.

Part of him wanted to ride back up the trail and see if he could run down Richard Stenck and find out what had happened to Vienna McAllister. But the most desperate part of him, the part that had killed Willie and had run from the war with his tail between his legs, just wanted to get back to town, to wash the blood off his clothes, and get some whiskey in his belly. He'd deal with Stenck later, in the light of day.

He shouldered the Henry and began walking back toward the scarp and the horses.

"You gonna tell me what all this is about?" Crosseye said behind him.

James only threw an arm up, beckoning his old

partner. He didn't answer the question until later, after they'd ridden back to town and stabled their horses in the same livery barn in which they'd stabled them before, and headed on back to the seedy hotel they were flopping at. There was a small saloon area in a side shed off the drafty, two-story frame building's right side.

Tonight, a weeknight, the saloon was occupied by two weary-looking whiskey drummers in shabby suits playing a desultory game of cards. A young Mexican whore, half-naked but with a frayed red blanket draped over her shoulders, sat near the room's sheet-iron stove, rolling craps die from a shot glass and muttering to herself as though to some ghostly opponent. The owner of the hotel, whose name was Burleson, was reading a yellowed newspaper atop the bar that ran along the room's far wall from the entrance, yawning frequently and loudly as though he wanted everyone in town to know how bored he was.

James and Crosseye sat at a small table near the entrance to the main part of the hotel, a whiskey bottle between them. James threw back the first shot quickly, then refilled his glass while Crosseye looked at him from the other side of the small, round, wobbly table, both his thick hands wrapped around his whiskey glass. His hat was pushed back off his age-spotted forehead, showing a large mole just over his bushy right brow.

James told his old partner the whole story of Stenck's interrogation in a few short sentences and then threw the second shot back and splashed out another one. He held the bottle up in front of Crosseye, glanced at the frontiersman's untouched glass that looked little larger than a sewing thimble sitting between his meaty hands with their cracked, yellow, shell-like nails.

"You savin' that for some special occasion?" James asked him.

Crosseye stared at him. Then he lifted the shot, threw it back, and set the glass back down on the table. James refilled it, set the bottle down, and leaned back in his chair.

"Hosses," Crosseye said.

James looked at him. "You wanna chew that up a little finer and spit it out slower?"

"I'm thinkin' we oughta get our Rebel asses down to Texas and start us a horse ranch. I hear there's all kinds of wild-assed Spanish-blooded broncs runnin' loco-wild along the San Felipe, in the Big Bend country. My cousin, Roy Handy, went down there years ago, and he ain't been seen since. I'm thinkin' the bastard got rich and didn't tell me!"

Crosseye's steady eye shone while the other seemed to be staring at the bulbous end of his nose.

James leaned over the table. "What the hell does that have to do with what I just told you?"

The barman, Burleson, yawned loudly as he leaned over the bar, slowly turning a page of his crinkly yellow newspaper.

"It has everything in the world to do with what you just told me, Jimmy. There's trouble here. We're fish out of water. What do we know about the West? Now, I say we haul our Reb asses the hell out of here tomorrow, pronto, and fog the trail to Texas and see if we can't find ole cousin Roy, finagle our way into his hoss ranchin' operation, and hole up from the whole rest of the world. Might even get rich. . . ."

James blinked at his old partner, incredulous. "You think I'm gonna let this slide? Stenck tried to trim my wick tonight. And what about Vienna McAllister?"

Crosseye sipped his shot delicately, then sucked the end of his soup-strainer mustache. "You done tried to find her, and all you found was trouble in the person of that Captain Stenck. Likely, if you stay here, you'll run into him again . . . and more trouble. Trouble's your way, Jimmy, and I'd like to help steer you clear of it."

Humor sparked in his good eye. He sipped his drink again, delicately, and scrubbed his mustache with his grimy shirtsleeve. "If the McAllisters was here, someone woulda heard of 'em. If they were ever here, they musta moved on. The war's jumbled everything up everywhere—you know that, Jimmy."

Burleson slapped the bar suddenly. It sounded like a pistol shot in the close confines, making the Mexican whore jerk her head up from her game with a gasp. Both James and Crosseye stiffened and dropped their hands to their sidearms.

"Damn, I almost forgot!" the barman said, looking at James.

James and Crosseye scowled at the fat barman as he plucked a folded slip of paper off a shelf behind the bar and on the left side of a dusty, sashed window staring darkly out on the night. "Someone left this here message for you earlier this evenin'," the man said, walking around behind the bar and dropping the folded paper on the table in front of James.

James stared at the note on which "For the Man

Inquiring About the McAllister Family of Denver" had been flowingly written in blue-black ink. "Who did?"

"Don't know. I just found it sittin' here on the bar when I come back from the privy. That'd be you, ain't it?"

James picked up the note. Burleson shrugged and walked back around the bar to his waiting newspaper. The whore rattled her die in her shot glass and tossed it onto her table. James opened the note, slowly unfolded it until he was looking at a small sheet of lined tablet paper, which read "See Mustang Mary at the Ace of Spades."

The note wasn't signed.

"What's it say?" Crosseye asked.

James told him. Burleson must have overheard. The barman gave a snort.

James looked at him. "You know Mustang Mary, do ya?"

"Heard of her," said the barman. "Never seen her. Not too many folks venture over to the Ace of Spades uninvited. It's on the far end of Auraria—Red Mangham's place."

James just looked at the man, as did Crosseye.

"What?" said the barman. "You don't know Red Mangham?"

The whore looked up from her dice, brown eyes wide between the thick wings of her chocolate curls.

"Red runs the Ace of Spades out on the Comanche Creek Trail. Caters to . . . a certain breed of hombre, if you get my drift. Few not of this certain breed venture over there unless they want their . . ." Burleson ran his index finger across his throat.

The whore hissed, clucked her disapproval of the

Ace of Spades, then returned to her game, still shaking her head.

"Outlaw lair," Crosseye said distastefully. "I'm too damn old for tanglin' with outlaws. Yankees was one thing."

"As long as I've known you, you've been too old," James reminded him.

"That's 'cause I've been old a long time. Older'n my years, and I'm gettin' older every day!" Crosseye wagged his head. "Steer around it, Jimmy."

James rose and looked at Burleson. "How do I get out to this Ace of Spades?"

Crosseye groaned.

Burleson looked at James skeptically. "You ain't gonna go out there, are ya, son? Most likely you're bein' led into a trap."

"I'm gettin' used to it."

Burleson sighed. "Head on over the creek to Auraria, and follow the main trail out of town to a fork. Take the right tine in the fork. Ace of Spades sits along Comanche Creek, a little line of bluffs behind it. Pay up before you go, though, will ya? If you're goin' out there, you prob'ly won't be comin' back again."

"Texas mustangs, I tell ya!" Crosseye said, leaning across the table.

James shoved a hand into a pocket of his buckskin vest.

"No point in goin' tonight, though," the barman said. "Red's only open on the weekends." He added grimly, "He and his pards are otherwise employed most nights durin' the week, ridin' the long coulees from here down to New Mexico an' back."

The whore clucked her disapproval once more and tossed her dice.

James sighed and slacked back into his chair. He poured himself another shot and threw it back.

"Why don't you take Estella upstairs?" the barman said. "I'll let you have her for an hour if you split me some more wood tomorrow. Don't look like I'm gonna be gettin' no more business tonight, anyways."

James had been splitting wood for the man in exchange for a discount on the room he shared with Crosseye, while Crosseye ran sundry other errands. They were low on funds and needed to find a steady supply soon.

James looked at the whore. She looked up at him expectantly. She wasn't bad looking as whores went out here—he didn't think she was much over twenty when most of the percentage girls he'd seen looked a hard forty—but his heart wasn't in it. He looked down at the blood staining his buckskin vest, shirt, and slacks.

"She'll wash that out for you, too," the barman said.

Crosseye threw the last of his drink back. "Ah, go ahead," the oldster said with a quick wave of his arm. "Help clear your head. She's too skinny fer me. I'd snap her like a stove match!"

James thought it over. The whore continued to stare at him, the corners of her mouth curved upward. She'd let the blanket around her shoulders fall open, revealing her threadbare chemise. Beneath the table, her slender, olive-colored right foot rested atop the other.

"Why not?" James stood, tossed a couple of coins onto the bar, and grabbed the bottle off the table.

"Hey, leave an old man his whiskey, you scalawag!"

"Buy your own," James raked out, taking the whore by the hand and leading her to the back of the room and up the creaky stairs to the second story.

"I saved your life tonight, ya ungrateful pup!" the oldster yelled behind him.

Chapter 10

James put the chestnut up the bank of the creek and drew back on the reins. He stared ahead toward a dark line of hills rising against the starry sky. At the base of the hills, the Ace of Spades Saloon sat amongst widely scattered cottonwoods, its windows lit against the night.

James had heard raucous sounds emanating from the place even before he'd taken the right tine where the trail forked half a mile out of Auraria. It had sounded like a wild Appalachian hoedown primed with corn liquor and stitched with fisticuffs and leg wrestling, and from this distance of a quarter mile, it sounded even wilder.

He touched heels to the chestnut's flanks and started ahead. He'd ridden only a few yards when he jerked back on the reins again and reached for the rifle in his saddle boot. He left the gun in its sheath.

A figure sat along the trail to his right, leaning back against a tree as though taking a nap. But the man had taken his last nap a long time ago, it appeared. A feather-fletched arrow protruded from his chest—or what remained of his chest after years of putrefaction. The man was a skeleton clothed in tattered duck trousers and work shirt and badly worn boots. The skeleton wore no hat, and the bleached skull was sickly pale, eye sockets twin pools of deep shadow in the light of a crescent moon. No doubt the poor jake had been found in a cave around here, maybe where he'd gone to die after being chased down by Indians, and someone had hauled him out near the trail, to welcome guests to Red Mangham's outlaw lair, the Ace of Spades.

The smile on the skeleton's face coupled with the sounds of raucous revelry emanating from the roadhouse caused snakes of apprehension to slither up James's long legs. Of course, whoever had left the note could be leading him into a trap, but it didn't stand to reason. Why lead him into a bushwhacking when they could have taken Stenck's more direct approach?

Crosseye had volunteered to ride along and watch the younger man's back, but James thought he had a better chance of riding unharassed into Mangham's den of curly wolves and finding Mustang Mary if he came alone.

Touching spurs to the chestnut, he continued ahead along the trail that curved gently toward the right. There were several corrals in the brush on both sides of the trail, but they were as bleached as the dead man's bones, and looked dilapidated. Obviously, Mangham's place had been a ranch at one time; there were more outbuildings off to the right, including a chicken coop and a large hay barn.

As James continued forward, he saw two more grisly indications that the place was a benign ranching operation no longer, for two men hung like fresh laundry from a cottonwood off the trail's left side, where it entered the yard. These weren't skeletons, for they still had hair on their heads. One had long black hair parted on one side. The other looked far too young to have come to such a grisly, premature end. Both men swung lazily from the ends of their ropes, hands tied behind their backs. The black-haired man had kicked a boot off, showing a pale sock. The holsters on both men's shell belts were empty.

James couldn't tell much more about the pair in the darkness, but they appeared to have been hanging there only a day or two, for they didn't seem swollen.

As the chestnut's hooves clomped slowly, James looked at the main, tall building growing before him. A large wooden sign over the long front stoop announced in large black letters ACE OF SPADES, with black spades abutting each end. "Red Mangham" had been written above the black letters in red. The building was a three-story, rambling, stone-and-wood affair from which the shouting and yelling grew louder amidst the rowdy strains of what sounded like a three-piece band and a woman singing loudly and vigorously—a woman with a good voice, ever so slightly touched with the rolling vowels and petal-soft consonants of the South.

The beat was being kept by someone banging a kettle, and by the crowd itself stomping their boots or clapping their hands. The windows upstairs and downstairs were all lit, and shadows moved in them. More shadows moved on the broad front porch, several hatted figures sitting atop the cottonwood pole rails. They were all smoking or drinking, the coals of their cigarettes or cigars glowing faintly in the darkness.

Saddled horses were packed nearly stirrup-to-stirrup against the hitch racks fronting the stoop, and more horses stood in a corral off to the right of the tavern, beyond a windmill whose blades spun slowly, nudged gently back and forth by changes in the breeze.

James walked his horse up to the corral, dismounted, and tied the reins around one of the pole rails, glancing warily toward the porch, a little puzzled that no one had contested his presence. If Burleson was right, and the Ace of Spades was indeed a hotbed of outlaw passions, it seemed doubtful that strangers would be welcome.

James resisted the urge to slide the Henry out of its saddle boot. Deciding that his Griswolds would have to do if he was turned away in a hail of lead, he adjusted the belt and pistols on his lean hips and strolled with feigned ease past the horses and up the squawky wooden steps of the porch.

Several men glanced at him, eyes narrowed with incredulity, but no one tried to stop him as he crossed the porch through a heavy cloud of tobacco smoke and the fetor of man sweat, horses, and leather and strode through the door that was propped open to the cool night air with a rock.

Inside were at least a dozen men sitting or standing in a semicircle around the band at the back of the long, low-ceilinged room lit by flickering oil lamps. Most of the crowd had their backs to James, and most were stomping or clapping to the beat of the band, the woman still singing though she'd moved onto another song. Most of the men were too interested in the comely young singer to pay much attention to James, though he was aware of several hard, unshaven faces scowling at him through the wafting smoke.

To a man, they were well armed with pistols as well as knives, and there were several rifles leaning against walls or square-hewn ceiling support posts. They likely weren't accustomed to trouble from outsiders here, as most enemies probably respected the boundaries and legends of such a place, but they were ready for it if it came.

One man stuck out of the crowd. Sitting on the bar planks on the room's right side, he was a middle-aged gent in a red serape and a broad-brimmed black sombrero trimmed with silver conchos. He was a white man, though he was also dressed in the fancily stitched deerskin slacks of a Mexican vaquero—*charro* slacks, James believed they were called. Over the serape he wore crisscrossed cartridge bandoliers over his chest, and two big pistols jutted from holsters attached to the bandoliers. Two horn-handled Green River knives were sheathed low on his thighs.

He was a hawk-faced man with blue eyes and long copper-red hair dancing against his shoulders as he laughed and whistled and clapped his hands in rhythm to the boisterous music. James felt his attention riveted on this man who emitted an almost palpable raw savagery—a wild brutishness that James had seen in wounded wildcats, but rarely in men even in the deepest Smoky Mountain hollows. That this was the proprietor of the Ace of Spades, and the leader of the cutthroats gathered here, couldn't have been more obvious had Mangham worn his name on a sign around his neck.

James raked his fascinated gaze away from the red-haired gent to scrutinize the room. He couldn't see much of the singer, but he could tell through the smoke that she was fine-featured, with coal black hair, in a light, peach-colored frock that left most of her milky torso bare above her breasts, her slight shoulders straight and smooth as delicately chiseled marble. A peach-colored choker, trimmed with an ivory cameo, encircled her neck. She was dancing, lightly stomping her slippered feet as she clapped her hands and sang, her lush raven hair flying around her face and shoulders, holding every male in the room enthralled.

She was singing an old Irish drinking song in a bewitching Southern accent that recalled for the young man from Tennessee balmy nights out on the big veranda at Seven Oaks, a band playing, young men and ladies waltzing and laughing, punch glasses clinking together, the air as intoxicating as blackberry brandy.

There were several other women in the place, James saw—a couple of brunettes, a blonde, and two or three Mexicans, perhaps one with Indian blood. Unable to determine which could be Mustang Mary, he decided to risk inquiring with the man standing to his right.

The man turned toward him, looking slightly annoyed. His dark, drink-bleary eyes raked James up and down, and then he turned his head forward, eyes indicating the singer.

The banjo and the fiddle fell silent as James slid his gaze to the front of the room and found himself gazing into the eyes of the black-haired singer, who was no longer singing but was staring at him across the crowded room. She had gray eyes. James hadn't seen her eyes before now, and so abrupt and shocking was his recognition that they were like twin sledgehammers slammed against his chest.

The man sitting on an overturned crate behind her stopped banging a wooden spoon against the bottom of the kettle he was holding, and looked curiously up at the girl, who continued to stare across the room at James.

He felt his lower jaw sag. He was glad he wasn't holding a drink, because he would have dropped it. His heart picked up its rhythm, and his palms grew hot.

By threes and fours, all the men in the room stopped stomping and clapping and yelling. Puzzled murmurs rose. Then all heads began swiveling toward James, until every man and woman in the room had followed the girl's gaze to the tall, dark-haired stranger, the men regarding him incredulously, angrily.

The man with the long red hair falling down from the silver-trimmed black sombrero glared at James as well, his hawkish face reddening as he said, "What for the love o' Christ . . . ?"

In the near silence, James heard himself rasp, *"Mustang Mary?"* He must have said it louder than he thought he had, because all at once, the beautiful young belle he'd known as Vienna McAllister turned away from him as though she'd been slapped across the face. Her ivory cheeks were touched with rose. A staircase climbed along the wall to her right. She made for it, grabbed the newel post at the bottom, then swung back around, her suddenly sorrowful gray eyes again seeking James out of the milling crowd.

"No," she said, shaking her head slowly. Even from

his position at the front of the room, he could see the shine of the tears in her eyes. "No," she said. "James, no!"

Red Mangham leaped down off the plank bar and closed his hands around the wooden handles of the pistols holstered low on his chest. He said nothing as he pushed through the crowd toward James. The long, slanted eyes set close against his long, hooked nose were shiny with wrath, lips pursed inside his red goatee and mustache.

Continuing to push toward James, he barked, "Mister, you just bought yourself a stretched neck and a wooden overcoat!" His voice was strangely high-pitched, almost girlish.

"Red, no!" Vienna cried.

She bolted away from the stairs and sidestepped through the crowd, pushing men out of her way—bearded, sun-leathered men who stood broad and sturdy as oaks in contrast to her small, pale, supple form. She approached James and looked at Mangham, placing a hand on his arm.

"No, Red, please," she said, her voice trembling. She slid her eyes almost reluctantly to James. "This . . . this is my . . . my brother. I fear . . . he's brought news from home."

James held her frightened gaze. Of course, she knew why he was here. What else but news of Willie's death could have brought him to her? But she didn't know it all, and the dread of telling her was more potent than the threat he felt of all the obvious killers now surrounding him and pummeling him with their dark, belligerent gazes, infuriated by the interruption in their revelry.

Mangham stared suspiciously at James, his nose working like some separate living thing on his face. "Brother? You sure about that, Mary?"

"Don't look like her brother," said a short, stocky man in a shabby bowler hat, sneering.

"Shut up!" Mangham shouted. "If Mary says he's her brother, he's her brother!"

The short, stocky gent in the bowler hat took one step backward.

"I'd like to speak to my brother in private, Red," Vienna said softly, gray eyes staring up at James.

Red snorted and scowled skeptically at the stranger, then jerked his head toward the stairs. "All right, I reckon. Since he's your brother an' all." As the girl began leading James through the crowd by his hand, Mangham grabbed James's other arm. "Don't be upset-tin' Mary, now, ya hear?"

James glanced at the man without expression, pulled his arm free, and followed Vienna through the crowd, feeling angry looks being hurled at him like razor-edged bowie knives.

As the murmurs of discontent rose behind and below him, he followed the long-legged, high-busted, raven-haired beauty up the stairs, wondering how in hell the beautiful young Southern belle he knew as Vienna McAllister had turned up here, half-naked and singing bawdy songs in this nest of human rattle-snakes, going by the name of Mustang Mary. . . .

Chapter 11

James moved up the stairs more slowly than Vienna, aka "Mustang Mary," for he turned around a couple of times to make sure no bowie or Green River knives were being hurled at him. When he gained the second-story hall, which was lit by a single bracket lamp beside a faded oil painting of a naked woman on a settee, James headed for an open door on the left. He went inside, doffed his kepi, and held it against his chest.

Vienna sat on the small room's rumpled double bed strewn with clothes of both sexes. A long duster hung from a peg on the wall. A pair of faded denims hung over it from the same hook. A fire glowed in a little monkey stove in the far corner, a stack of dead branches beside it. The room smelled of burning piñon, man sweat, perfume, and talcum. She looked up at him, long ivory legs crossed, one slippered foot hooked behind the other, wringing her hands together. Her gray eyes glinted worriedly. "It's Willie. . . ."

"Yes."

She sucked a sharp breath through her nose, pursing

her lips. Her face paled, and she turned her head to one side. "How?"

He sighed. It was mixed with a groan.

She looked at him, eyes widening a little with surprise.

James saw a chair in the corner to his left. He walked over, slacked into it, the dry wood creaking under his weight. His heart thudded heavily with the sorrow that lived in him, but even to his own ears his voice sounded dull, toneless, without any hint of emotion. "It was a dark night. Georgia. My outfit was trying to blow a bridge. Willie was there."

She stared at him, her lips opening slightly now, eyes skeptical, dreadful.

"I killed him," James said. "It was me, Vienna."

Her eyes widened as they bored into his.

"It's a long story, but I killed my brother in the darkness of Snake Creek Gap. Didn't know it was Willie until . . ." James let his voice trail off, drew a long breath. "He lived for half a night, wanted me to give you this."

He reached into the pocket of his buckskin tunic and extended to her the gold watch with the long chain of gold Confederate coins and the gold-washed fob at the end of it. She reached out and took it, drew it to her, and flipped the lid. Instantly, the tears came, and she sobbed, clutching the watch to her chest. She closed her eyes, lowered her head, and cried quietly for several minutes.

James felt heavy and weak. He sat back in his chair, knees spread, and listened to her. It felt like a penance he was paying, reliving over and over again the look in

Willie's eye when he'd withdrawn the knife from his brother's chest, and the blood had come, washing like red oil into the dark creek.

She wiped the tears from her cheeks and looked at him with anguished eyes. "I'm so sorry, James."

He hadn't expected such a reaction, and suddenly tears washed over his own eyes, and he leaned forward with a single sob, resting his elbows on his knees and lowering his head as though in prayer. Distantly, through the screeching in his own head, he heard bedsprings squawk, saw her crouch over him, run a hand through his long hair before wrapping that arm around his neck and drawing his head against hers. He let himself go then, and she did, too, both of them sobbing together, convulsing with shared sorrow.

Finally, she collapsed at his feet, drawing her legs beneath her, and rested her forearm across his knee. "That goddamn war! Is it over?"

James, a little taken aback by the language she'd picked up after heading west, shook his head.

The skin above the bridge of her nose wrinkled as he studied her. He didn't want to answer the unspoken question. He laid his hand against her smooth cheek, damp from her crying, and slid his thumb across her rich lips, remembering how he'd kissed her once, a long time ago, before Willie had won her heart with his music and poetry and passion for nearly everything under the sun, including politics.

James had been the true woodsman—the taciturn loner. Willie had been a lover. Remembering that now, he took his hand away from his brother's wife's face, and the question he'd suppressed for a time resurfaced: "What are you doing here, Vienna? Amongst these cutthroats?"

She lowered her head, cradling the watch in her hands. "That's a long story, James."

"What of your uncle?"

"He's dead. So is Aunt Elise and my cousin Kate." Vienna's voice hardened. "All killed . . . by Richard Stenck."

"Stenck?" James paused, wrapping his mind around the name. "*Stenck?*"

Vienna touched two fingers to her lips, then rose, walked over to the open door, and looked cautiously up and down the hall. Apparently finding no one lingering around her room, she closed the door quietly, then dropped to her knees before James once more and looked up at him from beneath her thin, chocolate-colored brows. Her eyes were hard and angry. "Stenck and my uncle Ichabod were in business together. The business of railroad speculation. But they needed money, so they decided to go down to Mexico and bring back a treasure that my uncle had heard about from a reliable source. Only, Stenck killed Uncle Ichabod for the treasure map."

James shook his head, puzzled. "Treasure maps . . . Mexico . . . ? That still doesn't explain what you're doing here."

"Stenck knows, or at least figures, I saw the killings in the McAllister House on Sherman Avenue in Denver City."

"I was on Sherman Avenue, and no one I talked to owned up to knowing the McAllisters!"

"That's because they're afraid of Stenck . . . just as they're afraid of my new *benefactor,* Red Mangham. The whole town—half of the territory—is afraid of Red and Stenck." She shook her head, causing her hair to slide across her bare shoulders. "Two outlaw gangs rule Denver City and all of eastern Colorado Territory. Stenck's . . ." She glanced cautiously at the closed door, then whispered, "And Red's. Red's an uncouth tyrant, born and bred here. Stenck comes from supposedly good breeding, but they're both equally dangerous . . . if you get on their wrong side."

"And Red is hiding you from Stenck?"

Vienna nodded.

"What about"—James looked at the gold watch in Vienna's small, pale hands—"the boy?"

A stricken look came to her eyes. She drew a hard breath and placed a hand on James's knee, gave it an urgent squeeze. "James, can you get me out of here?" She licked her lips and squeezed his knee again, anxiously. "Tonight?"

James could hear the low, menacing hum of conversation downstairs. There must have been twenty men down there.

"Tonight?" he said.

She squeezed his thigh. "James, please!"

James moved slowly down the stairs, raking his hand along the gray wooden rail. The three-piece band was playing where they'd been playing before, but almost none of the two dozen men in the room appeared to be paying much attention. They were all clumped around in the room haphazardly furnished with all manner of furniture from settees to horsehide sofas, upholstered chairs, and plain hide-bottom chairs arranged around scarred wooden tables such as one would find in any watering hole anywhere in the country. They were playing cards or conversing or roughhousing like boys on a schoolyard, but bleary-eyed and ragged-voiced from drink.

Red Mangham sat on the end of one of the room's two sofas, against the far wall. He was smoking a cigar while the man beside him sat with the Indian girl clad in a skimpy hide dress on his knee. Mangham had a tall, black, silver-tipped boot hiked on his own knee, and he looked dubiously toward James descending the stairs.

As James neared the first floor, Mangham rose from the couch and sauntered toward him, puffing the cigar in one corner of his mouth. The other conversations in the room grew quieter, and men swiveled their heads toward Mangham as he scowled at James and said, "You really Mary's brother?"

"That's right," James said as he stepped down onto the saloon hall floor.

He continued on past Mangham, who grabbed his arm as he had before, and said, "Was up there awhile."

"We haven't seen each other for a time. The war an' all."

"What news did you bring?"

"Ask her."

James pulled free of the man's grip.

"Hey!" Mangham said.

"I'm back," Vienna said, coming down the stairs, looking fresh after she'd composed herself, washed her face, and brushed her hair. She smiled broadly at Mangham, who'd turned his head toward her. "Let's get this party started again!"

A roar rose in the room. Men clapped and hollered, and the band member with the kettle beat it with a spoon. The banjo and fiddle lifted a jubilant albeit slightly off-key rhythm. With all attention now firmly focused on Vienna, James strode across the room and out the front door, where there were still four or five men smoking and milling on the stoop. They regarded him owlishly through the wafting smoke. He pinched his hat brim to them as he headed on down the steps, walked over to his horse, and stepped into the saddle.

He booted the chestnut into a spanking trot as he headed out of the yard, following the trail back in the direction of Auraria. When he'd ridden a hundred yards and was out of view from the Ace of Spades, he swung the chestnut into the brush on the trail's south side. He stepped down from the saddle, tied the horse to a branch, loosened its belly straps, and slipped its bit from its teeth.

According to his and Vienna's plan, he'd be here awhile.

He sat down opposite the side of the tree on which he'd tied his horse. He stretched out his long legs, crossed his ankles, and tipped his hat brim down over his eyes.

He could hear the music and Vienna's rollicking singing beneath the general roar emanating from the outlaw lair. She was a damn good actress. Her heart was broken and she was likely still stunned by the news of Willie's death, but she wanted so badly to get away from Red Mangham that she was putting on a good show for him and his men, assuaging any suspicions that James's appearance might have evoked.

He sat there against the tree, half listening, half dozing, for a long time. He himself was still stunned to have learned that "Mustang Mary" was Willie's sweetheart, and that she was singing in a roadhouse owned by a notorious desperado. Still, he had more questions so far than answers. Vienna had promised to tell him more, and about hers and Willie's child, but first James had to get her out of the place without getting them both killed.

He was wishing now he'd brought Crosseye along. The old frontiersman was probably pie-eyed in some whorehouse, sparking the fattest percentage gal he could find. James smiled at that, enjoying the momentary distraction from all the confusion, then closed his eyes and let himself doze. Occasionally he looked up to see the stars above the pale bluffs, the constellations switching positions, the moon arcing westward over Denver behind him.

Coyotes called. At one point, something sniffed and snorted in the brush off to James's right. He tossed a branch and heard the mewling of what he figured to be a bobcat—a creature he'd heard about but had so far not seen.

The West was a far different place from the Southeast. He had much to learn about the native flora and fauna, as well as its human inhabitants, most of whom seemed to hail from all corners of not only this country but Europe, Mexico, and South America, as well. It was rare to run into someone who didn't speak with a thick foreign brogue.

He dozed again. When he lifted his chin from his

chest and pushed his hat back up on his head, he looked around, listening. The night was darker, the moon having set, and, save for the breeze scratching the cottonwood leaves together, and the hooting of a distant owl, there was only silence.

Vienna had said that Mangham's killers didn't usually turn in on the weekends until after two a.m. It must have been after two now. James got up and moved around, getting his blood flowing. He milled in the trees with his dozing horse for another half an hour, giving Mangham's men plenty of time to drift off into drunken stupors.

He slipped the bit back into the chestnut's mouth, tightened the latigo straps on the horse's Texas-style saddle, and mounted up. He rode back through the trees, across the trail, and into the brush on the other side of it before swinging right and booting the horse toward the roadhouse.

Vienna had told him that Mangham rarely posted pickets around the roadhouse, as the law in and around Denver had learned to give the gang a wide berth. Mangham's natural enemy was his outlaw rival Stenck, but the two cutthroats had what Vienna had learned was an unspoken truce, leaving each outlaw captain's gang to do as it pleased as long as they didn't encroach on each other's territory.

She'd also told him that not all the men in the saloon belonged to Mangham's gang. The Ace of Spades opened its doors to several other gangs in the area— gangs with strong allegiances to Mangham, of course. Red made an excellent side living by providing them with liquor and women.

James felt he hadn't aroused too much suspicion, but he'd take no chances on being spied from the road-house. He kept to the brush wide of the trail, meandering around sage and buck brush clumps, the tang of the weeds rising on the chill air, the horse's shod hooves thudding softly. When he saw the murky silhouettes of the buildings ahead and on his right, he stopped the chestnut and swung down from the saddle.

He tied the horse to a gnarled piñon and slid the Henry from its sheath. Quietly, he levered a shell into the chamber, set the hammer to off-cock, and began walking quickly ahead, holding the rifle down low by his side. He moved carefully around the brush, so the stems of the sage shrubs wouldn't rake across his trouser legs and possibly give him away.

A low building grew ahead of him. It sat hunched on the north side of the yard, about fifty yards from the roadhouse. He continued around the squat, shake-shingled log structure and crept along its far wall before stopping at the front corner and dropping to one knee. He stared at the Ace of Spades, dark and forbiddingly silent in the deep night. Not even a glimmer of light shone in any of the windows. The horses had been put away for the night.

James waited there on one knee, pressing his right shoulder against the low building's rough wood. He heard the rush of blood in his ears. This stealing into enemy territory under cover of darkness reminded him all too much of the war, his several bloody forays behind the federal lines. He'd found himself living for the excitement of those missions, each one of which could have been his last.

How keen all of his senses had been then. How alive he'd felt.

Now he just wanted to get Vienna away from here, to somehow get her back safely to her family in Tennessee, if they were still there, that is, and if Rose Hill was still standing.

He waited, tense.

Inside the saloon, a girl screamed loudly, shrilly.

A man bellowed.

"No!" the girl cried.

A gun thundered.

Chapter 12

James jerked forward with a start, heart leaping in his chest, and began pounding toward the roadhouse.

He stopped suddenly. Inside, men were yelling, the shouts echoing woodenly. Boots hammered the floor.

He heard the wooden scrape and hinge squawk of the front door opening, saw a dark figure fly out onto the stoop, mewling and groaning. The figure dropped and then rose weakly, sobbing, and staggered forward, stumbling wildly down the porch steps and into the yard.

More boots pounded the stoop, and James, stepping back against the low outbuilding he'd been hunkered beside, hoping its shadow concealed him, saw another figure move out of the roadhouse and across the porch. The shadow, taller than the first, stopped at the top of the porch steps. Starlight glinted off steel as the second man extended a gun in front of him.

"I told you Lil was mine, McSween!" he shouted.

The other man ran, crouched forward, head hanging, dragging his boot toes, straight across the yard toward the windmill. He shouted something incoherent to James's ears, and continued running. James could hear breath rasping in and out of the wounded man's lungs in the night that had otherwise been as quiet as a held breath.

James jerked when the gun of the man on the porch flashed, a knifelike blade of red flame leaping from the barrel. The gun's thunder was like a thunderclap echoing off the dilapidated buildings surrounding the yard. Muffled whinnies rose from the horses in the barn.

For a moment, James thought the shooter had missed his mark. The man in the yard continued running toward the windmill. Only, his stride broke, slowed, but he kept moving until he stood at the edge of the stock tank for a full minute before his knees buckled and he tilted forward. His head and shoulders hit the dark water inside the tank with a muffled splash. The water rippled silvery in the starlight.

The wounded man remained bent forward over the side of the stock tank, sort of hanging there, the gurgling of the water dying gradually.

"Goddamnit—what'd I tell you about shootin' inside the premises?" another man shouted inside the roadhouse. "Was you born in a goddamn barn, Alvin?" Red Mangham's high-pitched voice owned a nasty, nasally, Yankee twang.

"Shit, I told McSween to leave Lilly alone twice tonight!" retorted the man on the porch as he lowered his pistol and walked back into the roadhouse, his voice muffled now as he continued with "I done told him if I had to tell him a third time, my smoke wagon would say it *fer* me!"

James dropped to a knee, his eyes raking the road-house that was filled now with the thudding of a single pair of angry boots. A shadow moved to the rear of the place. Starlight caught on something light and shiny—a straw sombrero. Then James saw the slender figure moving toward him, heard the soft tread of running feet. He couldn't see much more than the girl's shadow, but instinct told him it was Vienna.

He rose, hissed, "This way!" Then stepped back against the hovel once more, hidden by its inky shadow.

The figure swerved slightly, came toward him. In seconds, she knelt beside him, breathing hard beneath the low-crowned sombrero, the chin thong of which dangled against her chest. Her figure was lithe and curvy beneath a red-and-white-striped serape, which crawled down her sleek legs to her thighs clad in black denim trousers. Her hair was pulled back in a pony-tail. Vienna held a croker sack over her shoulder by its neck tied with twine.

"Been waiting long?" she asked, looking anxiously around her.

"No, but I figured that shot was meant for you."

"Not yet." She canted her head toward where the dead man hung half in and half out of the stock tank. "That sorta thing happens all the time. I've got so it doesn't even wake me up anymore. But in case you didn't hear, Red's up. I heard him clomping up the stairs when I slipped out the back door."

"That means he'll know . . ." James wasn't sure how to finish that.

Vienna wasn't near as squeamish about it. "He'll know he's bunking alone in about fifteen seconds."

"Let's go!"

James took her hand and ran back along the side of the building and around behind it. He figured Red wouldn't start to suspect that Vienna had flown the coop for at least five minutes. First, he'd think maybe she'd gone to the privy, or maybe to fetch wood for the stove in their room, as it was a cool night.

Still, James ran crouching through the sage. He released Vienna's hand when he saw that she was managing to keep up with him. What sounded like coins jingled in the sack—a good many of them. Glancing back at her, he flashed briefly on how he remembered her dressing back at Rose Hill or at dances at Seven Oaks—usually in cream taffeta and lace, her raven hair brushed to shining, trimmed with ribbons and hanging in delicate sausage curls along her peach-colored cheeks.

Never in anything like what she was wearing now— well-worn trail clothes of a Western cowpuncher. He wondered where she'd gotten the coins.

James had just spotted his horse about fifty yards ahead when a rifle thundered behind him and Vienna. Vienna gasped, fell, and rolled. The bag dropped, the coins clattering loudly. James wheeled to see the rifle flash once more—red-blue flames lapping toward him. At the same time that the slug tore up a sage shrub two feet to his right, the rifle's bark reached his ears.

"You'll never make it, you double-crossing little whore!" Red Mangham's voice added its echo to the fading echo of the long gun. Then, shrill with desperation: "*Marrrrrryyyyyyyy!*"

James raised the Henry to his shoulder, snapped off three quick shots—*Bam! Bam! Bam!* The heavy, thudding reports sounded like empty barrels rolling down a rocky hillside. The metal cartridge casings clinked to the sand and gravel over James's right shoulder. He'd purchased several boxes from a gun shop in Denver. Through his wafting powder smoke, he saw Mangham's tall shadow run crouching toward the far side of the shack as the *spang* of the last bullet added its scream to the dwindling echo of the blasts.

James wheeled toward Vienna, grabbed her arm. "You hit?"

"No, I just tripped!" She grabbed the croker sack that she'd dropped, and nimbly gained her feet.

James took the sack, so she could move unencumbered. Holding the sack in one hand, the Henry in the other, he continued running through the brush. "Let's go!"

Just then a rifle popped behind him and Vienna once more. A slug blew up dust and gravel well ahead and screeched off a rock. In the heavy silence that followed, James heard Mangham or one of the other cutthroats shout something. The chestnut was dead ahead, prancing and curveting nervously as James and Vienna ran up to it.

James slid his rifle into the saddle boot, then quickly tied the croker sack around the horn. The sack was heavy, the coins bulging through the bottom. Vienna stood behind him, staring back toward the roadhouse, where more and more shouts rose on the quiet night. There was the flash of Mangham's rifle, but the shots were dropping wide; because of the darkness or his own drunkenness, the outlaw leader had lost track of his quarry.

James stepped into the leather and then reached down and took Vienna's hand and swung her up behind him. "Where we going?" she said, a nervous trill in her voice as James ground his heels into the chestnut's flanks.

"Denver City!"

"That's the first place he'll look!"

"No choice—I left Crosseye there!"

"Crosseye?"

James didn't answer, for just then there was an especially loud string of shouted epithets that were quickly drowned by the rataplan of rifle fire—several rifles now fired quickly in the general direction of James and Vienna, though only a few shots kicked up dust and gravel anywhere near the fleeing pair. The chestnut was tearing up the ground in the direction of Denver, putting the cutthroats farther and farther behind them.

James turned left at the fork in the trail, and the dark structures of Auraria began appearing around him, cabins and corrals and privies hunching darkly. Then he rode between the taller business structures sheathing the trail from both sides of the wide trail that had become the town's main street. The chestnut's hooves clomped over the wooden bridge of Cherry Creek, the narrow stream of oily dark water glistening wanly in the starlight between the brushy banks, and then Denver pushed up around James and Vienna, the only sounds a couple of cattle braying from some distant stock corral.

All the houses and business establishments were dark—all, that is, except for one white frame house sitting along the right side of the town's broad main drag.

A window was lit in the house's second story, and from the same window James could hear a man talking drunkenly, slurring his words, while a girl bathed his voice in drunken tittering, as though the man were telling her the funniest story she'd ever heard.

He turned right and followed the north-angling side street for fifty yards. His and Crosseye's hotel sat on the right side of the trail, near where the side street dwindled off into the buck brush and sage of the prairie. The two-story adobe-brick building was dark. So, too, was the livery barn that sat on the opposite side of the street and nearer to James and Vienna by one block.

James turned the horse toward the barn. He'd stable the chestnut before taking Vienna to the hotel. True, Mangham's men would eventually look for them there, but James doubted that he and his men would do much searching tonight, when they were all drunker than peach-orchard hogs. They'd wait for morning to turn the town inside out, and by that time James intended to be gone—him, Crosseye, and Vienna. They'd have to find somewhere else to hole up until James could figure out a way to get Vienna back home to Rose Hill.

In front of the barn, James swung his leg over his saddle horn and leaped to the ground. He walked over to the big double doors and slid the left door open two feet before he saw a bulky figure standing before him, just inside the barn. James stepped back with a startled grunt and snaked his right hand across his belly for one of his cross-draw .36s.

He left the Griswold in its holster when he heard a familiar voice rasp, "Ain't safe here, Jimmy." Crosseye shoved the left door open wider, and then the starlight shone on his bulky, big-bellied frame and broad-nosed face under the pinned-up brim of his gray sombrero.

James's heart thudded. He'd never known a man, even men several inches shorter and a hundred pounds lighter, more furtive than Crosseye Reeves. "God-damnit, what are you doin' sneakin' around out here, you old miscreant?"

Crosseye grabbed the chestnut's reins and led the horse, with Vienna on its back, into the barn. James walked in with the horse. Crosseye quickly drew the door closed, then said softly in the darkness relieved by an oil lamp guttering at the far back of the place, silhouetting ceiling posts and stable partitions and hanging tack in front of it—"Stenck's at the hotel."

Vienna gasped as she swung down from the chestnut's back. "Stenck?"

Crosseye looked at her, frowning befuddledly as he looked her up and down, then, recognizing her, quickly doffed his hat. "Why, Miss Vienna . . . Law!"

"Hello, Mr. Reeves. It's been a while."

"Why, I ain't seen you since you was . . ." Crosseye held out a hand to indicate how tall she'd been when he'd last seen her.

Vienna cut him off with "Did I hear right—Stenck is at your hotel?"

"That's right, Miss Vienna," Crosseye said in the almost somber, faintly beseeching tone with which the mountain folks addressed the landed gentry. "You know Stenck, do you?"

"Only too well."

James peeked out the crack between the closed doors. "How many men does he have with him?"

"I saw ten ride into town."

"Ten, eh?"

"Don't worry—he has more than that. He keeps them spread out all over the place, mostly looking for gold shipments out of the mountains." Vienna looked at James, incredulous. "What's he doing in your hotel?"

"I didn't get time to tell you before," James said, "but I've already had the pleasure of making his acquaintance."

"Him and his men was ridin' up to the hotel about three hours ago, when I was headin' back there after . . ." Crosseye glanced at Vienna, winced, and added haltingly, ". . . After I was done seein' a man about a . . . uh . . . about a business proposition."

"I still don't understand what he's doing at your hotel," Vienna said again, persistently.

"It'd be nice to stand here an' palaver all night," Crosseye said, snugging his hat back down on his head and grabbing the Spencer repeater resting against a square ceiling post, "but we'd best light a shuck. He mighta seen the two of you ride into town."

"Where's your horse?"

"Out back."

"Let's go." James took his reins from Crosseye and followed the older man down the barn's central alley, the horse's hooves clomping on the hard-packed earthen floor. James could hear the livery barn's proprietor snoring off in a side room cloaked in darkness. Vienna hurried along beside James, sort of skip-hopping to keep up, her black ponytail curling forward across her shoulder.

They walked past the lantern hanging from a nail,

and followed Crosseye through the rear double doors and into the paddock beyond. There were several horses out here, and a couple snorted as the trio and the chestnut angled toward the side of the corral before Crosseye opened the gate, and they all moved through it. Crosseye closed the gate, then reached for the reins of his roan tied to one of the corral poles.

"There!" a man shouted.

James had just turned to the chestnut when he spied a shadow running toward him from along behind the dark buildings to the south. A gun flashed and roared. "*Oh!*" Vienna cried, grabbing her upper right arm and stumbling back against the corral.

"Goddamnit!" James rasped, gritting his teeth as he raked a .36 from its holster.

He clicked the hammer back and fired.

Chapter 13

The running man screamed, bent forward, fell, and rolled.

"Nice shootin', Jimmy. Someone taught you good!" Crosseye said, heaving his bulky frame onto his roan's back, the saddle squeaking beneath his girth. "How's Miss Vienna?"

"I'm all right," Vienna said, once more heaving herself to her feet and taking her right hand away from her other arm. "It's just a graze. Mostly tore my poncho."

"You sure?" James asked her quickly, holstering his pistol while holding his jittery horse's reins taut with his other hand.

Vienna nodded. He couldn't see her expression, but he took half a second to notice how unexpectedly tough this former Southern belle had become. Life with Mangham must have been to her what the war had been for James.

"More comin'," he said, stepping into the leather and hearing gravel crunching under running feet somewhere behind the man he'd just dispatched.

He took Vienna's hand and swung her up behind

him. She'd barely gotten seated before he curveted the chestnut and galloped off after Crosseye, who was heading straight out and away from the rear of the livery barn, past a long L-shaped stack of split firewood and a small log cabin attached Southern-style by a dogtrot to a stable.

The cabin door squawked open and an old man in a nightshirt and a night sock on his head looked owlishly out, holding a shotgun in his hands. "What in blue blazes . . . ?"

James hunkered low as the chestnut shot past the old man, then turned the horse right to follow Crosseye along a side street, mostly a two-track wagon trail amongst cottonwoods and frame houses positioned willy-nilly with buggy sheds and privies.

"You know where you're goin'?" James yelled.

"Does it *look* like I know where I'm goin'?" the older man returned.

Half an hour later, well south of Denver City, they slowed their horses and curveted them on the well-worn wagon trail they'd picked up once they crossed Comanche Creek, and followed it through a long, flat stretch of wild grass, sage, and prickly pear. A low, razor-backed ridge paralleled the trail on their left, shaggy with cedars and pines. They'd passed a couple of small ranches hunched in the darkness, but they'd seen no one out and about.

And the few times they'd stopped to check their back trail, they hadn't heard the telltale rumble of approaching riders. Now they continued riding ahead until they came to a dry creek bed. Leaving the tableland, they followed a game trail to the bottom of the ravine, and traveled along its winding course into a low jog of hills about four miles west of the wagon trace.

Their horses were blown out and sweat-lathered, so they set up camp against the ravine's high west wall. Light was beginning to show a wash in the west, beyond the razor-backed ridge. When they'd tended their horses, James went over to where Vienna sat with her back to the bank, arms wrapped around her up-raised knees.

"Let me look at that arm."

"Just tore my poncho's all."

James knelt beside her, touched a hand to her arm. The serape was torn, but it was also wet. She flinched.

"It did more than tear your poncho," he said in a castigating tone, removing his red neckerchief and tying it around the girl's arm, over the graze.

She stared straight ahead. In the faint wash of light, he could see that she had no expression on her pretty, fine-featured face. "How'd you get to be so tough?" he said, knotting the ends of the neckerchief.

"I'm not so tough."

"Tougher'n I remember, all decked out in them frilly dresses, ridin' in that leather buggy, twirling a parasol over your shoulder. You was even afraid of the sun, as I remember."

"*Those* frilly dresses, and you *were* afraid of the sun," she corrected him. "Willie was a better speaker."

"Willie was better at pretty much everything."

"But not better at fighting, I reckon," she said sadly.

James sat back against the bank, raised a knee, and rested his arm across it.

"I'm sorry, James." She slid a comforting hand up and down his upper arm. "I shouldn't have said that. It wasn't you who killed him. It was the war who killed him."

"No." James shook his head. "It was me, all right."

Vienna leaned her head on his shoulder. It seemed as though the weight of her head had joined his guilt, making a weight as heavy as the earth itself.

After a time, James heard footsteps, saw Crosseye's bulky figure moving toward him from the tableland they'd just traversed, holding his Spencer repeater straight down in his right hand.

"Any sign of 'em?" James asked.

"Nah. We might've lost 'em. Best hole up here for a time, though. Rest the horses." Crosseye turned and walked away. "I'll keep an eye out."

When the older man was gone, Vienna stood and, the hem of her long serape billowing around her denim-clad thighs in the breeze, stared over the ravine's bank toward Denver City. "Tell me how you know Stenck."

James told her about his involuntary visit to the man, and about how he'd been about to be shot like a chicken-thieving cur before Crosseye had saved his bacon.

"So he's still looking for me," she said of Stenck. "I'd thought he might be."

"What does he want, Vienna?" James rose to stand before her and placed his hands on her shoulders. "What's been happening out here? You, Mangham, Stenck . . . *Mustang Mary* . . . ?"

Vienna turned away from him and knelt down, untied the neck of her croker sack, rummaged around inside, and pulled out a book. She straightened and walked back over to James, holding up the cloth-bound tome. By starlight, he read the gold-embossed title on the cover—*The Count of Monte Cristo.* "My uncle Ichabod's favorite novel." She opened the book and pulled out a heavy sheet of parchment folded three times lengthwise. She handed the paper to James and set the croker sack and the book down beside her.

James opened the paper, scratched a sulfur-tipped match to life on his thumbnail, and looked it over. It was a crude but fairly detailed map, with simply but clearly sketched mountains, rivers, villages, trails, and canyons. There was a broken line at the top that indicated the border between the Arizona Territory and Mexico. The names labeling the land formations and villages were all in Spanish.

James's eyes briefly took in everything on the map except the box drawn beside a series of irregular triangles indicating mountains. Inside the box were a bell and the almost comical, horned face of a devil. At the bottom right corner of the page, a name was scrawled; it stood out not only because it was printed in bold pencil, whereas the rest of the map had been drawn in blue-black ink, but because of the nickname that preceded it—"Apache Jack" Davis.

"The treasure you mentioned at Mangham's," James said, tossing the match away suddenly when the dying flame nipped his fingers.

"It belonged to Uncle Ichabod." Vienna took the map, sort of waved it in the air for emphasis, her eyes regarding James with gravity. "It's for this map that Stenck killed him and my aunt Elise, cousin Kate, and their Indian housemaid, Verna White Feather."

Vienna swallowed and looked forlornly down at the map in her hands. "Uncle Ichabod couldn't afford a secretary, so I volunteered. This was before the baby came, and I needed something with which to occupy myself, to keep from worrying about Willie and the war at home. I couldn't just lie around in bed."

"You said your uncle was in railroad speculation?"

"He'd been out here since just before the war, trying to buy up land he thought the Union Pacific would eventually purchase for laying their rails on. He'd started in the business with his friend Jefferson Davis."

James looked at her. She nodded. "*That* Jefferson Davis. President of the Confederacy."

James whistled.

"Uncle Ichabod and Mr. Davis had a third partner," she said. "Richard Stenck."

"*Stenck?*"

"They all had been friends and business associates before the war. My uncle and Stenck had ended up out here, trying to raise money with which to buy up land they'd learned would soon be bought by the Northern Pacific Railroad. Of course, the war halted the railroad, and Uncle Ichabod found himself in hard times. He was about to return to the South and take a position in Mr. Davis's cabinet, when he heard from yet another adventurous friend, who was also the stepbrother of Mr. Davis—'Apache Jack' Davis. Apache Jack was the black sheep of the Davis family. He'd left the South many years ago to prospect for gold and to look for hidden treasure in Mexico. That's when he heard the legend of three golden bells, and he set his hat for those bells. Well, according to a letter and a map he sent to my uncle, he'd found the bells a ways from a little village in the Sierra Madre known as Tres Campanas, Three Bells."

Again, James whistled and kneaded his forehead, trying to absorb all facets of the complicated story.

"He wrote to his brother and to my uncle, asking for help in getting the bells out of Mexico. He intended to donate the bells to the Confederacy, to help out with the war effort."

James said, "Did anyone wonder if Apache Jack might have gone a little off his nut?"

"Of course," Vienna said. "But along with the map and a detailed letter to both my father and his brother, Jefferson Davis, he sent each a pound of pure gold, which he said he'd shaved off one of the bells. Uncle Ichabod showed me the gold."

"And you believe it's from one of the bells."

"I have no reason not to believe it. Uncle Ichabod believed it, and so did Mr. Davis. Enough so that Mr. Davis made my father a member of his cabinet, and brevetted him a major general, whose sole duty was to locate and retrieve those three bells and get them to Richmond. They speculated the bells would be worth around a hundred thousand dollars, even more in England where they intended to purchase guns and ammunition, as well as mercenary soldiers.

"Uncle Ichabod managed to fund one trip, but before he could find Apache Jack, he ran into some nasty Apaches of the more authentic, brown-skinned kind and lost four of his seven men. All were hideously tortured. He came home with the intention of raising more money for an armed party . . . and that's where he hitched his star to Richard Stenck."

"What went wrong?"

"Uncle Ichabod was a bit naive, I'm afraid. He didn't realize until they were finally acquiring the men needed to get the gold out of Mexico that Stenck had no intention of taking it to Richmond to help with the Confederate war effort. Stenck wanted it all for himself, to use for buying up every parcel of land he could between Denver and Julesburg, because that's where the Northern Pacific had intended to lay track before the war, and where Stenck still figured they'd lay track *after* the war. Thank God Uncle Ichabod hadn't yet given Stenck a copy of the map."

"So, when Stenck learned Uncle Ichabod wasn't going to give him the map . . ."

"And had no intention of going to Mexico with him . . ."

"Stenck killed him," James said.

"And he would have found the map if I hadn't gotten it first." Vienna shivered as if chilled, gripped her shoulders, staring down at her low-heeled boots. "When I think of that night . . ."

James waited. Crosseye had come over and sat on the other side of the ravine, smoking his Irish pipe, legs crossed at the ankles. His hat rested on his knee, Spencer rifle leaning against the bank to one side. James could see the old frontiersman's silhouette as the darkness gradually dissipated, see the glow of the pipe bowl when he drew the smoke into his lungs, the pale smoke then wafting around his bearded face and shaggy head and a tree root curling out of the bank over his left shoulder.

After a time, Vienna continued quietly with "I was upstairs, napping, when I heard the commotion downstairs. Uncle Ichabod and Stenck were arguing. Stenck had several men with him, and they were shouting and stomping around, and my aunt and cousin and the housemaid were screaming. Stenck ordered Uncle Ichabod upstairs and to fetch the map for him. I was in the library, and I hid under a liquor cabinet . . . and I saw the whole thing. Uncle Ichabod got his hands on a knife and was about to stab Stenck with it, but Stenck was too fast. He grabbed Uncle Ichabod's hand and rammed the knife through his heart."

Vienna sobbed. James wrapped his arms around her, felt the tears dampen his shirt.

"I don't remember what happened after that," she continued, sniffing. "I must have passed out. When I opened my eyes, the office was a mess. Stenck and his men must have ransacked it. Somehow, they didn't find me. When I crawled out from under the cabinet, I discovered that my uncle was still alive. Just barely. He told me where the map was, and he also told me to take it and run, not to wait for the city marshals, that I couldn't trust anyone, because many of the marshals were in league with Stenck. He made me promise to not let the map get into the wrong hands, and I did. His last words, whispered in my ear, were 'All for nothing. All for nothing.' And then he died. Heartbroken."

She sobbed again, quietly, then pulled away from James and sat on a rock, raising her knees and wrapping the bottom of her serape over them.

"How did you end up with Mangham?" James asked her as Crosseye continued to puff on his pipe, saying nothing, obviously as gripped by the story as James was.

"When I found the rest of the family and the house-maid dead downstairs, I took the map and a small bundle of clothes and I ran. I wandered the streets of Denver City for a time, holing up in abandoned miners' shacks, scrounging for food scraps. While I wandered around like one of the orphans, I learned that Stenck was looking for me. He knew I'd been my uncle's secretary, and he probably knew that I either knew where the map was or that I had it myself. I had nowhere else to go, no way to support myself, and that's when Red found me, working in a little watering hole along the east bank of Cherry Creek."

She looked pointedly at James. "I'd started calling myself Mustang Mary . . . and I did whatever I could to support myself." She paused and then said in a small, thin voice: "Strange, isn't it—our bodies' command to survive when our minds have long since given up the fight?"

"It is at that," James said, knowing exactly what she meant.

"All that happened over a year ago now," she said. "One of Red's men told me someone in Denver City was looking for me, and he described you, so I sent the note to your hotel. Something told me to take a chance you weren't one of Stenck's men."

"Wish I'd had better news," James said.

"Oddly, I felt relatively safe with Red . . . since he was Stenck's fiercest rival and they'd sort of called a truce of sorts. Red was devoted to me. I feel a little bad about that. But the Ace of Spades was a prison, and I couldn't wait to get out. I'd written letters home, but they were never returned." Vienna gave James a hopeful look. "My family . . . ?"

James moodily brushed dust from the knee of his twill trousers. "I don't know, Vienna. If it's anything like Seven Oaks, I reckon there's not much left. I'm sorry."

"Pa was very ill when I left," she said thinly, staring off. "I reckon if his weak heart didn't kill him, the Yankees did. I read in the paper how the federal troops were advancing farther and farther into the Confederacy." She sucked her upper lip. James saw more tears ooze out of her eyes and trickle down her cheeks. "I'd held out the hope that Willie would eventually come for me."

He knew she hadn't intended them to be, but the words were more knives stabbing James's heart.

No one said anything for a time. The dawn light grew in the east, relieving the shadows and dimming the stars. A coyote yowled mournfully. Birds were beginning to chirp raucously, flitting around the ravine.

"About the boy . . . ," James said tentatively.

Vienna hesitated, stretched her legs out before her, and folded her hands in her lap. "I gave birth in a shack by the creek. I would have died but for the help of a beautiful old woman, also alone, who called herself Aunt Sally." Vienna shook her head dully. "Still, little Thomas died. Didn't live a day, God bless him."

James doffed his kepi, as did Crosseye. Neither man said anything.

"Would you fellas be of a mind to help a lonely Confederate girl haul three golden bells to Jefferson Davis in Richmond?" she asked after a time, on the heels of a long coyote chorus. She smiled as if realizing how crazy it sounded even to her own ears, but liking the idea just the same. "I'd like to do that for Uncle Ichabod . . . and the South. I know Willie, even though he died for the other side, wouldn't mind. In fact, I think he'd right admire the romance of it."

James looked at Crosseye, whose pipe fell out of his mouth. They stared at each other for a time, and then James smiled and turned his gaze to Vienna, the smile growing broader. He felt a low fire of eagerness. Not for the treasure or for the South, which he knew was a lost cause, but for the hope and the distraction of a destination far, far away.

And for the lovely, raven-haired, gray-eyed beauty before him.

For the adventure.

Besides, they seemed to have worn out their welcome in Denver City.

"Why, sure, Vienna," he said softly. "Why, sure we will. Why the hell not?"

Crosseye groaned.

Chapter 14

Two weeks later, deep in New Mexico Territory, on a broad stretch of desert surrounded by high divides, James lay near the crest of a low hill, a pair of field glasses in his hands.

He was not looking through the field glasses, however. He was staring back over his shoulder into the small camp that he, Crosseye, and Vienna had set up at the bottom of the hill, in a nest of sun-bleached rocks, cedars, and yucca, also called Spanish bayonet. James preferred the spiky-leafed plants' second name, as no doubt Willie would have, too. Maybe he and his brother hadn't been so different, after all.

Crosseye had shot a jackrabbit earlier with a bow and arrow he'd fashioned from the limbs of an ash tree. They were trying to conserve their ammo as well as to move as quietly as possible, in case Stenck or Red Mangham was shadowing them. Vienna was just now skinning the rabbit on a flat rock near a low fire. Blood glistened on the knife and on her hands. Her shoulders jerked as she worked, hair jostling about her cheeks.

James regarded her wonderingly, still amazed by

how different she was from the girl that he and Willie
had grown up with in the hills of eastern Tennessee. If
someone had told him he'd find her skinning rabbits
out West in a few years, he'd have thought the speaker
fit for the nuthouse. He hadn't realized it before, but
deep down he'd always known she was different from
the other plantation girls; she'd displayed a tomboy
strength and frankness that she'd managed to keep at
least partly hid behind those hoop-skirted barbecue
gowns, sausage curls, and well-bred manners.

Or maybe even she herself hadn't known those
traits had lurked in her until she'd come west and had
endured what she'd endured, not the least of which
was being thrown into Red Mangham's camp.

And becoming Red's woman.

He couldn't imagine what that year with Mangham
had been like for her, but whatever it was, she'd sur-
vived it. And it seemed to have honed in her a steely
determination that James had seen in few men, let
alone a girl raised as Vienna had been raised, on balls,
piano recitals, and coming-out parties, all ensconced
in the frills of her high station. He supposed that's why
he'd been in love with her once, in his own shy, awkward way, before Willie had gained her heart with his
more direct brand of passion, not to mention his talent
for remembering and reciting poetry, and even writing his own for Vienna.

James also supposed that once Vienna had gotten
thrown into Red Mangham's camp, she'd had to learn to
survive—which apparently meant skinning rabbits
and probably whatever else the men hauled to the
roadhouse for supper—or risk being kicked out and

potentially falling prey to Mangham's "business" rival, Richard Stenck. Most girls of her station would have crumpled and died like autumn rose blossoms.

Vienna had not.

James continued to watch as she adeptly peeled the skin off the rabbit's pale carcass and began cutting the meat into chunks to roast on sharpened willow branches. An uncomfortable feeling gnawed at him, too nebulous to pinpoint. It was the same feeling, a raw tenderness moving slowly around between his belly and shoulders, that he'd been feeling over the past two weeks that they'd been riding down from Denver City.

Fear? Reluctance to go after the treasure? After all, he'd agreed to it—and had even volunteered Crosseye for it—when his veins had still run hot from their run-in with Mangham as well as Stenck. But that wasn't the source of his discomfort, he knew. He'd never turned his back on an adventure, however crazy and romantic. He'd grown up on them, in fact, and he loved the sound of this one—three gold bells in the fabled Sierra Madre!

But if the trek into such a foreign land wasn't gnawing at him, what was?

Hoof clomps rose behind him. James turned to peer over the crest of the hill and down the other side. Crosseye was loping toward him atop the speckle-faced roan. He held his Spencer straight up from his right thigh, and his big, gaudy Lefaucheux revolver jostled against his chest. The red, gold, and tan light of the setting sun played across his big frame, winking off his bandoliers, as he put the roan up the hill, meandering around rocks and patches of prickly pear cactus.

Crosseye had ridden out an hour earlier to scout around their camp. Neither had seen any riders on their back trail over the past two weeks, but they'd both been visited by the uneasy sensation that they were being followed. Now Crosseye's good eye was sharply incredulous as he put the horse over the crest of the ridge and drew up beside James, about ten feet down from it, so the sky couldn't outline him, and curveted the mount.

Sweat glistened on the oldster's forehead beneath his upturned hat brim.

"We grew us some shadows, did we?" James said darkly, well able to read after long practice the look in the old frontiersman's eyes.

"Five men holed up in a tavern about one mile away. I went in and had a drink, heard Stenck's name mentioned low and soft, like they didn't want to be overheard. Scouting party, I'd fathom."

James flicked the field glasses' leather cord pensively against his thigh, then turned to glance once more at Vienna. She stood beside the fire over which she'd spitted the rabbit, and was staring up the hill toward James and Crosseye, hands on her hips. Her hair glistened like warm molasses.

"Wonder what they want worse."

James glanced at his older partner. "What's that?"

"Miss Vienna or the gold."

"Maybe they figure they can have both." James looked at Crosseye, his eyes hard. His determination to avoid trouble at all costs had dissipated like smoke on the wind. There was no more avoiding it out here than there had been back East. Out here was just a different kind of war, but at least it wasn't brother against brother. "What do you say we go let 'em know they can't have neither?"

Crosseye narrowed his good eye with mock seriousness. "Now, I could have taken 'em all out my own self, but I figured ole Forrest's Rapscallion would want in on the dance." He grinned.

Crosseye remained on the side of the hill as James walked down to fetch his horse. Vienna watched him closely, the fire coughing and sputtering, the meat sizzling. "Stenck?" she asked, pitching her voice darkly. "Or Red?"

"Stenck's men." James walked past the fire and quickly saddled his horse. "Keep the home fires burnin', Vienna. We'll be back."

He slipped the Henry into its saddle boot and swung into the leather.

"James?" Vienna walked over to him, looked up at him worriedly, squinting her gray eyes against the last rays of the setting sun. "You be careful."

James looked at her. She flushed a little, taking one step back, and it made his ears warm. They both realized at the same time that she'd just asked the killer of her life's one true love to be careful. The terrible irony was lost on neither of them.

"Like I said," he muttered, shamefully reining the chestnut away from her. "We'll be back."

As he booted the horse up the hill toward where Crosseye waited, his Spencer's butt resting atop his thigh, his green neckerchief billowing in the wind, James realized with a chill and a hard thud of his heart what had caused that vexing gnawing inside him:

He was in love with his dead brother's wife.

* * *

Half an hour later, James and Crosseye followed a crease between steep, cedar-stippled hills and checked their mounts down.

A thin stream twisted from left to right before them, the water winking in the last, green light remaining at the top of the sky. The sun had set, and night birds cawed. Smoke issued from the chimney of the long, low, L-shaped log building in front of them—a stage relay station, Crosseye had said, having scouted the place.

A broad, rutted stage trail paralleled the stream. A log barn and a couple of stone corrals sat off to the left. Several horses stood still as statues inside one of the corrals, and five saddles were draped over the top corral slat. Behind the place, a high mesa rose darkly.

A girl's wild tittering emanated from inside the roadhouse.

James glanced at Crosseye, who said, "Believe the proprietor sells a poke now an' then. Might have partaken myself, but I knew you were waitin' on me."

"Thoughtful," James snorted and put the chestnut across the stream. He jogged the horse across the yard and reined up at the hitch rack on the right side of the three stone steps rising to a low, falling-down porch.

James swung down from the saddle and slid the Henry from the saddle boot. Quietly, he racked a shell into the chamber, then off-cocked the hammer. Crosseye checked the loads in his Lefaucheux and then in his Leech & Rigdon .36, then slid the .36 back into the holster pushed back a little on his right hip, the butt tipped forward. He left the Spencer in its boot, preferring his pistols for inside work.

James mounted the porch steps slowly, hearing a man now laughing along with the girl, and stepped cautiously inside the place and to one side as Crosseye came in behind him. James looked the place over. It was large for a relay station this remote, so it likely served as a watering hole for area ranches, as well.

This evening, however, the clientele consisted of only four men seated at a square table in nearly the center of the room. They were a shaggy, grubby-looking quartet, bristling with knives and pistols. A couple of pistols sat on the table before them, along with whiskey bottles, shot glasses, and beer mugs. All four were playing cards, but one of the men—a large man, even larger than Crosseye, and with a white streak through his heavy black beard—had a topless, dark-haired girl on his knee.

He and the girl were laughing while he rocked the girl up and down on his knee, causing the girl's small, pointed breasts to jiggle stiffly. He had a long, thin cheroot clamped between his teeth and occasionally the girl plucked it from his mouth, took a drag, then blew the smoke out her mouth and nose on a raucous paroxysm of coughing. James could hear another man grunting somewhere in the second story, and a girl groaning and sighing in rhythm with squawking bedsprings.

A tall, gaunt man with a tumbleweed of gray hair stood behind the bar on the room's right side. He had a mug of beer before him and a wild look in his eyes. Atop the bar before him, a long rattlesnake was coiling and uncoiling and shaking its rattle while the man held the snake's flat head in his right fist. James blinked, watching dubiously as the man appeared to be feeding the snake a green apple.

"Come on, now, dang ye!" the tall man intoned, his cheeks sinking into his face and quivering as he appeared to wrestle the snake down on the bar. "Take a good bite, now . . . a good long bite. *There ye go!*"

The man separated the snake from the apple, held both up high, the snake coiling and uncoiling frantically, wickedly. The man looked at James and Crosseye, his eyes glowing in the light from a half dozen lanterns situated about the shadowy place.

"Not to worry, friends," he said, grinning. He held the apple higher, and shuttled his gaze to it. "That's for the whiskey tub." He tossed the apple over his shoulder; it dropped down out of sight and made a splash. He looked at the madly coiling and uncoiling snake in his other hand. "That there . . ."

He held the snake down on the bar, picked up a meat cleaver, rapped it into the bar, then lifted the snake aloft once more. It was still writhing desperately though it no longer had a head. Its head was still on the bar, jaws opening and closing and showing long white, razor-edged fangs. "That there's for the stew pot!"

He tossed the snake onto the floor on the other side of the bar, near the table where the four men were playing poker while one also entertained the bare-breasted whore. All four men, seeing the snake jouncing around before them, leaped out of their chairs, the whore screaming as she tumbled off the black-bearded gent's knee, and grabbed their guns.

Chapter 15

Three or four pistols popped at once. The din sounded like a barrel being rapped with an axe handle. James gritted his teeth against the noise and squeezed his Henry in his hands.

"Hold your fire!" shouted the man with the tumbleweed head of gray hair. "Hold your damn fire—you're shootin' my stew meat all to hell!"

The four men—Stenck's men, or so Crosseye figured—stood in a semicircle around their table, the whore cowering on the floor between the black-bearded gent and the bloody snake. The guns stopped roaring. A heavy cloud of powder smoke filtered toward the low rafters. The shortest of the four men, wearing a paint hide vest and a funnel-brimmed black hat, waved a hand in front of his face and glowered at the gray-headed barman. "You poison-stupid old cuss. What was the meanin' of that? Are you plumb loco?"

"Ah, fer chrissakes—I was just funnin' with ya!" the gray-headed man said as he slouched out from behind his bar and walked over to the snake that was still writhing but in four or five separate pieces. "Can't you fellas take a damn joke? Oh, look what ya done!"

He got down on his hands and knees and began scooping the carnage up off the floor and setting it delicately atop the bar. "Oh, well," he said, chuckling, "I reckon it saves me from havin' to chop it up, eh?" He laughed at that and then turned as James and Crosseye sauntered toward the bar.

The four cardplayers regarded them suspiciously, sizing them up. Grunting owlishly and holstering their pistols, they sagged back down in their chairs. The black-bearded man crouched over the bare-breasted whore and drew her back onto his lap, cooing to her as one would a bereaved child. She wore a flour-sack skirt that had a long slit in it, showing a long brown leg. The black-bearded man began to chuckle again as he resumed bouncing the whore up and down on his knee, though she berated him with "You threw me on the floor, *bastardo!* That's no way to treat a *girl!*"

She slammed both fists against his shoulders, but he only laughed harder and bounced her up and down on his knee with more vigor.

As the others resumed their game, James bellied up to the bar, setting the Henry across the planks and keeping the four in the periphery of his vision. They continued to glance at him and Crosseye suspiciously. Meanwhile, the sounds of lovemaking in the second story had died, but he could hear the whore speaking in soft tones. The barman had walked around behind the counter, and now set the pile of ragged snake flesh on the bar top, wiping his hands on his apron.

"What can I set you gents up with? Name your poison." The barman laughed.

James glanced at the wooden washtub behind the man. The tub was about three-quarters full with what James assumed was the man's own particular brand of forty-rod. The venom-spiced apple was likely lolling around at the bottom, flavoring the whiskey—that and probably half a pound of gunpowder and only God and the barman knew what else.

"I hear the ale's good," he told the barman. "Set me up a mug of it, will ya?"

"Me, too," said Crosseye.

The barman set up two frothy beer mugs, tossed James's proffered coins into a wooden box, and began transferring the shredded snake into a cast-iron skillet sputtering on the range behind him, beside the whiskey tub. James drank down half of his beer in three swallows, then set the mug down on the bar and turned to face the four men who'd resumed their poker game though the black-bearded gent was paying more attention to the whore. He turned her around so that her back was against him, and he was nuzzling her neck while she closed her eyes and reached an arm up and back to tug at his ear, groaning with mock pleasure.

James stared at the other three. The man in the funnel-brimmed black hat glanced at him, dropped his eyes to his cards, then snapped his gaze back up to James.

"What're you lookin' at?" he wanted to know, nostrils flaring.

The others looked at James then, too. The black-bearded man lifted his face from the whore's neck and regarded James with marble black eyes. The whore opened her own eyes and shunted her puzzled, wary gaze between the men around her and the tall, brown-haired hombre facing her, his back pressed against the bar, his thumbs hooked behind the wide brown belt and the shell belt encircling his waist.

Crosseye tipped his head back, finishing his beer. Then he set the glass down on the table with a sigh, turned toward the room, and ran the back of his fat left hand across his beard. He'd removed the Lefaucheux revolver from the cord around his neck and stuffed it behind one of his bandoliers.

James said softly, letting his Southern brogue roll like warm water off his tongue, "You fellas been trailin' us. Here we are. Now, I don't see no reason why we can't keep things polite and you go on back to Stenck and tell him you didn't cut our trail."

The stalkers tensed, sitting up straight in their chairs. The man farthest to James's right opened his hands and let his cards fall onto the table near the Colt Navy before him, though he kept his hands where they'd been before he dropped the cards. A muscle twitched in the right one. The eyes of all the other men flicked to their own guns on the table, and the black-bearded gent raised his right leg slightly, as though to make the bowie knife sheathed there more accessible.

Silence hung heavy over the room. Over the entire relay station. Outside, a bird squawked. The stalkers held James's mellow gaze with hard, angry stares of their own.

"Hell, that wouldn't even be a lie," Crosseye said reasonably. "Not really. You didn't cut our trail, we cut yourn." His red cheeks above his gray-streaked red beard rose as he smiled, eyes glinting affably.

The cutthroat in the black, funnel-brimmed hat said tightly, "James?"

"That's right."

The man with the black hat nodded slowly. His gaze flicked toward the man on the left side of the table, then returned to James, the corners of his dark eyes narrowing slightly, bemusedly.

"I reckon you know we can't do that," he said.

"I reckon I do."

All four men reached for their guns at once, the black-bearded gent again throwing the girl to the floor, where she gave another indignant yelp and then rolled and wrapped her arms around her head. James and Crosseye ripped their own pistols from their holsters and from behind their belts, and ratcheted back the hammers a sixteenth of a second before they leveled the guns.

The killer in the black hat leaped to his feet, eyes cold but his jaws working as he shouted, *"Die, you dogs!"* But before he could get his own twin Smith & Wessons leveled, one of James's .36 balls ripped through the dead center of his chest, punching him straight backward. The man in the black hat drilled the man who'd been sitting on the opposite side of the table from him, nearest James, through the back of his neck, causing that man's own two triggered slugs to sail wide, punching into the bar to James's right.

James and Crosseye's own pistol work was so well coordinated after a dozen years of shooting both men and game together that five seconds hadn't passed between their first and last shots, and all four men were lying in bloody groaning piles around the table or, in the case of one, on top of it, arms dangling toward the floor, his own blood dripping off the table and onto the floor just inches from his extended fingertips.

The black-bearded man, lying on his belly near the still-cowering whore, reached for a blood-splattered pistol beneath an overturned chair. Crosseye's Lefaucheux spoke loudly, like the clap of two large hands, and the top of the black-bearded man's black-haired head virtually vaporized, blood and bone painting a seven-foot streak beyond him.

James heard a wooden squawk to his right and whipped around quickly, crouching, as a thin young man with sandy blond hair and a bowler hat triggered a pistol from the middle of the stairs that rose to the second story. The slug passed so closely to James's head that he could hear the bullet's wicked whisper in his left ear. He dropped the hammer of the Colt in his right hand, and the kid spun around on the stairs with a scream, ran two steps back up toward the second story before dropping to his knees. He screamed again, twisted around, the gun in his extended right hand making a heavy, awkward arc back toward James and Crosseye.

The two ex-Confederates fired at the same time. The kid howled loudly, like one of the coyotes James had been hearing, and slammed back against the steps, dropping his pistol. He tumbled down the steps, head and boots thudding loudly on the wooden risers, and piled up on his belly at the bottom. He howled again, coyotelike, and tried to gain his hands and knees before flopping back down to the floor with a groan.

James looked at Stenck's other men. None were moving, only bleeding. The whore sat on her butt, leaning back on her hands, looking around, shocked and dazed. James holstered one of his pistols and strode over to the kid lying on his belly at the bottom of the stairs, and kicked him onto his back. The kid's blue eyes glared up at him. His spindly chest rose and fell sharply, blood oozing from the three holes in his chest and belly, matting his pin-striped shirt.

"Bastard," the kid raked out, wincing, showing a mouthful of crooked, tobacco-stained teeth. "Ye kilt me . . . so go to hell. . . ."

"First things first." James squatted beside the kid, who had a demonlike, pale face with a long, hooked nose and close-set, soulless eyes. All he was missing was horns. "Where's Stenck?"

The kid seemed to think that was funny. His lips stretched a grin. "Who?"

"Is Stenck near here, or is he still in Denver City?"

The kid tried to spit at James, but he couldn't get the saliva past his lips. It was red with bubbly blood from his lungs.

James pressed the round barrel of his Griswold .36 into one of the kid's bloody wounds. The kid tipped his head back and screamed.

James pulled the pistol out of the wound. "I can make it hurt worse than that, junior."

"He's in Sand Creek!" the kid said, bawling. "He's there . . . waitin' on us."

"How many does he have ridin' with him?"

"Eleven, er . . ." The kid shifted his gaze to the rafters, blinked as he refigured, subtracting himself and his dead partners from the tally. "Six, I reckon."

He sighed raspily, his chest deflating like a balloon. His head smacked down on the floor, and his eyes rolled back in his head. James stood and turned to Crosseye standing at the bar behind him, deftly reloading his pistols with fresh caps, balls, nipples, and powder. "Five, huh?" the older man said. "Well, hell, that ain't too many."

James looked at the gray-headed barman, who stood well back behind the bar, looking worried, holding his hands high above his head.

"We mean no harm to you, sir. Just them."

The barman lowered his arms with a sigh.

"How far to Sand Creek?" James asked him.

The barman bunched his grizzled brows, thoughtful. "Twenty-five, thirty miles." He narrowed a fateful eye. "Is the Stenck you mention the same Stenck from up Denver City way?"

"One and the same," James said, wiping his bloody pistol off on the dead kid's wool vest.

"Had a feelin'," the barman said, sounding none too happy.

James holstered his Griswold and narrowed an eye at the barman, who was looking around the bloody, smoky room and shaking his head. "If you help us get these hombres on their horses, you can have whatever you find in their pockets and keep all the hardware they got on 'em, too. How'd that be?"

Crosseye looked at him curiously.

"Why not send Stenck a message?" James said with a shrug. "Maybe if he sees he's lost half his men, he'll turn tail just like he did back home and run on back to Denver where he belongs."

Why spill more blood when there was a chance you wouldn't have to? He'd seen enough of the stuff.

"Hell," Crosseye said, shoving his pistols butt-forward into the holsters on his broad hips, "worth a try."

His tone gave the lie to his words.

Just the same, he, James, and the barman dragged the dead men outside and tied them belly-down over their saddles. The barman had gone through their pockets and taken all their weapons, so they were considerably lighter than they'd been when they'd ridden into the station yard hoping merely to have a poke and to down some cheap whiskey, cutting the trail dust before heading out after their quarry again in the morning.

James slapped the horses back in the direction from which they'd come. Stenck would likely find them the next day. What he'd do with the grisly message was up to him.

James and Crosseye pinched hat brims to the barman, and gigged their horses on back to their camp.

Chapter 16

The country the three Tennesseans rode through as they made their way toward Mexico was like that from some child's book of fables. It inspired fantasy and wild, boyish conjurings in the former Confederate, James Dunn.

James was accustomed to low mountains thick with trees and brush, shrubs, and berry brambles of a thousand different varieties, and of foggy hollows and mossy canyons as colorful as God's own garden, jeweled with lazy waterfalls. In the south, the sky was often obscured by a low, hazy cloud-cover, but it made the grass and leaves a rich tropical green, the air as soft and damp as wash freshly hung on a line.

But in the arid west, the sky was mostly cobalt blue stretching from horizon to horizon like the lid on all the cosmos—earth, moon, sun, and stars. The sunlight here was a rich copper or brassy color, the air as clear as a lens. Not as much grew out here, but what did grow owned its own spare, sometimes severe beauty.

James's party rode through sandy, rocky deserts on which little grew but small tufts of wiry brush and dangerously spiked cactus plants. When they climbed slightly higher in elevation the sparse grass and cactus gave way to cedars, fragrant junipers, and piñon pines. The trees were not very tall and not crowded together the way they were in the South, but spread out so a man could see through them and sometimes beyond them, almost as though they'd been arranged for this very purpose.

The ex-Confederates and Vienna McAllister crossed shoulders of pine-clad mountains and traversed several deep canyons through which muddy streams meandered through wiry brush and stirrup-high, dun-colored grass, the stream banks scored by the tracks of many Western beasts, including coyotes, porcupines, and mountain lions. In the vast distances that opened nearly as wide as all the universe were breathtaking vistas of steep, sloping mesas supported by coppery, crenellated sandstone walls.

There were also what appeared to be old volcanoes surrounded by black lava rock and gravel, and sudden escarpments rising like the spines of long-dead, partially buried dinosaurs. The broken, rocky terrain climbed to high plateaus. But even these formations were dwarfed by massive sierras looming beyond them, often in all directions. The bottoms of these ranges were hidden in a light blue mist, causing them to appear like islands hanging from the sky, with many thrusting peaks shaped like the teeth on a saw blade, some of these teeth so white they looked as if they'd been dipped in paraffin.

It was good, being out here. The air was thinner, so thin it sometimes made James feel that he couldn't

catch his breath, and he sometimes felt his head suddenly throbbing. But the air spiced with sage and cedar
was clean, and there were few people, and all was
refreshingly new and exotic. James felt the bloody war
slipping farther and farther behind him, making him
begin to imagine starting a new life for himself here on
the western side of the Mississippi.

A life with Vienna?

He found himself vaguely considering the possibility in a wishful, speculative sort of way. Her earthy
beauty was intoxicating, and having a woman for company in this strikingly vast and lonely land would be a
rarified comfort for any man. Listening to her voice,
watching her move, admiring the way the light of a
crackling fire played in her hair made James feel unde-
niable male stirrings that he tried hard to ignore, even
going so far as trying to keep his eyes off her for long
stretches of whatever trail they were following.

For even if Vienna had showed any interest in him
at all—interest beyond that of a mere trail partner and
treasure-seeker—which she hadn't, James knew it
wasn't in the cards. They'd always have Willie and the
war between them.

One night a troubling thing happened. Unable to
sleep, he rose from his blanket roll and walked down
to the river that they'd camped beside and which lay
beyond a short stretch of willows and knee-high grass.
As he did, he heard slow, languid splashing sounds.
He knew right away that it was her, but he couldn't
stop himself.

He took several more steps, slid a branch aside. She
stood naked in the stream, the light of the nearly full

moon glistening like liquid gold on the dark, rippling water and on the lush ivory curves of her naked body.

She had her hair pinned to the top of her head, but several strands dangled toward the water. The strands danced as she suddenly turned toward him. He released the branch and stumbled back to the camp with the back of his neck on fire.

They continued south and west, not relying so much on maps—for the few maps they could consult were in land and assay offices or frustratingly unreliable stage relay stations—but on directions from passing strangers and from ranchers and cowpunchers.

The land was almost startlingly empty, with most of the able-bodied men off fighting the war in the East. Outside of towns and small ranches, they saw few white men, but they saw several bands of roving, dark-skinned riders on small, rangy mustang ponies often trimmed with tribal designs and colors.

These men, who James and Crosseye assumed were the native Apache or Navajo of one band or another, wore colorful calico bandannas and shirts and deer-skin breeches, with bows and arrow quivers hanging down their backs. Some wore strange hats of what appeared to be woven bird feathers and capes of animal hide. Pistols and knives jutted from sashes. While James's group saw several small packs of these distinctly wild natives—every bit as feral as the wolves, panthers, and grizzlies they'd spotted in the deserts and mountains they'd traversed—they kept their distance, wily as coyotes. James had the uneasy feeling that he and his two trail partners hadn't seen a third of the natives who'd been watching them, maybe even trailing them from a cautious, curious distance.

One night in the mountains above the Mexican *pueblito* of Tucson, in the Arizona Territory, where they hoped to acquire supplies for their pull into Mexico, Willie came to James in a dream. He saw Willie's face in that moment just after James had thrust the knife into his brother's chest and saw that blue eye that was like looking into a mirror. Recognition shone in that lone, pain-racked eye at the same time that James screamed his brother's name and pulled the knife out as quickly as he'd shoved it in.

"Willie!"

He heard the scream echoing around the rocky canyon, as though it had been shouted by someone else from a distant ridge. Only then, a second later, when he opened his eyes and heard his own labored breaths raking in and out of his lungs working like a bellows, did he realize he'd screamed it himself. He was bathed in sweat, his clothes glued to his skin beneath the double wool blankets of his hot roll.

Instantly, Crosseye and Vienna were kneeling beside him, Crosseye wheezing, "Good Lord, Jimmy!" and Vienna calling his name as though trying to summon him back from a great distance. Sitting straight up, back taut, he shifted his gaze from Crosseye's bearded, cross-eyed face to Vienna's fine, pale, perfectly feminine one, framed in mussed chocolate hair, and he drew a deep breath as he sagged back onto his elbows.

He blinked slowly as the image of Willie hovering

just behind his retinas sagged slowly back into the misty, black water of Snake Creek, mercifully gone from his sight though the dream's memory remained, nearly as real as the memory of the actual event.

"He's gone, James," Vienna said. "He's gone, and you didn't mean to kill him. It was the war. You're here, and Crosseye and I are here, in the West, and now we're all that matters." She smiled weakly but encouragingly, then slid her face to his and pressed her lips to his temple.

He knew she'd meant the kiss to be comforting, but it only aroused a welter of conflicting emotions inside him, and he felt as though he'd somehow stuck that knife into his own lung.

"Thirsty," he said, throwing his blankets aside, and rising. "Gonna take a walk."

He stomped into his boots, grabbed the Henry repeater that he went nowhere without, and stumbled off into the brush and the rocks beyond the soft, umber glow of their fire. He walked through some willows, saw the stars arching between toothy black mountain peaks, and drew a deep draught of air into his lungs. He shivered against the mountain chill.

Maybe he hadn't come as far as he'd thought he had. How far did you have to travel to outrun a memory?

He stood out there for a time, taking deep breaths, then sat on a rock and lit a black cigar he'd bought at a mercantile in a mountain crossroads town and mining camp called Payson. He smoked it halfway down slowly. When he'd smoked half of it, he peeled off the coal, returned the cheroot to the breast pocket of his shirt, then walked back through the brush toward the fire's low glow.

He passed under a willow branch and stopped suddenly at the edge of the firelight. His heart thudded. He brought the Henry down in both hands, but held it against his chest, the barrel up, as someone shouted incoherently—it sounded like a mixture of grunts and clipped, hard consonants.

Three figures in addition to Vienna and Crosseye were gathered about the low, quiet fire. One stood to the left of it. Another knelt behind Vienna, who sat up on her bedroll, facing James from the other side of the fire. Crosseye sat with his back against a rock to the fire's right side, holding his thick hands high above his head, one leg extended, the other leg and cavalry boot angled inward.

James could see only the silhouettes of the three stocky figures, and their colorful headbands and red or green sashes. He could also see the knife in the hand of the one crouched behind Vienna, the steel tip of which was pressed taut to the underside of the girl's chin. The man near Crosseye was aiming an arrow nocked to a bow at Crosseye's face. The Apache nearest James, on the left side of the fire, was aiming a nocked arrow at James.

Crosseye said while keeping his head turned toward the native nearest him, "Damn, but they were quiet, Jimmy."

This first man was the one who'd spoken, if you could call it speaking. He cut loose with the grunting and spitting snarls once more and gestured with his bow and arrow. James lowered the Henry in one hand, looking once more at the knife held in the hand of the Apache crouched behind Vienna. She stared straight over the fire at James. The fire's dark red glow was reflected in her shadowy eyes.

James set the Henry down against the tree to his right and raised his hands palms out. His heart slowed, his anxiety ebbing like the last waters down a flooded streambed. Funny how a nightmare could drive him to the brink of madness but moments of true terror slowed time down for him, steadied him, lightened his limbs, and honed his vision, preparing him for battle.

The Indian nearest him spoke again loudly, sharply, and gestured with the arrow, making the bow's drawn-taut sinew creak. James stepped to the left, away from the Henry, for the native who'd spoken was obviously after the rifle. As the man moved toward him, James glanced past him toward the knife held against Vienna's neck. Too close. If James or Crosseye made any kind of an offensive move at all, he'd lay Vienna's neck wide open.

The possibility chilled his blood, but his heart continued its slow, steady, insistent rhythm, his mind working through his options.

"You want the gun?" James said, keeping his hands raised. "All right. Take the rifle."

The first Apache lowered the bow and arrow, glancing at the others and spewing out his guttural tongue, likely telling his partners to stay alert. James heard one of his party's horses give a nervous nicker from where they were tied back in the brush.

"You think they speak English?" James said.

The Indian nearest him looked at him sharply as he picked up the Henry. James could tell by the Indian's expression that he hadn't understood. He kept his wary, vaguely puzzled, dark brown eyes on James a moment longer, then lowered his eyes to the rifle in his hands, impressed. He studied the sixteen-shooter closely, obviously never having seen such a weapon before. He ran his hands down the loading tube and barrel, then held the piece close to his face, inspecting the receiver.

James felt the nerves in his ankles twitch. Should he make his move? He glanced at the savage with the knife. The man was also looking at the rifle in his partner's hands, but the knife was still pressed against the underside of Vienna's chin.

Maybe not as tightly as before . . . ?

James slid his eyes toward the Apache nearest Crosseye. He couldn't see the native's eyes, but his face seemed turned slightly toward the one with James's rifle.

The one with the rifle toyed with the hammer, then held it up and inspected the cocking mechanism, frowning. Finally, he took the rifle under his arm, pulled the lever down slowly, then just as slowly shoved it back up under the stock. He'd seen the shell slide out of the receiver and become lodged beneath the hammer, which was now cocked.

James had a sinking sensation. That cocked repeater in the hands of this precocious Apache was like giving a razor-edged pocketknife to a baby.

Crosseye must have been reading James's mind. "I reckon if we're gonna make our move, now'd be a good time," the older man said.

James said, "What about our friend with the knife?"

"That's a problem," Crosseye admitted, keeping his

eyes on the Apache nearest him, who spoke loudly in his guttural tongue, jerking his cocked bow at Cross-eye. Apparently, he didn't appreciate his prisoners' idle chatter.

The Apache nearest James held up the rifle to show the others. The one with the knife smiled. He lowered the knife from Vienna's chin and slid the flat of the blade down across her shirt and over the tip of her right breast. He squeezed her other breast with his other hand.

James jerked forward, but stopped when he saw that the native nearest him had the cocked Henry aimed at his head.

Chapter 17

James stared down the rectangular maw of his own Henry repeater. The Apache's rawboned, broad-nosed face hovered over the other end of it, grinning, dimpled cheeks twin pools of shadow.

James stood frozen, every nerve in his body twitching, his heart now quickening. He watched with another sinking feeling as the Indian's right index finger closed over the Henry's trigger and began tightening.

Vienna gave an angry grunt. "You bastard!" she shouted.

In the periphery of James's vision, he saw her throw an arm up and over the right one of the Apache groping her, and reached for her assailant's knife. As the Indian holding the Henry on James shifted his eyes slightly toward the struggling pair, James lurched forward, whipped his right arm up, and knocked the Henry sideways. It barked loudly, the concussion of the report like a fist hammered against his ear. At the same time, James slid his Green River knife from its sheath on his right hip and thrust it into the belly of the Apache before him.

He pulled the knife out quickly and glanced toward Vienna. The second Apache had her on the ground before him, struggling as the warrior raised the knife over his head, blade angled straight down.

With one quick flick of his right wrist, James's own knife was hurling end over end through the darkness, disappearing for a moment before reappearing with a crunching thud in the dead center of the chest of the second Apache at the same time that the savage started to thrust his own blade down toward Vienna's neck. The native's knife hand froze, and he jerked back with the Green River knife in his chest, dark blood boiling up around the blade.

He fell back on the ground and mewled, lifting his head, lips stretched from his teeth, to glare at the knife that had all but killed him.

James picked up his rifle and turned to where Crosseye's thick frame was jostling around in the shadows beyond the far end of the camp. James pressed the stock against his shoulder and tried to draw a bead on the Indian whom Crosseye was struggling with. It appeared to be a bizarre dance. Then Crosseye swung to the left, and the Indian was twirled to the right, screaming. Crosseye lunged toward the brave and slammed his big head into that of the Apache, making a solid *smack!*

James lowered the Henry as the brave dropped, limbs slackening. Crosseye snarled like an angry grizzly, stepped toward the brave on the ground and slid the Lefaucheux from behind his belt. The big pistol roared. The brave's head bounced off the ground, the right temple ruined, and lay still.

Crosseye looked around. He met James's gaze.

"Don't you ever tell me I smell bad again, Jimmy," he said with a growl. "I don't smell half as bad as these fellers!"

James walked over to where Vienna was climbing to her knees. He held the Henry straight out from his right hip, aimed at the Apache who was still groaning and flopping around with the Green River knife sticking straight up from his chest.

"You all right?" he asked her.

She heaved herself to her feet, dusted off her pants. She was breathing hard. Sweeping her hair back from her face with a forearm, she said, "Not the best night for sleeping, is it?"

James moved off into the shrubs toward where the horses were picketed. He knew that Crosseye would scout the other side of the camp, as James searched this side. Where there were three Apaches, there could be more.

The horses were spooked, drawing back on their hackamore ropes that were tied to the picket line strung between two cottonwoods. Spooked in a way that told James, accustomed to the manner of horses in all shades of battle, that no further Indian trouble was likely imminent. If there were more Indians out this way, the horses would likely have scented them and be kicking up a bigger fuss.

At least, he thought they would. He was at a disadvantage out here in this alien territory and having no previous experience with the Western brand of native. He'd heard much about the Apaches—that they were fierce nomadic warriors giving up their traditional lands at great cost in white blood, but until tonight he'd never seen one up close. As far as he could tell, they were all elemental rage packed in dark, stocky vessels of hard muscle and steely sinew—born and bred for fighting.

James ran a hand down the neck of Vienna's horse, a grullo they'd traded with a rancher for. Vienna had bought the horse and a packhorse for the party with twenty-three gold dollars she'd produced from her croker sack. She'd never said where she'd gotten the loot, and James hadn't asked. He figured it was money she'd stolen from Mangham, which was just fine with James. She'd likely earned every penny.

Calming the grullo's taut nerves, he stared off toward the high, rocky, talus-strewn ridge that rose about fifty yards away, its base a gauzy, black jumble of ironwood, stunt cedars, and boulders. Taking his Henry in both hands, he moved out away from the horses and padded soundlessly through the brush and gravel to the base of the ridge.

He stood there for a full five minutes, looking around and listening, hearing nothing but the occasional cry of a night bird and the faint muttering of a spring bubbling out of the rocks and into a sandy-bottomed pool. Finally, he walked east along the base of the ridge for nearly a hundred yards, setting each low-heeled cavalry boot down carefully. He turned and walked back the way he'd come and past the spring for another hundred yards.

Still, no sounds but the birds and the single, mournful howl of a faraway wolf.

He walked back toward the camp, stopped when he saw a silhouette standing between him and the dark shapes of the horses.

Vienna's voice: "James?"

"Yeah."

He moved toward her. She stood there in the darkness, tense, turning her head slowly from left to right, looking around. James put a hand on her arm. "You're shivering."

"Spooked me," she said, and swallowed. "I'd just started drifting off to sleep when . . ."

"They had to be damn quiet to sneak up on Crosseye." He could feel the fluttering of her nerves and muscles under the serape she'd dropped over her shirt. "Did he hurt you?"

Vienna looked up at him. He could see her face in the shadows, the sheen of her gray eyes and her lips. "No, just put the fear of God into me, I reckon. Denver City was all new to me. This place . . . out here." She placed her hands on her shoulders and looked around once more. "I guess I didn't know what I was getting us all into. It wasn't fair of me to ask you to come here, to do this."

"Hell," James said with a rueful snort, "Crosseye and me don't have anywhere else to go. Besides, I . . . uh . . . I like helpin' you."

"You do?"

"Yes."

She stared up at him. Her lips were slightly parted. Her eyes stared straight into his. He could smell her— warm and slightly fragrant, like blackberry blossoms along the creek running along the southern border of Seven Oaks. Her skin was pale as flour in the deep night. He wanted to press his lips to the smooth curve of her neck beneath the thick hair tumbling over her shoulder.

There it was again—the fluttering of his heart, the twisting of his gut. Before he knew it, he'd drawn her to him with one hand. With the Henry's barrel, he nudged his Confederate gray hat back off his forehead and pressed his mouth against hers.

To his vague surprise, she did not pull away from him. Rising onto her toes, she opened her lips. He felt the wet tip of her tongue curling against his own, and it was like a warm hand caressing his loins. He turned his head, grinding his lips against hers, drawing her harder against him, until he could feel the hammering of her heart against his ribs.

He had to have her. There was no denying the need.

She pulled her head back from his, jerked her arm from his hand, and stepped away, almost stumbling, gasping. Looking down, she swallowed, shook her head. "Not yet, James," she said softly, shaking her hair back as she looked up at him once more. "It's too soon."

"Nothin's ever gonna change, Vienna," he said hoarsely. "I'll always have killed Willie."

"Not because you killed Willie, James, but because you can't let him go."

He stared at her. "Can you?"

She drew a breath, let it out slowly. Her voice was quiet, steady. "I already have."

Footsteps sounded on James's left. He wheeled.

"Crosseye," came the oldster's low, gravelly voice, announcing himself. "See any more of them devils?"

"No."

"Musta grown up right out of the rocks," Crosseye said in disgust, "or I'm gettin' too damn old."

As the old frontiersman moved forward, James looked at Vienna. She was still gazing up at him, as though there'd been something else she'd wanted to say. But now she turned and walked back around the horses toward the camp.

Crosseye walked up to James and stared after her. James could hear him breathing, his broad, rounded chest rising and falling slowly behind the crisscrossed bandoliers he rarely removed even to sleep.

"Hope I didn't interrupt nothin'." Crosseye grinned.

"You got bats in your belfry, old son." James strode off toward the camp.

The next day around noon, stone and plank shanties sprouted up out of the desert along both sides of the stage and freight road that James, Crosseye, and Vienna were following, Crosseye trailing the packhorse by a lead rope.

The air was cool, but the sun rained like liquid brass out of an arching, periwinkle sky. A weathered wooden sign appeared along the trail's right side, leaning toward the one-armed saguaro standing to its right. The paint on the sign was so badly faded that James had to scrutinize it carefully before he could make out the ghostlike lettering: TUCSON, ARIZ. TERR.

He glanced behind him, toward the mountains they'd ridden down out of before reaching this relatively flat expanse of desert. The trail meandered through saguaros, paloverde trees, mesquites, and ironwood, disappearing into a tangle of brush fifty yards away. They hadn't seen any Apaches or even Apache sign all morning, and that made him nervous. He'd heard from cowpokes and ranchers on the way down here that not seeing Apache sign was often the worst sign of all.

"You feel it, too?"

James looked at Crosseye, who was hipped around in his saddle and looking behind, as well, squinting. "I feel somethin'," the older man said.

"Yeah." Vienna's grullo was dancing in the trail as she stared straight back toward Mount Lemmon rising in the north. "I feel it, too. Like something's about to happen."

"Apaches been bad since the war started," Crosseye said, repeating what they'd heard from a relay station attendant somewhere in western New Mexico. "The federal soldiers are all off fighting *us*, so the red devils out *here* is like mice when the cat's away."

"I'll feel better in town," Vienna said, reining the grullo around and booting the horse on up the trail.

James followed suit, and Crosseye fell in behind him with the packhorse. As they followed the trail's westward curve through the desert, more shanties and stock pens appeared, and James heard the ringing clangs of a blacksmith's hammer, a mule braying, a dog barking. A stout old Mexican woman stood in a barren yard outside a mud-brick shack, feeding a baby goat with a milk bottle. A dead hog hung from a paloverde tree near a stock pen beyond the shack. The bucket beneath the hog was filled nearly to its rim with dark red blood steaming in the cool, late-autumn air.

James turned his head forward, then glanced once more at the Mexican woman. She followed him and Vienna and Crosseye with her eyes, her expression for some reason adding to James's uneasiness.

They followed the trail past more small houses and stock pens and privies, then turned right onto what appeared the pueblo's main business street. More shacks here, but also false-fronted business establishments that hunched silver-gray in the harsh sunlight.

A blocklike sandstone church stood about halfway down the street, with a six-foot adobe wall around it. A short Mexican priest in a brown robe and rope-soled sandals stood on a red-clay walk in the churchyard, watering some spindly flowers from a tin can. As James's party walked their horses past the church, lifting small dust streamers, the padre turned toward them, straightening his back and following them with his own oblique gaze.

Espinoza's Mercantile stood on the left side of the street a block beyond the church. It was a two-story adobe-brick building with what appeared to be a warehouse with broad wooden doors on the first floor. A wide loading dock running the length of the building stood on cottonwood stilts before the main story, with whipsawed plank steps running up from the street. A slender Mexican man with thick, wavy salt-and-pepper hair stood atop the loading dock, holding a broom in his hands. He wasn't sweeping but watching the trio of riders angle toward his store.

As James reined the chestnut up near the steps, he pinched his hat brim to the man he figured was Espinoza. "Afternoon."

Espinoza just stared at him darkly, his eyes flicking around beyond James and the others before returning once more to the tall, dark-haired stranger sitting the chestnut rabicano before him. "*Sí, sí,*" he said with an impatient air.

James pulled a scrap of paper from his shirt pocket and handed it up to the man, who reached down to take it. "Can you fill this list?"

The man looked at the list, then turned away, leaned his broom against the front of the building, behind a barrel bristling with picks, shovels, and rakes, and walked into the store. James dismounted, as did Vienna, and looked at Crosseye.

"You best wait out here, keep an eye skinned."

"Just wish I knew what I was keepin' an eye skinned for." Crosseye looked behind, where a small brown dog was crossing the street and regarding them as warily as the human had. "Doubt them 'paches would follow us into town."

"I reckon we don't know the Apache."

"Don't care to get to know them all that well, if you wanna know the truth, Jimmy."

James went back to the packhorse and removed four nearly empty supply sacks from its back, draped the sacks over his shoulder, and mounted the loading dock steps behind Vienna, following her into the store. Inside, Espinoza was moving around the stacked shelves of dry goods, glancing occasionally at the list. He scooped coffee beans from a wooden bin into a small burlap pouch and set it on the counter, and then he did the same with sugar and flour.

He added several boxes of metal cartridges for James's and Crosseye's rifles, and caps, balls, nipples, and paper cartridges for their pistols, to the growing pile of goods on the counter. Meanwhile, Vienna walked along a display of bolt cloth, holding her hat down in front of her. Occasionally, she reached out to finger a length of brocade or muslin. How far she'd come from such fineries, James thought. How far they'd both strayed from home and all that was familiar.

Only, Vienna could eventually go back. He never could. Even after the war, he'd be considered a deserter in most folks' eyes—including those of his father. He'd be an enemy in his native land.

"How do I look?"

He turned to see Vienna holding a powder blue silk dance gown in front of her. There were no sleeves and the neck was cut low, and the red-and-white-stitched ruffles along the hem were in the Mexican style. She smiled over the dress at him, a glow in her cheeks, which had taken the harsh Western sun well, turning from the pink of an initial burn to a dark olive color.

"Miss Vienna," James said, letting the Tennessee accent roll gracefully off his tongue, dipping his chin slightly, "you ah a sight foh these soh eyes."

She gave a regal bow and partial curtsy. "Why, thank you, suh. Perhaps someday, I'll have occasion to wear such a frivolous affayah again."

"The soonah the bettah."

She laughed and returned the dress to its rack. As the mercantiler continued to fill their order, and

Vienna continued to browse, James turned to stare out the large front window left of the door.

Crosseye had dismounted and now stood out near the middle of the street, cradling his repeater in his arms. James caught movement just beyond Crosseye, in the second story of an adobe-brick, brush-roofed building sitting kitty-corner to the mercantile. A man's hatted head slid slowly out a window over a wrought-iron balcony rail. A rifle followed stealthily, its barrel slowly being angled toward Crosseye, who had his head turned to peer down the street in the direction from which they'd entered Tucson.

James jerked one of his Griswolds from its holster with his right hand and slapped the window with his other hand, shouting, "Crosseye—*mind the other side of the street!*"

Chapter 18

He hadn't finished shouting the warning before Crosseye, who must have spied the movement in the periphery of his good eye, stepped straight back and swung around toward the building in which the shooter was now bearing down on him. The rifle flashed and boomed, the slug tearing up dust near Crosseye a quarter second before Crosseye's cocked and aimed Spencer roared.

The would-be bushwhacker jerked back against the open shutter behind him, then fell forward out the window, turning a somersault before landing crossways atop a stock trough with an audible cracking of bone and wood. His head, arms, and legs flapped madly; his boot heels struck the street with a wash of tan dust. His rifle landed beside him with a clattering smack.

The three horses standing around the trough sidestepped wildly, one loosing an angry whinny.

As Crosseye worked the Spencer's trigger guard cocking mechanism, seating another metallic cartridge, another rifleman stepped out from an alley mouth on the far side of the two-story building the first cutthroat had fired from. James heard two shots as he bolted out the mercantile's front door, shouting, "Vienna, get down!" and saw two more men moving quickly toward the mercantile from the right, crouching along the adobe wall fronting the church.

James crossed the loading dock in two long strides and leaped down the steps as the two men in front of the church opened up with their rifles, one bullet narrowly missing Vienna's grullo and plunking into a post. Another screeched past James's left ear.

As three of the horses whinnied and tore loose of the hitch rack to go galloping down the street, James dropped to a knee and fired two quick shots at his attackers, both slugs hammering the wall behind and between them. His chestnut was just now pulling its reins free of the rack, whinnying shrilly as one of the riflemen's bullets clipped its left rear hock and blew up dust beside it.

James lunged for the horse, keeping the jostling mount between himself and the shooters, and slipped the Henry from its saddle boot. As the horse galloped away after the others, James racked a round into the Henry. A bullet flung from one of the shooters nipped the side of his chin, then hammered the front of the mercantile. James cursed as he raised the Henry and, cutting loose with a tooth-gnashing Rebel yell, venting his own mad rage and intending to confuse and terrify, opened up with the sixteen-shot repeater.

He dropped the man on the right, punching him back against the wall with a shriek and tossing his rifle against the wall, as well. Another shot chewed through the knee of the man on the left and the next one plunked through the same hombre's thigh just above the bloody hole in his knee. Cursing shrilly, he fired his Spencer from his butt until another of James's Henry rounds plunked through his forehead just above his left eye.

James had no sooner fired that last, killing round than another head and another rifle peeked out around the side of the opening in the adobe wall. The man's rifle roared twice. James knew the cutthroat had him dead to rights, so he bolted up off his heels and dove behind a stock trough as two of the shooter's bullets spat into the dust at his heels and another crunched into the stock trough before yet another *zipped* into the trough's straw-flecked water.

James crabbed to the far end of the stock trough, snaked the Henry around it, and, propped on his right shoulder, triggered three more quick rounds. Two plunked into the wall to the right of the shooter, while the third puffed dust from the man's bull-hide vest as it hammered his shoulder.

"*Shit!*" the man shouted as the bullet drove him straight back away from the opening, partly hidden by the wall.

James fired two more rounds that merely blew up dust around the man, who was scrambling to his feet and running toward a dry fountain between the wall and the church. As he threw himself behind the fountain—a statue of Mother Mary and the baby Jesus—James squeezed the Henry's trigger once more.

The hammer pinged on an empty chamber.

"Diddle yourself, you bastard!" the shoulder-wounded

cutthroat shouted as he bolted out from behind the
fountain and ran, limping, toward the church's stout,
steel-banded front door.

James lowered the Henry's butt to the street and
pulled the rifle's loading tube out from beneath the
barrel. He'd practiced loading the modern piece many
times during the trek down from Denver City, and it
took less than half a minute to pluck shells from his
cartridge belt and thumb them into the tube and then
shove the tube back into place beneath the barrel.

He racked a fresh round into the Henry's chamber,
gained his feet, and looked in both directions along
the street. To his left, Crosseye was hunkered down
behind a wagon on the far side of the mercantile, swap-
ping lead from a shooter beyond him, on the same side
of the street. Not surprisingly, the old mossyhorn was
holding his own, so James ran through the opening in
the adobe wall and on up the churchyard walk past the
dry fountain to the heavy oak door.

He paused to listen at the door. Hearing nothing on
the other side, he grabbed the iron handle and drew the
door open only halfway before releasing it and throwing himself to the left behind the church's outside
wall.

As his instincts had somehow anticipated, guns
thundered on the other side of the half-open door,
slugs pounding the door and throwing slivers through
the opening. The flashes of the guns were reflected on
the inside of the door itself.

The echoes of the shots hadn't died inside the
church before James stepped into the open doorway
and fired the Henry from his hip—jacking and firing

five times, swinging the rifle from left to right and back again, tracking the jostling shadows. Men screamed and groaned and grunted, and rifles clattered onto the church's stone floor.

James pressed his back against the wall, racking another round and staring through the wafting powder smoke and into the church, whose stained glass windows on both sides did little to relieve the heavy shadows. Three men lay twisted and bleeding just in front of the door, one man's boots shaking as though he'd been lightning-struck.

Heels clacked and spurs sang as the wounded man in the black bull-hide vest moved down the center aisle between the benches, stumbling and grunting as he ambled toward the altar and wooden cross and the door in the back wall. James raised the Henry and fired. Just then the man stumbled sideways, and the bullet ricocheted off the altar and plunked into the back wall left of the small wooden door.

James ran a dozen yards down the aisle, stopped, and raised the Henry once more. "Stop or take it in the back, you son of a bitch!" The wounded man's stooped silhouette ducked through the back door, and was gone.

Boots thumped outside the church's front door, and James turned to see Crosseye running toward him in his bandy-legged way, the old man's bearded face red from exertion. He had a pistol in each hand. The oldster bounded into the church, stepped sideways, and pressed his back to the door, squinting.

"Jimmy!"

"Here," James said, knowing Crosseye couldn't make him out clearly in the semidarkness. "Check on Vienna!"

He continued running down the aisle to the front of the church and out the back door and into the gravelly graveyard beyond. Raking his eyes around, he saw the wounded man bolt out an opening in the adobe wall to James's left.

James took off running, leaping gravestones and wooden crosses. He crouched behind the wall to the left of the opening and looked through the gap. Seeing no one, he dashed to the other side of the gap and looked through it again.

Deciding he wasn't about to have the same reception as he'd gotten from inside the church, he bolted through the opening in time to see the wounded man ambling into an alley mouth on the other side of the trail that ran along the side of the church—between it and the second-story adobe building from which the first shooter had fired on Crosseye.

James ran across the trail and into the alley mouth. Again, he glimpsed the wounded man as he stepped into the rear of a building abutting the second-story structure on its far side. James ran to the door, but took his time entering, holding the Henry straight up and down before him.

He found himself in a dark room that owned the molasses odor of good spirits and wine, his back pressed against the wall left of the door. Beyond, another door stood open to show several feet of dark red carpet. James crossed the rear room and darted through the open door to find himself in what appeared to be a parlor room well appointed with fancy furniture and wall hangings, including a Japanese brush painting of two women pleasing a muscular, amazingly well-endowed bald man with a long black queue.

The room was empty except for a mulatto girl in a sheer black robe curled up on a dark blue settee smoking a brass-bowled pipe, the gray smoke rife with the musky-sweet aroma of burning opium.

The girl spoke softly, slowly, her black eyes not focusing: "What in . . . *tarnation* . . . is all that . . . *shootin'*?"

A stairway rose on James's right, and he climbed the carpeted steps slowly but taking two steps at a time. Blood streaked the rail and the varnished pinewood wall to the left of the stairs.

"*Stenck!*" a man screamed somewhere above him. "Stenck, the son of a bitch has nine lives, Stenck!"

James turned to his right on the first landing and stared down a hall lit with two flickering lanterns and a window at the hall's far end. Frightened women's voices murmured behind closed doors. Halfway down the hall, the man in the black vest, leaning against the hall's right wall, turned with a groan toward James. A pistol winked in the lantern light.

"Stenck!" he screamed, eyes sparking fiercely, as he thumbed his pistol's hammer back.

James fired the Henry twice from the hip. The man in the black vest jerked twice, the back of his head smacking the wall twice before he dropped the pistol and fell in a twitching pile at the base of the wall.

James walked slowly down the hall, his eyes burning from his own powder smoke. Silence had fallen behind the closed doors. James glanced down at the dead man, whose eyes were open and lips moving though his chest was still. James looked at the purple-painted door beyond the fast-dying hombre. He stopped beside it, near the dying man's head, and pricked his ears, listening.

Hearing nothing, he tried the doorknob. Locked. He kicked the door open and stepped into the room before the door could swing back against him. He stood crouched, aiming the cocked Henry from his hip.

Before him lay a rumpled, brass-framed bed. The sheet was drawn up over a quivering hump. On a small table to the left of the bed stood a bottle and a shot glass. A half-smoked cigar lay smoldering over the tip of a dirty water glass whose bottom was littered with gray ashes. On a matching table to the right of the bed stood another shot glass and another half-smoked cigar, this one hanging over the edge of the bed, also smoldering.

The air in the room was rife with the smell of sweet perfume, cigar smoke, and sex.

James heard a whimper. He turned to the quivering lump on the bed, walked slowly around to the bed's right side, and pulled the sheet down to reveal a plump, naked blonde, her thick hair piled atop her head. Her large, pale, pink-mottled rump faced James. She was curled up and shivering, and as the sheet fell at her feet she gave a yowl and glanced up at James from over her shoulder.

"Leave me be! I didn't do nothin' to nobody, so you leave me be!"

A breeze stirred the open window on the left side of the bed. From beyond the window, James heard the squawk of straining wood and a grunt, and then the thud of someone landing in the street outside the bordello. There was a pained curse.

James had just started to move back around the bed, heading for the window, when a closet door on the opposite side of the bed burst open. A naked man bolted out the door with two Remington pistols in his hands, raging like a teased grizzly bear. The man's pistols roared a half second after James cut loose with the Henry, the .44 slugs plowing through the man's bony, floury white chest and blowing him back into the closet, where he sat down with a clipped groan and a *chuff* of expelled air. One of the man's slugs had plunked through a window, the other hammering the frame beside it.

As the blonde sobbed into her pillow, shoulders shaking, James racked a fresh cartridge and continued around to the other side of the bed. He swept a purple curtain away from the window and poked his head outside. Beyond the shake-shingled awning roof before him, a tall, thin man clad in only a gray Confederate cavalry hat and carrying a bundle of clothes in one hand, with a holstered pistol and cartridge belt looped over his other shoulder, ran awkwardly toward a horse tethered on the opposite side of the street.

The man's thin, straw yellow hair jostled around his shoulders, and James could hear him grunting and wheezing painfully, unable to put much weight on his left foot.

James raised the Henry. "Turn around or take it between the shoulder blades, Stenck!"

As he reached the cream gelding tied to the hitch rack, Richard Stenck glanced over his shoulder, showing his white teeth beneath his sickly yellow mustache, then turned his head forward and jerked the cream's reins free. James raised the Henry, but as he drew a bead on the cowardly ex-Confederate's spine, just beneath his neck, a loud grumbling growl rose from behind him.

James whipped around in time to see the man he'd fed a half pound of lead weakly raising one of his Remingtons in a quivering fist and narrowing one copper-colored eye as a thick gob of blood oozed out of his mouth to paint his spade-bearded chin. James triggered two more rounds into his chest and another through his forehead, throwing him back into the closet for what James hoped would be the last time, then returned his attention to the street.

Stenck was straddling the cream and batting his bare heels against the horse's flanks as the horse galloped off up the street to James's right. "Hyahh, you mangy cayuse!" Stenck bellowed.

"Hold it right there, you son of a bitch!" came Crosseye's voice.

James glanced to his left. His burly partner was running down the middle of the street from the direction of the mercantile. Vienna stood on the loading dock, shading her eyes as she stared toward Stenck's diminishing figure. James turned back to Stenck and triggered two rounds quickly, but both slugs merely blew up dust several feet behind the cream's pounding hooves. Horse and rider disappeared around a bend in the street, the thuds of the cream's hooves dwindling.

James looked down at Crosseye, who was staring after the Confederate cutthroat down the barrel of his aimed Spencer repeater. "That was Stenck!"

Crosseye looked up at him, squinting. "I figured."

"Well, if you figured, why in hell didn't you shoot him?"

Crosseye hiked a shoulder, then, lowering the carbine, scowled off along Tucson's main drag after the now-fled Stenck. "Beats me." His voice acquired a speculative pitch. "I reckon I just couldn't shoot a nekkid man, Jimmy."

Chapter 19

The cat's head with pricked ears appeared for just a moment between buffeting waves of windblown dust and sand—a black face with two coal chunks for eyes and small, ominously curved white sabers for teeth shown in a feral snarl.

Then another wave of sand obscured the black cat, and when the wave had passed, the notch in the rocks where the cat had been was as empty as the eye sockets of the ancient, bleached skulls that littered this long-forgotten canyon.

Conquistador skulls, James figured. Or maybe Apaches or Yaquis or one of the half dozen other Mexican tribes that had long called this vast, empty, rugged stretch of southern Sonora home and had fought a bloody, pitched battle here in this rocky barranca, leaving their bones to the wildcats and the ages.

Keeping an eye on the notch where he'd seen the head of the strange black feline, James backed the chestnut out of the small box canyon into which he'd ridden after deciding to investigate an angry snarl he'd heard. The horse's left rear hoof clacked, and James turned to see a skull rolling off away from him to settle against the base of a large, flat-topped boulder. There was a ragged-edged hole in the skull's forehead, just above its right eye—an arrow wound, possibly.

He stopped the chestnut to look around at the steep, rocky slopes that nearly surrounded him, climbing to ridge crests he couldn't see for the sandstorm. The wind howled like a thousand maniacs as it funneled through the rocks and was ripped and torn along the edges of the precipitous shelves, pillars, and narrow ledges. He imagined what a battle would have been like in here, and he had to suppress a shudder—he, who'd fought in some of the worst battles and skirmishes of the War of Northern Aggression.

But it was more than the thought of that ancient battle that needled him. It was the black cat, as well. Back in the Appalachians as elsewhere, a black cat was the grimmest of omens. He'd known a slave family who, upon spying a black cat, would boil up several cottonmouths with persimmons and roots, and dribble the broth in a tight circle around their cabin to prevent evil conjured by the cat's hex from crossing their threshold.

The cat he'd seen had not been of the common barnyard variety. He'd spied several mountain lions on his trek deep into Mexico from Denver City, but he'd seen no black ones. This one, however, had appeared to be the size of the more common rock-colored lion. But, then, there were many things James had yet to learn about the West. And of Mexico, as well.

It had been six weeks since they'd left Tucson after wiping out Stenck's entire gang except Stenck himself.

James, Crosseye, and Vienna had last seen him high-
tailing it buck-naked out of Tucson, his cartridge belt
and pistol flopping from his shoulder, sickly yellow
hair blowing out behind him in the wind. Since that
time, they'd seen no sign of the Confederate scourge.
Without his gang, it wasn't entirely unlikely that
Stenck had given up the hunt for the treasure map and
had returned to Denver City. The cowardly captain
had never had much stomach for fighting.

For six long weeks, the trio of Tennesseans had
dusted the trail down from Tucson, following the
rough map that had been sketched by the long-lost half
brother of Jefferson Davis who was now going by the
name of Apache Jack somewhere in Sonora. It had been
no Sunday ride through the laurel thickets, either.
They'd fought two small packs of bronco Apaches, narrowly missed losing their "topknots," as scalps were
called in the colorful West, and endured an apocalyp-
tic rainstorm that had turned all near arroyos into
seething mountain rivers, for two full days making
travel impossible. They'd also had a nasty run-in with
a small band of banditos who'd been out for the party's
horses as well as its *"bonito chiquita."*

That had been a pitched battle in and of itself, inside
an ancient church ruin where James, Crosseye, and
Vienna had sought refuge from another though lesser
tempest. At the end of the skirmish, when the howling
and yelling and gunfire and the clash of knife blades
had died, Crosseye had harvested two ears with his
Green River knife and added a pronounced strut to his
walk.

The old Confederate now wore the ears strung from

a rawhide thong around his neck, with the Lefaucheux. He'd thought that the ears, worn with the bear claws that already adorned the thong, would give him a certain cache down here south of the border—similar to a bronco stallion's battle scars—where such trophies were obviously admired and respected. The bandito who'd belonged to the ears had worn a similar necklace himself, though Vienna had pointed out that Crosseye himself hadn't respected him for it.

Still, the old potbellied frontiersman had dried and strung the ears in hopes they might provide for him and the others smoother sailing in this alien, mysterious, and savage land, darker than the darkest Appalachian folktale James had ever heard.

"You see that critter, Jimmy?" Crosseye's voice had sounded little louder than a whisper beneath the howling wind.

James turned to see the old frontiersman and Vienna sitting their horses on the trail behind him, Crosseye holding his Spencer carbine barrel up against his thigh. James nodded, pitched his voice casually, as there was no point inflicting his superstition-fueled apprehension on the others. "Just a cat like any other," he said, reining his horse away from the rocky ridge and the canyon mouth, and booting it on up the trail that wound along the base of it.

"Huntin' durin' the day?" Crosseye said, sort of yelling it to be heard above the wind.

"Maybe it couldn't sleep!"

Keeping his head down and squinting against the windblown grit, James put the chestnut up a gradual rise, curving around the side of the mountain.

Tumbleweeds and willow leaves blew across the trail, shepherded by the snarling wind.

He'd ridden another mile before spying another steep, rocky sierra rising on his left, like a massive ocean wave that had somehow turned to jagged stone. In the path of the stony wave lay what appeared to be a village of adobe brick, stone, and plank shacks sprawling across the sage and blowing tumbleweeds. The shacks and corrals and barns were nearly the same color as the rocks and sand, making them almost indistinguishable from the desert itself. They sprawled down across the slope under the formidable, stony eye of the formation looming over them.

The trail rose and curved several times as it entered the town, which a wooden signpost along the trail identified as Pueblo de Cordura. James could smell the stock pens and privies and goats, but he could see no one on the curving street except a few goats, a pig, and some chickens that appeared to be fighting the wind for the seeds they were foraging in the gaps between the buildings.

James was looking around for a barn in which to stable their horses when a large wooden door opened on his left, and a little man with long black hair stepped out and whistled, beckoning. The barn was unmarked, but it turned out to be a livery barn, and the little, long-haired liveryman with a face like a prune seemed happy to stable the *norteamericanos'* horses for two pesos each in advance, though the Americans learned this mostly through gestures and sign language, as none of the three could speak Spanish and the little liveryman appeared to understand no English.

The other stock in the barn appeared content and comfortable enough that the Americans saw no reason not to trust the man. They paid him, shouldered their saddlebags, rifles, and bedrolls—they'd discovered few Mexican hotels that furnished more than rough grass pallets for beds—and started out the door. James stopped and turned back to the man and inquired of a fellow American going by the name of Apache Jack. If the little man understood, he didn't show it, but James thought he'd detected a strange apprehension in his dark, red-rimmed eyes as he shrugged and turned away.

James followed the others off in search of food, drink, and lodging. They found such a place off a side street—a typically seedy-looking cantina from the outside and even more typically seedy on the inside. Smoke from a cook fire hung as heavy as the dust outside. It was touched with the additional smoke of marijuana and ground peyote. A barefoot young boy in the white pajamas of a peon sat on a stool near the back, shucking corn and grunting melodramatically with the effort.

There was a small bar of planks spread across two rain barrels, and about five tables, three of which were occupied. Five men sat in a separate area, beyond a broad, arched doorway, with three *putas*—all looking like the proverbial three sheets to the wind, one hombre passed out on a rickety sofa that was now more wooden bones than the original horsehair it had been covered with.

All that the trio from Tennessee could get to drink, as had been the case for the past two hundred miles, was the native Mexican brew, pulque, an astringent concoction of the fermented sap of the maguey, or century, plant. The thin, milky brew was kept in a stone jug atop the bar and ladled into clay cups.

The first time James had imbibed the liquor, he'd felt as though he'd been smashed in the head by a brute wielding a sledgehammer. He'd drunk too much too quickly, and Crosseye and Vienna had put him to bed.

Now he merely sipped the brew, having grown to respect its potency as well as to enjoy its slightly sour taste and heady effect. But he dug into the roasted goat meat, frijoles, tortillas, and even the slightly crunchy fried ants and peppers, all smothered in sweet syrup, with the untethered vigor of a hungry coal miner.

The bartender was a withered old lady with Indian-dark skin in a red calico basque and gray *reboza*, her coal black hair piled in a bun. She came over with a pitcher to refill the trio's glasses, and James said slowly, "Pardon me, ma'am, but have you heard of an Apache Jack hereabouts?"

She set Vienna's refilled cup down, then picked up Crosseye's, merely glancing at James skeptically while pursing her incredibly thin, dark pink lips.

"Apache Jack?" he said. "Friend of ours. Amigo. We're looking for him."

"If that's all the Spanish you've picked up so far," Vienna said dryly, lightly kicking James's shin beneath the table, "let me try."

Haltingly but impressively, she spoke in Southern-accented Spanish, James only recognizing "Apache Jack." The old woman merely shrugged impatiently, prattled off some Spanish, then shuffled on back behind the bar.

"Well," Vienna said, "he's got to be around here somewhere, in one of these villages. Uncle Ichabod said he'd be waiting for him near the bells, and going by the map, we're reasonably close to the bells."

"Hard to judge distance on that map," Crosseye pointed out. "We might still be a hundred miles from 'em."

James chewed a chunk of meat and tortilla lathered in syrup and washed it down with the pulque that continued to grow on him. The liquor had a way of mercifully soothing saddle sores and any other kind of discomfort. "If he's alive and still in Mexico, we might find him in Tres Campanas. According to the map, that's the last village before the cache."

Crosseye belched into his fist. "Hard to know how far Tres Campanas is, too, goin' by that map. Could be twenty miles, could be a hundred, and with our Spanish we'll never find out!"

"Quit bein' so damn negative, old man," James said.

"What he needs is a woman," Vienna said, giving the old frontiersman a lopsided smile. "It's been a while."

Crosseye leaned toward her with a look of mock admonishment. "Now, Miss Vienna, I'm old enough to be your pappy!"

Vienna snickered. James kicked the oldster under the table. "Ow! What's that for?"

James grinned as he chewed. "Just shinin' my boot."

Vienna stared down at her empty plate, thoughtfully turning her clay cup in her hand. "If we can't find him, we've come for nothing. The bells could be no more than a hundred yards from Tres Campanas, but we'll never be able to find them. The map isn't that detailed."

"Don't worry," James said. "We'll find 'em with or without Apache Jack."

The romance of their adventure, however teeming with danger, had grown on him. The trek reminded him of his solo journeys into deepest Appalachia when he was still a shaver outfitted with only a Kentucky rifle, a powder horn, a knife, and the education in woodsmanship that Crosseye himself had bestowed upon him. He didn't care how long it took; he'd find that gold. Every man needed a reason for pulling his boots on every morning, and the Bells of El Diablo were currently his.

Part of him hoped they didn't find the treasure too soon, as he was enjoying the journey.

He forked another portion of roasted goat meat onto his plate, then reached for a tortilla. Just as he'd closed his index finger and thumb around the edge of the tortilla, something whispered in the dark, smoky air of the place. An object streaked toward him, arcing.

And then an obsidian-handled stiletto was suddenly jutting from the table, pinning the tortilla he'd been reaching for to its wooden plate.

Chapter 20

James followed the arc of the knife back to its starting point—a tall, rangy Mexican in a low-crowned sombrero and a shabby black suit coat over a frayed silk shirt, a red sash around his waist.

Giggling girlishly, the knife thrower rose catlike from his place on the threadbare sofa. The whore who'd been sleeping against his shoulder groaned and blinked her eyes indignantly as the Mexican gained his feet a little unsteadily and, still snickering girlishly beneath his drooping mustache, walked toward the arched doorway. He leaned a shoulder against the wide stone arch support and covered his mouth bashfully as he continued to laugh

James sagged back in his chair, dug a cheroot and a lucifer from his tunic pocket, and glanced at the knife handle that had just stopped quivering where it jutted from the plate in front of him. "Good one, amigo. Very good. *Bueno.*"

He struck a match to life on his cartridge belt and touched the flame to his cheroot, puffing to work up a good, glowing coal, drawing the peppery Mexican

tobacco deep into his lungs. The Mexican stopped giggling and snickering. His heavy brows drew down
over his eyes, as though he didn't like the gringo's off-
hand reaction to his display of south-of-the-border
machismo. It had been James's recent experience that if
these bean eaters didn't have you trembling at the first
flash of a knife blade, they clouded up and rained like
chastised three-year-olds.

The man pushed off the stone arch support and
came slowly toward the table. Through the cigar smoke
puffing around his head, James glanced at Vienna. She
sat with her back to the approaching Mexican, a tight
look on her face, her eyes boring into the table before
her. Crosseye stared across the table at James, the old
frontiersman's eyes looking dark but ready for the inev-
itable . . . if it came to that, as it so often did down here.

The Mexican stopped at the corner of the table
between James and Vienna. He scowled down at
James, his demeanor dark and rigid with coiled menace. On his hips were two big Walker Colts; another,
larger knife was sheathed over his belly, the scrolled
handle jutting up over his sternum. His brown, long-
fingered hands were bunched at his sides.

James drew on the cheroot and blew the smoke out.
"Can I offer you a drink, amigo? Ain't been down here
long. Don't have too many friends."

The Mexican wasn't looking at James. He was looking at Vienna, his eyes glassy, heavy-lidded, and ab-
solutely riveted on the woman, her thick raven hair
swirling across her shoulders clad in the red-and-
white-striped serape.

The Mexican's black eyes slid toward James. His

right nostril flared slightly, his long jaws hardening, and then he turned back to Vienna and grabbed a fistful of her hair. Vienna grunted and glared up at the man, her gray eyes spitting defiant fire from beneath her straw sombrero.

"This one I take!" the Mexican said, spitting the words out harshly and pulling the stiletto out of the table. He slid its nastily thin blade toward Vienna's throat. "Or I cut!"

James leaped to his feet. The Mexican released Vienna's hair and swung her around to face James, the blade in his left hand angled toward James's belly. Only, James's own right hand was wrapped firmly around the Mexican's knife wrist. The Mexican looked down at it, eyes winking in the lamplight, puzzled. As he tried to push the blade toward James, he made a deep-throated groaning sound. His wrist didn't move. He hadn't been prepared for the sudden, decisive reaction of the tall, dark, blue-eyed gringo, and he looked down in growing fury as James twisted his wrist back and sideways, making the little bones in the appendage pop and crack.

The Mexican stepped back haltingly, and James followed, increasing the destructive pressure on his wrist, until the man's back was pressed up against the opposite stone arch support of the one he'd been leaning against a few minutes ago.

With an agonized cry, he released the stiletto. It clattered to the floor. Raging, he reached for one of the Walker Colts. It was in James's hand first, and the tall Confederate hammered the butt against the Mexican's right cheek.

The Mexican flew sideways and hit the earthen floor

with a thump. He groaned, body tensing, long legs crossing, then uncrossing. Making a deeply pained expression, he fell back against the floor, unconscious. Blood trickled from the three-inch gash in his cheek and around which the skin was purpling.

Holding the Walker Colt butt-first in his fist, down low by his side, James looked around. The other Mexican males in the room remained where they'd been when the tall Mex had thrown the stiletto. They regarded him now dully, droopy-eyed, heads wobbling drunkenly on their shoulders. The little boy who'd been shucking corn stared at James, his eyes wide, lower jaw hanging. The old woman who ran the place was peeling potatoes into a skillet and regarding James with only a vague look of disapproval, apparently accustomed to such carryings-on and, likely, far worse.

"Well, I'm glad you made us some more friends, Jimmy. Can't have too many friends—that's what I always say!" Crosseye heaved his burly bulk up from the table, adjusting the pistol hanging down his chest and the cartridge belt around his waist. "With that, maybe we should find somewhere else to hole up out of the wind."

They found such a place down a cross street nearby. It was marked HOTEL but it was merely a second story with straw pallets above a goat stable. The pallets were partitioned off from one another with ropes strung from ratty striped blankets, all smelling of must and goat.

Behind the stable was a small living area where the young couple who ran the place lived with several children of all ages. One of the children, an infant, was crying as James tried to sleep on his own pallet sand-wiched between Vienna and Crosseye, each separated from him by blanket curtains. Occasionally, the child's cries were drowned by the moaning wind, but every time sleep reached up for James, the wind would die or the child would wail louder.

Crosseye apparently had no such difficulty. To James's right, the graybeard was snoring peacefully. That, too, would have kept James awake if he hadn't grown accustomed to the raucous sawing long ago. To James's left, there'd been no sounds for a time, and he'd thought Vienna must have gone to sleep, as well, but now he heard water being poured from a pitcher. Unable to sleep, she must have decided to wash.

Soft splashing sounds continued to emanate through the curtain, as well as the light sucking of a sponge being squeezed. They somehow drowned out Cross-eye's long, luxurious snores and the wind's caterwaul-ing. James lay on his back, hands behind his head, squeezing his eyes closed and fighting the images that kept shaping themselves behind his retinas.

His loins burned. He gritted his teeth and was about to roll over onto his belly and bury his head in his sad-dle when the curtain to his left suddenly drew back.

Vienna pulled a hand away from the curtain and sat back down on her pallet. She wasn't wearing a blouse but only her denim trousers. They were unbuttoned. She turned sideways to him, drew her knees up, and wrapped her bare arms around them. Before her was a rusty tin washbasin and a clay pot of water. A sponge lay beside the basin.

Vienna shook her hair back from her face. Her voice

was husky as she said, "Would you like to finish for me, James?"

He stared at her firm shoulders and long, slender arms. He could see half a pale, full breast beneath her arm, mashed against her upraised right knee. Despite the hammering in his chest and the searing agony of lust in his loins, James hesitated, vaguely repelled by the offer.

His mind swirled until his head ached, and then he found himself climbing to his feet, staring down at her stonily, his broad chest rising and falling heavily as he kicked out of his boots. He unbuttoned his shirt, tossed it down on his saddle. In a minute, the rest of his clothes were there, as well—pants, long-handles, red neckerchief, socks.

He moved to her stiffly, his goatish male need for her fairly dripping off him, and sat down behind her. He wrapped his arms around her, around her knees, and nuzzled her neck, intoxicated by the touch of her smooth skin, by the smell of her, the caress of her silky hair on his cheek. She turned her head, and his lips found hers, hot, wet, and pliant. Her tongue was waiting for his at the edge of her mouth, and as he mashed his lips against hers, her tongue retreated, teasing, before jutting forward to entangle itself with his.

He pulled away from her but kept his head very close to hers, their lips almost touching, and cupped her breasts in his hands. He lowered his head, ran his lips down her neck and her right breast, and stopped. He slid his eyes toward her cleavage at the top of which lay a small tattoo in the shape of a bucking bronc, tail curled upward.

James stared at the horse above her heaving breasts.

"Oh, that," Vienna said, running her hands through his hair, her voice pitched with passion. "Just ignore it, James. That's from a life I've left behind."

She thrust her breasts against him, and he continued moving his head down, kissing his way down the upturned orb to the jutting nipple.

"James," she whispered later, half groaning, a single tear rolling down her cheek when they collapsed together, spent. "I'm in love with you, James."

Something tugged on James's big toe.

Instantly, he was awake to find his Griswold already in his hand, his thumb ratcheting the hammer back. He was on his back, Vienna curled against him, her head on his chest. He looked up, focusing his sleep-bleary eyes, to see the boy from the cantina lurch back against the blanket curtain behind him, throw his hands straight up above his head, and yell a terrified Spanish plea.

Vienna gasped and jerked her head up from James's chest, clutching one of the blankets they'd shared against the stormy chill to her naked bosoms. James looked around, listening, hearing only Crosseye grumbling on the other side of James's own now-vacant sleeping crib to his right. The kid was alone.

James depressed the Griswold's hammer and lowered the weapon, his ear tips warming with self-consciousness. He glanced at Vienna looking incredulously up at the boy, her hair mussed, shoulders bare, and then he returned his own grumpy gaze to the kid. "What the hell, boy?"

The kid pressed a finger to his lips and turned his head as though listening, wondering if his own scream had been heard in the living area below the hotel. Finally, he turned sideways, canted his head, beckoning to James—an oddly adult gesture in one so young, probably not over ten—then pushed back out the blanket curtain.

"What in tarnation?" came Crosseye's sleep-gravelly voice from James's right. The oldster was stomping into his boots. "Jimmy, what's poppin' over there, blame it!"

James pushed off his elbows and heels and slipped back into his own sleeping area to see Crosseye poking his shaggy head through the curtain on the opposite side. The old man's sleep-bleary eyes raked him up and down, puzzled by the younger man's nakedness.

"You mind if I have a moment?" James snapped.

As if he suddenly understood, Crosseye's big cheeks above his beard flushed and a grin tugged at his mouth corners as he pulled his head back through the blanket. James dressed quickly, then carried his boots and rifle out to where the kid stood in front of Crosseye, whispering in Spanish and gesturing wildly with his hands, pointing out the small, sashed window in the adobe wall at the far end of the little sleeping area.

The wind continued to blow sand against the hotel's walls and rattle the thin, cracked windows in their frames.

"What is it, kid?" James said, squatting so his head was level with the shaver's.

The boy looked out from under a neatly cut shelf of straight blue-black bangs, made a frustrated expression, shaking his head. A thin white scar slanted across his nose. He began walking toward the stairs that led down to the goat pen, beckoning.

James looked at Crosseye, who returned the favor. "Trap?" the older man said.

James looked at the kid who stood over the open stone stairs, beckoning and prattling on in Spanish. Somewhere in the tangle of incoherent Spanish, the words "Apache Jack" jumped out like a zebra in a herd of whitetail deer.

James glanced at Crosseye and then at Vienna, who stood to his right, buttoning her blouse and staring wide-eyed at the little boy by the stairs. Quickly, James set his rifle against the wall, removed his shell belt and holsters from where he'd hung them on his shoulder, and wrapped the belt and twin .36's around his waist.

When the others were ready, the three of them leaving their bedrolls in their respective cribs but all donning their hardware, including Vienna, who wore a .36 Remington for the cross draw on her slender hips, they followed the boy down the crumbling stone stairs and into the stock pen below.

The goats brayed and scurried away, hooves thudding softly on the manure-and-straw-strewn floor of the stable. The boy ran toward a small wooden door in the east wall. "Apache Jack," he whispered, opening the door, peeking cautiously out, then regarding the three gringos behind him, and beckoning. "Apache Jack—*vamos!*"

Chapter 21

"Viene esta manera!"

The boy beckoned again as he ran across the narrow side street obscured by blowing dirt, sand, and tumbleweeds. James, Crosseye, and Vienna followed, looking both ways up and down the cluttered, abandoned street. James wondered who the kid was watching for.

The old woman from the cantina?

He got an answer to the question a few minutes later when they were angling amongst the scattered hovels toward the town's far southwestern edge, on the far side of the massive stone wave standing sentinel over the village. The boy stopped running suddenly, looked toward a trail following a near arroyo, then motioned for the others to hurry. A minute later, the kid, James, Crosseye, and Vienna were hunkered down against the bank of the arroyo, staring through the spindly brush at the lip of it toward the trail.

Horseback riders were moving along the trace, entering the town from the desert on James's left. As they came nearer, all five riders hunkering low over their horses' necks against the wind, James saw that they were clad in dove gray uniforms with high black boots with silver spurs, heavy pistols holstered on their hips or thighs. One wore a leather-billed forage cap, long, curly brown hair blowing out around the cap in the wind. The other men's gray felt sombreros buffeted down their backs by their chin thongs. One rider was holding aloft a wind-torn, powder blue guidon depicting a buffeting golden eagle with spread wings.

James had seen the guidon before, as well as such uniforms as the riders were wearing. Mexican *rurales*. Rural Mexican policemen. Being foreigners here, and on Mexican soil for admittedly nefarious reasons, he and the others had swung clear of them. The boy seemed to think it important to swing clear, as well, as he waited until the riders had passed his and his three charges' position before clambering up out of the arroyo and dashing across the trail and into open desert.

"Where in the hell we goin'?" Crosseye groused, breathing hard. "If I woulda known we was walkin' this far, I'd have ridden my hoss!"

"Looks like we're there," James said, following the boy from about ten yards back and seeing a blocky sandstone church rise before him.

A ruined stone wall surrounded the church and the long, L-shaped adobe brick building behind it. The boy led his party across another shallow arroyo and then across a cart trail that angled toward the church from Cordura, and around the church's front corner toward the shabby addition flanking it. Beyond the addition were stock pens, a garden with irrigated ditches, and a sprawling cemetery.

The trio of Confederates followed the boy to a stout

door beneath a brush arbor. Wind-whipped paper lanterns hung beneath the arbor, and a clay water pot called an *ojo* in these parts lay shattered on the cracked flagstones near the door. The boy rapped the heel of a hand on the door and shouted something. After a few seconds, the door opened, and a young woman in a nun's habit poked her head out. While the boy spoke to the young, fair-skinned nun in Spanish, she regarded the three dusty visitors warily, curiously, before nodding once curtly and pulling her head back inside.

The boy beckoned as he moved through the door, remembering to doff his straw sombrero and hold it against his chest. James and Crosseye removed their hats, and Vienna tossed her sombrero back off her head, letting it hang from her neck by its chin thong.

Inside a dark entrance hall lit by one small window near the door, the nun glanced at each of her visitors in turn while the boy stood respectfully to one side, head tilted back, a small rooster tail swaying at the crown of his head as he looked around at the nun and his three incredulous charges peppered liberally with dust and grit from the windstorm. From deep in the bowels of the building, a scream sounded.

A man's scream, at once raspy and guttural and filled with primal fear. The agonized lament lifted gooseflesh between James's shoulder blades, but neither the nun nor Pablo reacted.

"Pablo says you've come to see Apache Jack," the nun said in a heavy Irish brogue. "Is this true?"

Vienna spat sand from her lips, brushed it from her eyebrows. "He's here?"

"What is your business with Jack?"

The scream came again, garbled by distance, as though the screamer was a long ways away, in another part of the building. It was answered by an angry shout, as though the screamer was being admonished.

"His brother sent us," Vienna said.

"And who is Jack's brother?"

"Jefferson Davis."

The nun absorbed the response without expression aside from the merest hint of a flush rising in her pale cheeks as she stared directly at Vienna. Then she ran her still-skeptical eyes across James and Crosseye standing near the boy before she swung around, the black skirt of her habit giving a sibilant rustle.

"Follow me."

The nun led the party through the entrance hall. She turned right and followed a long, dingy corridor paneled in pine, her sandals slapping on the grime-encrusted flagstones. The hem of her skirt lifted wisps of dust in her wake.

The screams continued, as did the shouting, though more distantly now. Doors lay along each side of the hall. Most were open. Near some of these doors, or between them, ghostly figures stood ensconced in pale light and shadow. Some of the figures were men, some women, all dressed in the plain cotton garb and shabby ponchos of the Mexican peon, though some appeared to be American. They were of all ages. Some were missing limbs or were otherwise disfigured—there was a hunchback and someone suffering the ravages of leprosy. But in most that James passed, he saw in their eyes the dark shimmering light or hollow, vaguely terrified casts of insanity.

What haunted James even more than the twisted figures around him was the possibility that he'd come all this way only to visit a madman with a crazy, made-up story of the devil's gold. As he walked, following the nun and the boy, James glanced at Crosseye and Vienna in turn, and he almost chuckled at the dark humor of the possibility of their journey ending here, in a Mexican madhouse.

Well, it was fitting, wasn't it? The world on the eastern side of the Mississippi was mad, so it only stood to figure that the one west of it would be, too. The whole damn world, in fact. There was no escaping it.

Near the end of the long hall, the nun stopped before a door that stood partway open. Voices emanated from inside as did the clink of a glass. The nun glanced at James.

A crispness entered her voice. "Wait here."

She pushed through the door and immediately cut into loud, fluent Spanish. From the hall behind her, James saw a thick figure nearly lurch out of his boots and swing wide of the woman, who turned to continue directing her tirade his way, as he made his way to the door, sort of hop-skipping, limping. James saw that one of the big man's bare feet was much larger than the other, and that the ankle bulged hideously. The man, clad in white pajama bottoms and a long, dark brown serape tied at the waist with a rope, bounded past James and the others and went skip-hopping down the hall in the direction from which James's party had come.

The nun had turned her attention to a man lying in a bed on the small room's right side. Her voice was gentler but still admonishing. The man lay with his back against two pillows propped against the far wall, to the right of a window of animal hide scraped thin as waxed paper; it rippled in the wind, tossing dull javelins of gray light around the otherwise dark room.

This hombre's bald head was bullet-shaped, with tufts of wiry gray hair sticking out on the sides, with more wiry tufts protruding from over his eyes and from out of his overlarge ears. His face was long, angular, and craggy—at least what James could see of it below the white bandage that had been wrapped around the top half of it, covering his eyes. Over his eyes, the bandage was liberally spotted crimson.

In one big, gnarled hand he held a clear bottle. In the other, he held a loosely rolled corn-husk cigarette. The smoke curled up from the lit end of the quirley, unspooling in the air above his head. He was holding his own with the nun in Spanish before suddenly turning his head toward the door and saying in English weighted in the lush, rolling accents of the American South: "Visitors? I have visitors? Who is it—that bastard Salsidio again? What'd he come for now? My *balls*?"

He dropped the cigarette on the heavy quilt covering him, reached under the bedcovers, and hauled out an enormous Colt Patterson revolver. His thumb ratcheted the hammer back, but he did not get the big popper leveled at the newcomers before the sister shoved it down with one hand while retrieving his cigarette with the other.

"It is not Salsidio, Jack. These people said your brother sent them! Pablo brought them!"

"Pablo?"

"*Sí*," the boy said, adding a few sentences in Spanish.

Apache Jack jerked his chin up and called, "Who's there? Name yourselves."

Vienna moved into the room and said her name.

Apache Jack's lips spread with a faint smile. "A girl . . ." He held up his right hand, curling his thumb and index finger until the tips of each were half an inch apart. The nun slipped the cigarette between them, and Jack drew the quirley to his lips. "Who you got with you, girl?"

"James Dunn," James said, moving into the room as the nun stepped back away from the bed, making room for the visitors. "And this here's Crosseye Reeves."

"I like the sound of your voice, son. Southerners. But I've been expecting a man named Ichabod McAllister."

"My uncle," Vienna said, adding, "He's dead. I've come in his stead."

"How'd he die?"

"He was killed by a man named Stenck."

"Stenck?" Apache Jack said, his tongue flicking along his leathery lower lip. "Stenck's the other man I been expecting. My brother told me to expect them both at the head of a good-sized party of seasoned shooters."

"They were indeed due to come together with a company of men," Vienna said, "but my uncle Ichabod grew suspicious of Captain Stenck's motives. There was no better validation of his suspicions than Stenck's bloody murder of my uncle's entire family as well as a maid."

Apache Jack was nodding slowly as he puffed the cigarette lodged in one corner of his mouth, as though he was surprised by none of what he was hearing. As though he'd almost expected such a grim turn of events.

"What about you?" Jack asked.

"I was my uncle's secretary. I witnessed the murders but made away with the map. I've spent the last year hiding from Stenck and his men, biding my time, waiting for an opportunity to come here in my uncle's place and locate you and secure the gold for the Confederacy."

"I'll be damned." Jack continued to puff the quirley, absorbing the information. "Your voice sounds sweet as pecan blossoms, but your words wear pants, girl." Smoke jetted from his nostrils as he worked the quirley to the other side of his mouth. "Tell me about the two you got with you—this Dunn and Reeves."

"They're from home. Both soldiers in the Confederacy."

James noted how she used the present tense.

"Ah," Apache Jack said with approval. "How is the Confederacy these days? Have we kicked Grant's drunken ass back to Washington with his consarned tail between his legs? Got that ole tyrant, Abe, tarred and feathered and run back to Illinois on a greased rail?"

Jack laughed at that, rocking back and forth and nearly losing his cigarette.

James and Crosseye shared a look. "Not quite," James said. "In fact, when Crosseye and I left, the federals were marching toward Atlanta."

"Devils!" Jack took a pull from the bottle. "That's likely why I ain't heard from my brother in a while.

He's gonna need money for rifles, new cannons, maybe mercenaries from Europe, to drive them yellow-fanged Yankees back up north where they belong."

"That's why we're here, Jack," said Vienna, brushing his chest with her right hand, lending comfort. "Can I call you Jack?"

Jack smiled and lifted his chin, ran his tongue along his thin, dry lips sheathed in gray-brown beard bristles. "Honey, you can call me anything you like. You're purtier'n a speckled pup. I can hear it in your voice." Jack took a deep breath. "And you smell like woman!" He paused, smiling almost ethereally, then spoke with mock furtiveness behind his hand. "Sister Larena has taken a shine to me, but she smells like candle wax!"

He cackled like an old woman. Sister Larena lowered her chin, color touching her cheeks.

Jack broke into a coughing fit. When it had passed, he said, "But I do answer to Apache Jack. The Mescins gave me that handle on account o' how I slip in and out o' them mountains to the south—a spur range of the Mother of Mountains, the Sierra Madre—silentlike. Silent as a damn, wild-assed, savage Apache!"

That last fairly exploded out of Apache Jack's chest, his face swelling up and turning beet red, his brown hand closing around the bottle so tightly that James thought he'd shatter it.

Sister Larena gasped. "Settle down, Jack! Don't get yourself all heated up again, or you're going to give yourself a heart seizure for sure!"

"'Paches done this to me," Jack said, when he'd settled down, his voice quiet but heavy with remembered misery. "Last time I was out there, two months ago, they run me down finally. After all these years of me headin' up into the Shadows, the Lipan Apaches' sacred range, they finally caught me. Must have figured I was up there for a reason, searchin' for the bells. And they was right. And they figured they could keep me from showin' anyone else the way to the canyon them three beauties are in by searin' my eyes out with stone arrows heated till they glowed like little suns over a hot fire."

Apache Jack gritted his teeth between quivering lips, as though reliving the agony of the Apache torture. He drew a breath, kept his voice pitched low with foreboding. "Didn't kill me. No. They wanted me to show others what happens to them that go trampin' around up there in the Shadows—Las Montanas de la Sombra—their sacred range. Sons o' pagan bitches! So they throw me over a horse, ride me right up to the edge of Cordura, dump me in the dirt, and ride away."

"What were you doing up there?" Vienna asked, shaking her head. "You already knew where the bells were. You'd drawn the map."

"Oh, you look at those bells once, twice, even three times, and you can't but wanna look at 'em again!" Jack laughed, cackling madly, causing the hair at the back of James's neck to rise. "They're beauties. All three. Sittin' there in that cave just like the Father, the Son, and the Holy Ghost on a cracked black boulder!"

The nun lurched forward, dropped to a knee beside Jack's bed, and wrapped both her hands beseechingly around his forearm clad in the sleeve of a threadbare underwear shirt. "But they're not, Jack. You know they're not. There's nothing holy about them. They're the devil's work! The Apaches themselves have *cursed* them!" She whipped her brown eyes around, fixed them on James. "Anyone who goes near them dies the most horrible death imaginable!"

She gained her feet, and her stare became even more piercing. *"And that's just the start of their misery!"*

Chapter 22

"Well, I'll be hanged," Crosseye said when Sister Larena's tirade had finished reverberating around Apache Jack's tiny room. "I think I'm ready to go home now."

"Hold your water," James told his partner, turning to Sister Larena and then to Apache Jack. "What's all this about? The devil's bells, Apache curses . . ."

"That's the legend," Jack said. "Don't listen to the sister. She's just superstitious, that's all. And for some reason she's got it in her head she's gotta watch over me. Maybe I'm better lookin' than I thought I was." He snickered, shoulders jerking, and took another pull from the bottle.

"The devil is not a superstition," the nun said softly, still down on her knees and staring at Jack. "And while the Apache curse might be, the Indians themselves are still a force to be reckoned with. You found that out for yourself, Jack."

"That I did," Jack said with a long, ragged sigh.

"Hold on, now," Crosseye said from the open doorway. "If Apache Jack's been blinded by them Apaches, there ain't no way we're gonna get back to that canyon in them Shadow Mountains to where the bells is at. Ain't that right?"

James and Vienna looked at Jack.

"Pablo still here?" Jack said, then repeated the question in Spanish.

"*Sí.*" Holding his sombrero against his chest, Pablo slipped between James and Vienna to stand next to the bed, right of the nun. Sister Larena merely shook her head in defeat, rose, and, crossing herself, strode out of the room, muttering a prayer.

"Pablo knows where the gold is," Jack said, placing a hand on the boy's head. The hand was gnarled and long enough to nearly cover Pablo's entire scalp. When Jack repeated the sentence in Spanish, the boy looked at the blind man gravely and nodded once, nearly dipping his chin all the way to his chest.

James shook his head. "No way. We can't put the boy through that kind of danger. Look what happened to you."

Pablo had tipped his head far back, staring up at the tall ex-Confederate, wide-eyed, trying to fathom what he'd said.

Jack took a deep drag on his cigarette. Ashes drifted down to his narrow chest, and Vienna brushed them away.

"Pablo is full-blood Apache. His grandmother married a white man. She runs the cantina the boy works in. Pablo's father was killed fighting the Apache's fiercest enemy, the Yaqui. That gives Pablo a certain cache." Jack shook his head and turned his blind eyes toward the boy, smiling fondly. "They won't hurt him. They'll hurt us . . . if they find us . . . but they'd most likely haul Pablo back home to his grandmother with their blessing."

Crosseye's voice sounded like the slow scrape of stone against stone. "While they roast the three of us slow over low fires. Yeah, I've heard how they work."

"They'll likely do worse than that," Jack said. "If they find us."

Vienna said, "Pablo's grandmother might have something to say about Pablo traipsing into the mountains with us . . . on so dangerous a mission."

Jack shook his head. "Pablo goes his own way. His grandmother doesn't keep him tied to her apron strings. He's his own man—ain't ya, Pablo?"

"Wait," James said. "You said *us*?"

"You don't think I'd let you go out there by yourselves, do you? Hell, I don't even know you. Now, the girl sounds like a she-saint in flowered silk, and I'm cursin' every second I can't lay my lusty ole eyes on her. I'm sure she's as pure as a Virginia rain. But you boys . . ." Jack shook his head cunningly. "You might just rob me blind, take that gold for yourselves when it's meant to go to Richmond."

He snorted and then took another pull from the bottle.

"So, what's it gonna be?" Jack said, wiping his mouth with the back of his hand holding the bottle. "We gonna go after the gold . . . *together* . . . or we gonna leave it up there for the Apaches, who won't do nothin' with it but steer clear of it and keep everyone else away, to boot?"

James looked at Crosseye. The old frontiersman

turned his dark, wary gaze from Apache Jack to James. "Injun curses aren't nothin' to mess with, Jimmy."

James looked at Vienna, who kept her own eyes on Apache Jack. "If we find the bells, how will we get them all the way to Richmond?"

"Don't have to," Jack said. "There's a Confederate mint in New Orleans. It kills me to say it, but we can get them purty ladies melted down into coins there, and a company of Confederate soldiers will make sure they get back to brother Jeff in Richmond—hopefully not too late to do some good."

Vienna looked at James. "I'm in," she said.

James hadn't come all this way to let a couple of curses, one Christian, one pagan, detour him. In fact, all of this smacked of just the kind of adventure that kindled his inner fires . . . though he hoped that was the only kind of fire that got kindled, and none that the Apaches kindled themselves under his naked ass.

James looked at Crosseye. "If you're scared, I reckon you could find a fat whore to hole up with till we get back."

"Ah, shut up," Crosseye grumbled, hitching his pistol higher on his hips and flushing. "It's the curse I don't like. Them Injun curses ain't nothin' to mess with, and you can fun me all you want!"

Apache Jack held out his bottle and they drank to their partnership.

"When do we go?" Vienna asked after she'd gotten the rotgut down and was keeping it down.

"Early bird gets the worm," Apache Jack said, grinning. "Is tomorrow mornin'—oh, say around four— too late?"

* * *

James felt as though he'd chugged some secret elixir brewed by the old Scottish mountain people near Seven Oaks—a concoction that didn't so much inebriate him as touch him with a raw, powerful energy and optimism. Something with sweet sicily in it. Maybe some partridge berry and Indian pipe thrown in. And camel's hump. God knew what else—maybe the dust from a raven's wing.

The concoction liberally scooped into a cup of piping black coffee.

It wasn't so much the prospect of gold that had his blood up, but of riding off tomorrow into the craggy, dark mountains that Apache Jack had pointed out from his own window in the mission house. The wind-blown sand made them appear even more mysterious than their formidable shape and their distance from Cordura.

James watched them now in the periphery of his vision as he, Crosseye, and Vienna followed Pablo back toward Cordura, not retracing their previous furtive steps but taking a more direct route while avoiding the cart trail. The Bells of El Diablo. He liked the way the phrase rolled off his tongue as he whispered it to himself, the wind keening too loudly for the others to hear.

He'd always heard that a man couldn't run from his problems. Hog tripe. He didn't think he'd ever feel alive again after Willie's death, but down here in Mexico, on a trek to seize three gold bells and haul them out of the Shadow Range, he felt the hunger of living awakening once more. The Apaches considered the range their sacred home and would fight tooth and nail to protect it from interlopers.

Of course, Crosseye didn't see it the way James saw it. He respected Indian curses, as he'd respected Negro legends and hoodoo lore back home in Tennessee. But Crosseye wasn't running from anything. James was running from his brother's murder, running as fast as he could until he could forget that horrific night altogether.

He didn't see anything wrong in what he and Apache Jack and the others were doing. They merely intended to take three gold bells that the Apaches had no use for—treasure that was there for the taking by anyone brave or crazy enough to take it—and send them back home to help the Confederates defend themselves against the scourge of Yankee imperialism.

What about Vienna?

He looked at her now as they tramped into the outskirts of Cordura, her hair blowing behind her as she walked with her head down, sombrero flopping down her slender back. She was so different now in this foreign land so far from home that somewhere along the trail he'd ceased thinking of her as Willie's. Now she was her own woman. And if she decided again to give herself to James, he'd take her.

Vaguely, he remembered the tattoo nestled between her breasts, and just then she glanced at him. As though reading his mind, she gave a faint smile, blinking slowly, and he felt the pull of her down deep in his loins. He spat to one side to distract himself but couldn't help yearning for the next time they'd be together.

When Pablo returned to his grandmother's cantina,

James, Crosseye, and Vienna found another cantina on the other side of Cordura—one where they hoped no more trouble would find them. It was nearly suppertime, and dusk was falling over the windblown town.

Apache Jack had told them they could secure trail supplies farther south, in another pueblo nearer the Shadow Range. There, they'd also purchase pack mules for hauling out the bells.

James pushed through the batwings of the cantina whose name Vienna had translated as the Carnival of Happiness and removed his hat, sand immediately sifting off the crown. He swiped it against his breeches and looked up to see, to his surprise, a blonde in a skimpy pink dress and a matching choker smile at him from where she leaned against the bar.

Her blue eyes roamed across the breadth of James's shoulders, then up and down before she waggled a knee under her skirt and said, "Well, look what the wind blew in."

Crosseye and Vienna filed in behind him, stomping their boots and dusting the sand from their clothes. Vienna tossed her head, causing her hair to fly in a delicious black cloud, and it became obvious that despite the male attire, she was very much a woman. Her rich black hair danced about her shoulders as she shook her head again, dislodging the grit from the storm, then threw it back, her gray eyes meeting those of the blonde regarding her incredulously.

"Just pulque will do, honey," Vienna said, hooking her arm around James's elbow and heading for a table to the left of the bar.

The blonde made a sour expression before glancing

at the Mexican barman, who started ladling the tangle-foot into tin cups. James sagged into a chair near a crackling sheet-iron stove, on the far side of the table from the bar. Vienna sat beside him, her back to the wall, and Crosseye lowered his heavy bulk into the third chair, on the far side of the table from James. From here, they could keep an eye on the entire room.

There were several other patrons gathered around two tables to James's left—all dressed in the colorful shirts and the deerskin, gaudily stitched and tooled *charro* slacks of the working vaquero. They wore silk neckerchiefs; one wore a red leather vest under a short bull-hide jacket with large brass buttons.

No work today on account of the wind, so the cow-boys were drinking and playing cards. Another vaquero, with a gray beard that hung to his chest, sat alone at a table nearest the stove, a red-and-black-striped blanket draped over a spindly shoulder. He was playing a man-dolin very softly, his bent and calloused fingers mov-ing fluidly over the strings, singing very quietly to himself.

The other, younger men had turned their attention to the three newcomers, their brown eyes especially riveted on Vienna. Now as the blond barmaid carried a small tray of drinks to the trio's table, most of the Mexican punchers returned their attention to their respective games. A few snickered, cracked some obvi-ously lewd jokes while glancing at Vienna, and chuck-led amongst themselves.

James felt his ears warm in offense, but he sup-pressed his anger. He'd heard such cracks before when Vienna had been present, but now, after their tumble above the goat pen, he felt a proprietary protectiveness despite him and her having made no promises. Still, the goatish lack of manners directed at a woman he now realized he considered his own burned him, and he had to remind himself that this was these men's territory and that he was a foreigner here. He didn't want a repeat of what had happened in the first cantina they'd visited here in Cordura.

The bargirl stole another glance at James and smiled, revealing gaps where two teeth should have been. One of her eyes was slightly discolored, as though it had recently been visited by the knuckle end of a fist. She set the tin cups on the table. "Four pesos, *por favor*," she said, extending the tray over the table toward Vienna with a haughty, faintly mocking air.

"Why, you speak *americano*!" said Crosseye.

"You ain't the only *americanos* in Mexico, honey," the blonde said coolly, arching a surprised brow as Vienna plucked coins from her pocket and tossed them onto the tray, giving the blonde a too-friendly smile.

The blonde looked at the coins suspiciously, then bounced the tray, plucking the coins out of the air with one plump, pale fist. "Me—I married up with a prospector who fell on a rattlesnake, swelled up big as a hog, and died, leavin' me here to fend for myself any way I can." She glanced at James once more, then wrinkled her nose at Vienna, and turned to Crosseye, curling a lascivious smile. "Got any ideas, sugar?"

Crosseye laughed and pulled the blonde onto his knee. "Well, I can think of a couple right now, but if you got a quiet room somewheres, I'm sure I could come up with a few more!"

James sipped his drink, the cool, slightly pungent liquid popping and crackling as it burned pleasantly across his tonsils before stoking a friendly fire in his belly. From outside, voices rose. Several pairs of feet stomped, and spurs rang. A man moved through the batwings, stopped, and swung his gaze across the room. The man who'd accosted Vienna with a knife earlier now clutched his bandaged right hand to his belly and flung an arm out, jutting an angry finger.

He shouted shrilly in Spanish as several more men, all wearing the dusty gray attire of the Mexican *rurales*, stormed in behind him, rifles raised. He shouted again, and the *rurale* at the head of the six-man *rurale* pack stepped forward, his gaze holding on the three gringos and the blonde sitting on Crosseye's knee.

He was tall, with long, thick curly hair tumbling from his leather-billed kepi stamped with a colonel's insignia. He wore a long machete on his left hip, behind a holstered pistol. A brushy dark brown mustache mantled his mouth, and a large mole sat off one end of it, like a punctuation mark.

"This one here, huh, Toli?" the colonel said, tearing his gaze from Vienna to settle it on James. "This is the gringo who broke your wrist?"

"*Sí, sí, el Colonel!*"

"Ah!" The colonel laughed and clapped his hands in front of his face. "The same one who just paid a visit to *mi amigo* Apache Jack!"

He laughed again—harder, more menacing.

Chapter 23

As the colonel sauntered slowly toward the gringos' table, a hush fell over the room. He canted his head slightly to one side, muttered orders in Spanish, and the five other *rurales* hurried up behind him, formed a semicircle around James, Crosseye, Vienna, and the whore still on Crosseye's knee, and cocked and raised their muskets.

Beneath the table, James loosed his right-side .36 in its holster. Then, leaving that hand over the pistol's wooden grips, he raised the other one chest-high, palm out. "Whoa, there, amigos! I don't see why we can't all be friendly."

"Gringo *bastardo*!" said Toli, standing up close to the colonel and clutching his bandaged hand to his belly. His cheek was swollen and blood-crusted where James had torn it open with the man's own gun. "You broke my wrist, blackened my eye!"

The colonel indicated Toli with a delicate turn of his hand—a curiously gentlemanly gesture in a man with eyes like a rabid wildcat. "Is this true, senor?"

James closed his hand more tightly around his

Griswold's grips and smiled. "True enough. Toli, allow me to buy you a drink."

"Diddle yourself and your drink, gringo," said Toli, whose glassy eyes and wet, hanging lower lip showed that he'd had enough.

The colonel looked at the blonde on Crosseye's knee. "Found one of your own, eh, Kate?" Glancing at the vaqueros who had all stopped playing cards to turn their attention to the loud doings at the gringos' table, he grabbed the blonde's hand and jerked her off Crosseye's knee. "What—with them here, you're too good for the *Mejicanos*?"

He swung her back behind him and she hit the floor with a scream and went rolling. Crosseye bellowed and bolted out of his chair, quick as a ten-year-old, and buried his ham-sized left fist in the colonel's belly. Just as the colonel jackknifed forward with a scream of his own, Crosseye pulled his left fist out of the man's belly and slammed his right one against the side of the man's head. The colonel hit the floor like a half-ton bale of cured tobacco.

The whole thing happened so fast that the other *rurales* didn't have time to react. James, bolting up out of his own chair, bulled forward with his arms spread wide and plowed into two of them, knocking them both backward as they triggered their old blunderbusses into the cantina's ceiling. As he hit the floor on top of both men, he saw out the corner of his right eye a rifle butt slam down against the side of Crosseye's head.

The big frontiersman groaned. His eyes drifted up in their sockets just before the lids closed over them.

James scrambled to one knee, hearing the colonel and several other *rurales* shouting and seeing the vaqueros leaping to their feet in astonishment at the sudden dustup. Just as James gave a wild Rebel yell, every shred of sanity suddenly leaving him and the old fiery-blooded Scotch-Irish impulses firing unrestrained, he began sliding both his .36's from their holsters, clicking back the hammers, ready to start shooting—and let the devil take the hindmost!

But before he could get the pistols leveled, a rifle butt smacked him from behind. The pistols turned heavy as lead. He heard them hit the floor as the cantina before him slid around crazily, all lamps dimming at once.

The *rurales* were regathering themselves, the colonel climbing to his feet, hatless, hair in his eyes, blood dribbling down from his torn right ear. Toli was bent over, laughing hysterically, tears running down his cheeks, but James couldn't hear his guffaws. The colonel opened and closed his mouth, javelins of fury stabbing from his eyes. He was shouting, but James couldn't hear what he was saying, either. Just as James saw Vienna dart into the scene, dropping to a knee by Crosseye, then casting her terrified gaze toward James, the floor came up to smack James's knees.

As if from miles away at the bottom of a deep well, he heard the colonel's voice shout something in Spanish and punctuate it with *"Vamos!"* as he swung around, stuffed his hat on his head, and strode out the cantina's louvered front doors.

James was about three-quarters conscious, so he was aware of being picked up by his arms and being dragged out of the cantina and into the dusk-dark street. He couldn't see Crosseye or Vienna, and that worried him until total darkness enveloped him for a time, though he was aware of being moved around, sometimes painfully, and hearing distant voices speaking and yelling Spanish.

Something slammed against his right cheekbone, sending a knife of pain through his face and down through his shoulders, that Scotch-Irish fury boiling upward once more. His eyes opened, and he saw the *rurales* again, though they were in a darker, smaller place lit by the wan, shifting light of several lanterns. Animals moved around on the floor—chickens and goats. James heard the grunts of pigs, though he couldn't see them. He could smell them, however—as well as the chickens and the goats. He smelled hay and straw and the musky sweat smell of the *rurales*. And spicy cigar smoke.

The *rurale* standing in front of him, blocking his view of the place they were in—a barn?—smacked him on the other cheek. Raw, senseless fury roared again inside James, and he tried bringing his own right fist up in an effort to smash it as hard as he could against the big, broad, pitted nose of the man before him grinning at him, showing two chipped front teeth.

But James then realized his arm was already up. Both his arms were secured above his head, and, try as he might, he couldn't bring either one down much less fling them at the insufferable, ugly face of the *rurale* pig in front of him.

"Cut me loose, and we'll make a time of it, you chicken-livered cuss!"

"James!"

The female voice was familiar. He turned to his left. Vienna stood beside him. Her arms were also pulled taut above her head. Her handcuffed wrists were chained to large, steel eye-rings high in the stone wall above and behind her, just as James's must have been. Someone had removed her serape; it lay at her knees. Her blouse was partway open, revealing the swell of a breast.

"That's enough," Vienna said, her face taut with anger.

Beyond her, Crosseye leaned forward, knees bent. He was passed out and half hanging by his shackled wrists that were chained to eye-rings above his head. The old frontiersman was missing his hat. His head drooped toward his chest, and he wasn't moving beyond the regular rising and falling of his broad, lumpy chest. Blood matted the gray-brown hair at one side of his head, just above and behind his ear.

James looked up to see the same shackles on his own wrists. The links of the chains were log grade. He wasn't going anywhere soon.

He looked again at the man in front of him grinning at him, taunting, holding his fists balled tightly at his sides. The colonel stepped up from behind him and gently pushed him aside with the back of one hand while the *rurale* colonel's crazy eyes bored once more into James's. Dried blood crusted his ear and made two dry rivulets down his neck. He held a cigar and a brandy snifter in his left hand, like a man of leisure preparing for bed.

Around him, amongst the chickens and the goats,

stood half a dozen other *rurales*, all holding muskets up high across their chests. They stood in silhouette or only partly lit by the weak light from the lamps hanging from posts. Double doors stood open to the night on James's right. The wind had died. James could hear the chickens clucking peevishly as they plucked seeds from the churned dung and dirt of the stable floor.

On the other side of the stable, a narrow, open doorway revealed stone steps rising out of sight but lit by a near lantern.

"From the American South, I take it?" the colonel said knowingly, puffing the cigar and squinting through the smoke at James. "Confederates?"

James opened his mouth to tell him to do something physically impossible to himself, but then he glanced once more at Vienna. She stared at him hard, her breasts rising and falling heavily behind her red and black muslin blouse.

James turned back to the colonel. "I reckon you have me at a disadvantage."

"Colonel Basilio Salsidio."

"Ah." James remembered the name mentioned by Apache Jack.

"And you . . . are . . . ?" Salsidio turned from James and walked over to where Vienna stood suspended against the wall, arms above her head. He stood before her, looking her up and down with open, lusty interest.

"Dunn," James said. "James Dunn. You're right— we're from the South. Nasty war goin' on. Thought we'd come down here, see if we couldn't find us some good broncs to start a ranch with in Texas. Oh, we'd be buyin', ya understand. Not stealin'."

Puffing on his Perfecto, Salsidio walked over to Crosseye, took the cigar in the same hand with which he held his brandy snifter, and lifted Crosseye's big, blocky head by his hair. Crosseye groaned. James could see him blink his eyes, stretch his lips. "Get your hands off me, you greaser bastard!" he intoned through a burly growl.

Salsidio released his head and stared at him with a repulsed expression. Wiping his hand daintily against his blue wool trousers that had gold stripes running down the outsides of the legs, he sighed, then turned and walked back to study Vienna some more. She stared up at him, jaws hard, meeting his goatish gaze with a defiant one of her own. He turned his cigar over and touched its wet end to the small mustang tattooed above her cleavage, then lightly along the side of her half-exposed breast.

"And who is this delectable creature?"

Vienna shook her hair out of her eyes and said crisply, "Vienna McAllister." She canted her head toward the big man groaning beside her. "That's Crosseye Reeves. Yes, we're from the Confederacy. Now, what Crosseye did to you was wrong, but hardly warranting"—she jerked on her chains, making them clink raucously—"this!" She added, trying to sound contrite but unable to keep the demanding tone from her voice: "Won't you please let us go?"

"First, a little information." Salsidio sipped his brandy and walked back over to James. "What are you doing in *Mejico*, amigo?"

"We told you, we're lookin' for—"

Salsidio swung around suddenly, smashing the

back of his hand against James's left cheek. A ring on the man's little finger caught James just above his eye. He felt the sting of a cut; blood oozed. The hammering in his tender head turned to the explosions of three Napoleon cannons, and he ground his teeth against it, seeing triple. He grabbed the wild dog of his rage before it could get away from him, and caged it.

"No more lies," the colonel said quietly, taking a sip of his brandy, the Perfecto smoldering between his fingers. "I know you visited Apache Jack, led by the sneaky little Apache urchin, Pablo. I saw you in the arroyo." He grinned, delighted with his shrewdness. "We waited until you'd left, and then we paid Jack a little visit."

James's belly filled with bile as he wondered what condition they'd left Jack in.

"After the proper amount of screaming, just before he died writhing on the floor—along with his most unwise protector, Sister Larena—he told us you were here to help him retrieve the treasure he'd found in the Montanas de la Sombras."

Vienna expressed the words that James had just started forming, her voice shrill with emotion. "You killed Apache Jack? You *bastard!*" That last came out on a sob.

"I killed him because he's been lying to me for years," said Salsidio, walking back over to Vienna. "That became most apparent when the Apaches hauled him back to Cordura with his eyes burned out. Lying about the treasure and hiding behind the skirts of that Irish nun who has no more business here than you do. Now, if you don't want me to kill you, too, *chiquita* . . ." He leaned forward until his mouth was only four inches from Vienna's. ". . . You must tell me, or show me on a map, the exact location of Las Campanas del Diablo."

"Jack just told you what you wanted to hear," James said. "He likely figured you pestered him long enough. We ain't here about no treasure. We saw Jack about horses, Colonel. We heard from Pablo that a fellow American was stayin' around here—one who knew Spanish better than we do, and . . ."

James let his voice trail off. Salsidio had taken his cigar and his brandy in his left hand. He'd drawn a stout bowie knife with his right, and he now used the nastily upturned tip to cut another button off Vienna's calico blouse.

"Huh?" Salsidio cut another button off Vienna's blouse, exposing both breasts heaving behind a thin chemise. She stared at him, jaws taut, stubborn eyes wide with fury. "You want to continue with the lies . . . at the detriment of the *chiquita* here . . . ?"

Toli was giggling between the barn's open doors, a chicken rooting around at his feet. The other *rurales* were shifting around and making lusty grunting sounds, a couple shuffling forward to get a better view of Vienna's torn blouse.

"It's the truth." Vienna glanced sharply at James. "Don't worry, James. There's nothing this pig can do to me that hasn't been done before."

Salsidio cut through another button, and then another, and the blouse fell back to the sides of her breasts. "That is what you think, *chiquita*."

"That's enough," James said, grinding his teeth and pulling futilely at the chains. "The game's yours, Colonel. We're here for the gold."

"Shut up, James!" Vienna barked, whipping her face toward his, her blouse falling back and a chemise strap falling to lay one shoulder bare. It glowed like varnished oak in the lamplight.

Salsidio arched a brow at James.

"She has a map with her gear," James told the man, staring at the knife, the point of which was caught in the top of Vienna's chemise.

"No, James!" Vienna stared at him, eyes flashing fire. "Think of your home. *Our* home! Think of what the Yankees will do to us if they win that war!"

"It's too late, Vienna. The war's all but over. Besides, in case you hadn't noticed"—he pulled on his chains again with a grunt—"we're not goin' anywhere." He looked at the colonel. With Apache Jack dead, no one was going to find the gold. The map wasn't detailed enough, though obviously the colonel didn't know that. James doubted that Jack had told Salsidio about the boy. He'd have taken that secret to his grave, no matter how much pain he'd endured first. "I'll get you the map, but first you gotta turn me and my friends loose."

Salsidio tossed back the last of his brandy. He set his cigar in the empty glass with a soft sizzling sound, gently set down the glass on the earthen floor, then quickly cut a notch in the top of Vienna's chemise.

"*No!*" the girl screamed as Salsidio dropped the knife, then ripped the chemise down the middle with a savage tug of both his hands.

He pressed his face between the jutting orbs of Vienna's breasts, drew a long, deep breath, as though drawing in the very essence of her, then pulled his head away from her chest and smiled at James. "That's not good enough, amigo. If you don't tell me where I'll find the map in the next five seconds, I and my men will do something most foul to your precious *chiquita*, and then we'll throw her and you and your fat friend over there to my hogs!"

Toli had been laughing hysterically, bent forward at the waist, resting his good hand on his knee. But he stopped laughing so suddenly that all eyes in the barn turned toward him. He groaned and stumbled forward, and his lower jaw dropped as he raised an ear-rattling scream to the rafters.

He fell forward, howling and writhing, and the handle of what appeared to be a corn knife to James's Confederate eyes jutted up from between his bloody butt cheeks.

Chapter 24

All the *rurales* including Salsidio jerked toward the shrieking Toli—looking around, tensely incredulous. Salsidio barked orders and the *rurales* glanced around at each other, hesitating. Salsidio barked more loudly, angrier, and the six lower-ranking *rurales* ran out the front of the stable into the street, looking around warily, dropping to a knee, and raising their rifles, some turned one way, others another.

Salsidio walked up in front of Toli, whose wails were growing softer as he writhed belly down on the stable floor, reaching back with both hands as though to dislodge the knife sticking out of his butt. Salsidio shouted something at his men, who merely stared up and down the street, shifting around, rifles jerking.

James glanced at Vienna, who arched a curious brow at him. If she felt self-conscious about having her breasts and the mustang tattoo bared, she didn't show it. Crosseye spat. "Sure wish that son of a bitch would quit screamin' so I could hear myself think. Pardon my French, Vienna."

"Why, when you speak it so well?" she returned

softly, staring out the open doors, where ambient light reflected off the *rurales'* gray uniforms.

As though on command, Toli stopped screaming, dropped his head to the dirt, and lay still.

The colonel stepped around him, unholstering a pistol, the ratcheting of the hammer being cocked sounding loud in the sudden heavy silence. He moved cautiously, one step at a time, into the street, holding the pistol barrel-up. His boots crunched softly in the dirt and straw.

James stared, waiting, wondering . . .

Something flashed brightly. It looked like the moon exploding. A quarter second after the first flash, a thunderous rattling sounded. It was like a thousand sticks of dynamite rolling down a rocky cliff, exploding.

Only a Gatling gun could kick up that much racket.

The ground beneath James's boots shook. He tightened his jaws against the raging cacophony. The *rurales* in the street jerked and screamed, some doing a bizarre dance pirouette, tossing their rifles in the air and jerking as though struck by lightning. Salsidio dropped to a knee and fired his pistol to the right, in the direction from which the flashes came, but then he, too, was stood up and blown back to the left of the doors, his boot heels rising a good two feet above the ground.

James didn't see him drop, but he heard the dull thud and the clipped groan.

And then, as fast it had started, the rattling stopped.

A *rurale* lying twisted in the street groaned. The Gatling gun went *rat-tat-tat!* and the *rurale* was rolled over and silenced. Smoke wafted like mist, faintly obscuring the stars. James stared, riveted, heart thudding anxiously.

Boots lifted a rataplan in the street. A silhouetted figure in white slacks ran toward him from the street's other side—a hobbling, shuffling figure in what appeared a long serape and a steeple-crowned, straw sombrero.

James's gut tightened apprehensively as the figure half dragged one awkward, lumpy foot around a dead *rurale*, then disappeared behind the stable's wall to the left of the doors. When he reappeared a moment later, crouching, he was holding a bloody bowie knife in his right hand. Blood dribbled down from the red-coated steel. The light revealed the rawboned, sweating face of the clubfooted friend of Apache Jack whom Sister Larena had berated for bringing Jack a bottle of forty-rod in his room at the mission church.

Clubfoot's open serape revealed two more knives wedged behind a burlap sash, another jutting from a sheath sewn inside the poncho's left flap. He had an oddly shaped, apish face with a single black brow. He looked around quickly, eyes wide, as though expecting more *rurales* to descend on him from the shadows.

James heard the hoof thuds and the clatter of a wagon rising somewhere out in the dark night. A man yelled, "Free the Rebs, Vincente!"

The command caused James's heart to leap, and, jerking on his chains, he looked at the clubfooted gent, whose eyes had now caught on the bare-breasted Vienna. "Check Salsidio for the key!" James yelled, jerking on the chains once more, unable to restrain himself.

Their knife-wielding benefactor limped back behind the front wall of the stable once more. In the meantime, two mules appeared, angling toward the barn's open doorway. The mules pulled a stout-wheeled, spruce-green wagon with a Gatling gun jutting like a giant mosquito above the box. Driving the wagon was a hulking form in what appeared to be a short bearskin vest and a low-crowned black sombrero trimmed with silver talismans. James blinked at the man riding to the left of the hombre in the bearskin vest, eyes riveted on the bloodstained white bandage wrapped around the old, wizened fellow's eyes, beneath a red bandanna wrapped over the top of his head and knotted on the left side, the knot hanging over his ear.

"Jack?" James blurted.

"Dunn? That you, boy?" Apache Jack stood uncertainly up in the driver's boot as the hulking creature in the bearskin vest reined the mules to a stop just outside the stable. The big man had long, drooping black mustaches, coal black eyes beneath the black sombrero's brim. A long, thin cheroot drooped from a corner of his broad mouth, the coal glowing as he drew on it.

Vienna leaned forward, smiling with relief. "Salsidio said he'd killed you!"

"Is that that purty Vienna—belle of the ball?"

"Yes!" the girl cried as the clubfoot, Vincente, moved as quickly as he could toward her, ignoring James, who was chained nearest the door.

"Come on, Vincente, get them folks loose. There's another *rurale* outpost about a mile out in the desert, and the night's so damn quiet they might've heard my friend Chulo's Gatlin' fire!" He turned his head this way and that, listening. "Where's Pablo? I told him to fetch your horses."

The boy's voice rose on the night somewhere to the left of the open doors.

"Pablo, you little scudder!" Jack intoned, cackling like an ancient witch and nearly falling out of the driver's boot. He placed a hand on the shoulder of the big man in the bear vest to his left and looked over his right shoulder. "You got the Rebels' mounts?" He repeated the query in Spanish.

"*Sí, sí!*" came the excited, high-pitched reply.

A horse whinnied. James heard hooves thudding, sandals slapping. Vicente openly ogled Vienna's breasts between the flaps of her torn blouse as he unlocked her shackles, then stepped back with a ragged sigh, glancing at her once more and then turning away, sweat dribbling down his broad, oddly shaped face.

Vienna shook back her hair, grabbed the key out of Vincente's hand, and quickly unlocked James's shackles. He drew his arms down, rubbing his wrists.

"Are you all right?" she said, drawing her blouse closed.

James gave her a quick peck on the cheek, then grabbed the key and ran over to Crosseye, who was staring at Apache Jack and the hulking man in the bearskin vest as though not sure his eyes weren't deceiving him. "Been through a lot—you an' me, Jimmy," he muttered as James unlocked the big oldster's left-hand shackle. "But I don't know quite how to play this one."

"I reckon it'll come to us," James said as the frontiersman's beefy right fist dropped from the shackle. The younger man crouched, wrapped Crosseye's right arm around his shoulders, holding him up. "Can you make it?"

"Hell, I can make it." When James released him,

Crosseye staggered backward as though drunk. Getting his feet under him, he groaned and touched a hand to the back of his head, where the *rurale* had kissed him with his rifle butt.

James looked around. Vienna had just dropped her serape down over her head. Now she slid her hair up out of its neck to let it fall down her back and glanced at a support pole on the far side of the stable. "Our guns!"

James followed her gaze to the post. He was still seeing nearly double from the braining he'd taken. He ran over to the post, stumbling, chickens scurrying out of his way, and saw his and Crosseye's and Vienna's gun belts hanging from the same rusty spike, pistols jutting from their holsters.

Crosseye's Spencer repeater leaned against the near side of the post. James's Henry rested against the post's opposite side. The new weapon must have looked so foreign to the *rurales*, more accustomed to the older, cruder muskets they'd been wielding, that none had appropriated it.

James quickly wrapped his Griswolds around his waist, positioned the holsters low on his hips, and grabbed the Henry. Crosseye had draped his bandoliers over his chest, the Lefaucheux around his neck, and was checking the loads in his Leech & Rigdon .36, making sure the caps and nipples were still set and ready to fire.

"Come on, you Rebel devils!" shouted Apache Jack, hooking an arm to beckon them toward the doors. "We ain't got all night! Pablo's done brought your hosses!"

The hulking man in the bear vest was backing the

mules away from the barn. The Gatling gun jounced in the box, squawking on its unoiled swivel. As the formidable-looking driver turned the wagon around to head back in the direction from which he and Jack had come, James ran on out of the stable to see little Pablo sitting a beefy mule and holding the reins of the Southerners' mounts, including those of their pack-horse.

"How in the hell did the kid know which horses were ours?" James called, shoving his Henry down in his saddle boot.

"Pablo knows everything there is to know about everyone and every*thing* in Cordura!" Apache Jack replied, laughing.

As though he'd understood, Pablo grinned, showing his large white teeth against his dark face beneath his straw sombrero, and tossed James all four sets of reins.

"Gracias, amigo!" James tossed Crosseye and Vienna the reins to their respective mounts and climbed into his saddle, wincing at the throbbing the maneuver kicked up in his head. Vincente was already sitting a steeldust stallion near Pablo, holding a Maynard carbine barrel up on his thigh and staring cautiously down the dimly lit main street of Cordura.

Apache Jack and the hulking man in the bearskin vest rattled eastward along Cordura's main street, and Vincent turned the steeldust to ride just off their left rear wheel. Pablo yelled at his mule and batted his sandals against the beast's ribs, and the animal lunged into a ground-eating gallop with a single bray.

Vienna ground her heels into her own mount's

flanks, and Crosseye did likewise as James glanced around at the dead *rurales* littering the street and the mostly dark buildings hunched beneath the glittering stars. No one seemed to be out and about, but most likely there were more than a few spectators peering out from dark windows or even darker alley mouths.

Chickens clucked and pecked and one of the goats sniffed a hat of one of the dead men.

Satisfied no one near had taken umbrage with the demise of Salsidio and his contingent of *rurale* policemen, and was about to start flinging lead at his back, James put the chestnut on up the trail. He caught up to the others as they followed a bend around the trail that formed a pale line through the brushy, rocky desert in the darkness, the hooves of the galloping mounts hammering loudly in the quiet night.

The wagon rattled raucously, the Gatling gun bouncing around in the box, and James was worried the cacophony would draw every Apache within fifty miles. He supposed they didn't have much to worry about, however. The Gatling gun was a formidable weapon, and James wondered where Apache Jack had acquired it.

The big man slowed the wagon's two-mule hitch after a short time, and they rode at a little more leisurely pace. Vincente continued to ride beside the wagon's left rear wheel. Pablo followed directly behind the wagon. James, Crosseye, and Vienna rode about fifteen yards behind Pablo.

No one said anything. There were plenty of questions, but they figured they'd get their answers soon enough, when they'd put enough distance between themselves and any further trouble back in Cordura.

When they'd ridden for half an hour, the big man whom Jack had called Chulo pulled the wagon off the trail's left side and into the mouth of a steep-walled canyon. He stood in the driver's boot and grunted loudly, bizarrely, as he whipped the reins against the mules' backs, trying to get them moving on the rougher trail. When the wagon was bouncing along at a regular pace, the stout, iron-shod wheels ringing off rocks, James looked around to see the cliffs on each side of the trail rising darkly, ominously.

They must have been nearly two thousand feet high in places. On the right side of the trail was an arroyo sheathed in boulders and paloverde trees.

The trail rose gradually, and short, wiry pines began to appear. The night air grew cooler. There was a distant, angry screech of a pouncing wildcat.

After another hour of hard riding, the wagon stopped near the base of a towering sierra, the steep slope of which the starlight showed strewn with large boulders. About a hundred yards out from the mountain's base, a stone hovel crouched, its brush roof touched with the light of a rising sickle moon. A corral flanked the cabin. Lights shone in the shack's windows—at least the two from which the shutters had been thrown back. Shadows moved behind them.

James walked his horse up to the side of the wagon and stopped just off its right front wheel. Apache Jack and the big driver sat facing the shack, the big man studying it carefully, nostrils expanding and contracting like those of some stalking beast. Jack had turned his head to one side, listening.

"It's occupied," he said to the big man, who sat with

his elbows on his knees, holding the reins lightly in his gloved hands.

The big man said nothing. James could hear him breathing. Something told James he couldn't speak, though he apparently understood English.

"La Croix's bunch," Jack said, making a sour expression. "I can hear that striped skunk's voice from here . . . goin' on about his latest woman." The old desert rat spat a tobacco quid over the side of the wagon; a good bit of it dribbled down the wheel. Turning back to the big man, he said, "I reckon you know what to do, Chulo. But don't use up too much ammo. We're gonna need it for the Apaches."

Chulo nodded, then flicked his reins over the mules' backs. As the wagon continued forward toward the cabin, Apache Jack turned to James and the others, grinned devilishly, ran a hand across his mouth, and said, "Wait here."

He repeated the order in Spanish for Vincente's and Pablo's benefit.

James sat the chestnut, letting the mount crop grass around the base of a boulder and watching the wagon jounce and rattle slowly into the yard. When it was thirty yards from the hovel, Chulo turned the mules back around to face James and the others, while the Gatling gun faced the cabin. When the wagon had started turning, Jack started shouting in Spanish, and men in the cabin began shouting back at him, their shadows jostling in the windows.

Jack jumped down and stood beside the wagon box, gesturing broadly as a tall man stood crouched in the cabin's low door. They made several friendly-sounding exchanges in Spanish, laughing with a little too much exuberance, before the man in the doorway stepped out into the yard, canting his head to one side as he walked slowly, a little apprehensively, toward the wagon.

Three more men came out of the cabin and spread out in front of it, near the door, two holding rifles, one holding a pistol down low along his right leg clad in silver-trimmed leather chaps. They were dressed in various types of serapes and dusty Mexican trail clothes, with pistols and knives hanging off their hips and jutting from the wells of their boots.

None was wearing a hat. They'd settled in for the evening.

When the tall man had come to within twenty feet of the back of the wagon, he stopped suddenly and pointed angrily at the Gatling gun he must have just then picked out of the shadows in the wagon's rear. He prattled off a handful of curses. The others lurched forward, also cursing, and began bearing down on the wagon with their weapons. Jack threw his head back, laughing, and a half second later the Gatling gun began its ugly song.

Knives of fire careened from its maw.

The men standing between the wagon and the brush-roofed hovel had no chance at all. They did a dance similar to that of the *rurales*, and in less than five seconds three of the four were heaped on the ground, the fourth one having been blown back into the cabin through its open door.

Vincente, sitting his steeldust, cut loose with a short, victorious, coyotelike yowl.

Vienna muttered an exclamation as she drew back on the reins of her startled horse.

Holding his own reins taut, James stared, incredulous, toward the dead men. Smoke wafted above the wagon. He heard the squawk of the Gatling gun's tripod swivel, saw the nose of the gun rise, as did the man called Chulo, from his position behind it. His boots scraped in the wagon bed.

As James and the others booted their mounts toward the wagon and the cabin, Jack said something to Chulo in Spanish, and the hulking creature, who seemed more beast than man, leaped down off the wagon and walked around, prodding the down men with his boot toes.

Jack turned toward the Southerners and Pablo as James said with a wry chuff, "Friends of yours?"

"Ha!" Jack slapped his thigh, cackling. "*Bandidos* of the worst stripe. The tall fella there, Madrino, and Chulo got along like two bobcats tied to the same plank. Ya see, Madrino made Chulo's sister heavy with child and left her to fend for herself." Jack cackled again, wagging his head. "My friends from the Confederate States of America, welcome to Mexico!"

Chapter 25

When Jack stopped laughing, he reached under the wagon's seat for a bottle, pulled the cork, and glanced over at Chulo and Vincente, both of whom were now looting the bodies of the dead, closely inspecting the cadavers' arsenal of knives, pistols, and rifles. "Ladies and gentlemen from Tennessee," Jack said, "meet my friends Chulo and Vincente. Chulo and Vincente, these here good folks is Miss Vienna McAllister, Mr. James Dunn, Mr. Crosseye Reeve, and, well, you know Pablo."

Pablo was busy unhitching the mules from the wagon.

If Chulo and Vincente had heard the introductions, they didn't acknowledge them. Vincente was pulling the right boot off one of the dead men while Chulo was hefting a revolver in his hand, testing the weight.

Jack wiped the lip of the bottle off on his pants and extended it to Vienna. "Ladies first . . . if you've a mind for a libation, Miss Vienna."

"After this day, I could drink it all down myself." Vienna threw back a healthy slug of the tanglefoot, choked down a cough, and extended the bottle to

James, who took it and glanced at Chulo and Vincente. "Where'd they come from, Jack?"

Keeping his voice low, Jack said, "They help out around the mission when they ain't up to no good, stealing horses and robbin' banks an' such. They've helped me with my prospectin' from time to time, though they haven't never seen the bells."

"They understand English?" Crosseye asked, throwing back a drink of the tonsil-burning tequila.

"Just Chulo. Don't speak a lick of nothin', though." Jack smiled and passed his index finger across his throat.

James continued watching the big men, Vincente moving awkwardly on his clubfoot. He was a full head shorter than Chulo, but broader and even more powerful-looking through the shoulders. He seemed more interested in the dead men's knives than their guns; just now he was running his thumb across the blade of a six-inch, wooden-handled skinning knife.

James turned to Jack. "Can we trust 'em?"

Jack threw back another drink and sucked air through his teeth, shaking his head. "Nope. Once we get to the bells and get 'em down out of the mountains and past the Apaches, we'll have to kill 'em."

James and Crosseye both just stared at him, James wondering if the man was joking and deciding he wasn't. Jack jerked a jeering finger at him and Crosseye. "You two don't know Mexico yet, but you're about to get to know it real well!"

Vienna said, "I don't understand, Jack. Salsidio said he'd killed you."

"He was playin' a bluff, tryin' to get you to open up about me an' my ladies." Jack chuckled. "Salsidio was

more *bandido* than *rurale*. Like most of 'em are. Oh, he
paid me a visit, all right. Seen you leave, I reckon. He's
been after the bells for years himself. Got close but never
found 'em. Somehow, months back, he started to figure I
had. He musta tracked me once or twice, and got savvy.

"Anyway, when he seen you gringos in Cordura, he
figured you were here to help me get the gold out. He
came to pump me about it, threatened to kill me, of
course, but he never would. Not on holy ground, leastways. Salsidio was many things, and a good, hell-fearin'
Catholic was one of 'em. God rest his soul." He spat in
disgust, chaw dribbling down his gray-bristled chin.

Crosseye was leaning against the wagon, staring at
the Gatling gun. "Where'd you get this bullet belcher,
Jack?"

"Chulo and Vincente got drunk one night and stole
it off ole Salsidio himself! They been hidin' it out in the
desert!"

Jack wheezed a laugh and passed the bottle again to
James. He turned to Vienna. "Darlin', would you help
a blind old man into the cabin? I need to sit a spell,
have another drink or two. Then we'd best turn in. Got
a lot of rugged country to cross next several days."

Vienna walked forward and took Jack's skinny arm
and began leading him toward the cabin. Both Chulo
and Vincente rose from where they'd been crouching
amongst the dead men and ogled Vienna openly, their
animal eyes dark and wanton, Chulo's nostrils working.
James noticed that Chulo had a long, thin scar across his
neck. As Jack had indicated, he'd had his throat cut.

James didn't like the looks the two Yaquis were giving Vienna. Apparently, Jack sensed the looks, as well,

and berated both men in Spanish, gesturing wildly. Both Indians cowered like curs, flushing and looking sheepish, and quickly began dragging the dead bodies out away from the shack.

James put his back to the wagon, staring after Apache Jack and Vienna. Through the open door and the window to the right of it, he could see them moving around in the cabin.

Standing beside him, arms crossed on the side of the wagon, Crosseye said, "What do you think, Jimmy? Is Jack crazy?"

"Oh, he's crazy, all right."

"And I'm thinkin' them three bells might be all in his head."

"If so, he's got his brother, Jeff Davis, fooled, and we'll be taking a dangerous trek into Apache country with a blind man for nothing. But remember, Pablo's seen the bells, too."

"So Jack says."

"Right." James nodded. "We don't really know what he's said to the sprout, do we?"

"Nope." Crosseye paused, staring back over his shoulder at Jack now sitting at a crude wooden table on the other side of the front window. Vienna had taken a pot off the fire and was dishing the dead men's supper onto a plate before the crazy, old desert rat.

"How we gonna play it, Jimmy?" Crosseye asked.

"One hand at a time." James walked over to where he'd left his chestnut. "And my first card's gonna be tendin' my horse and cleanin' my guns." He grabbed the chestnut's reins and began leading it around the cabin toward the corral in the back.

* * *

The entire party threw down on the cabin floor. Most were asleep against their saddles within half an hour of tending their horses and eating some of the dead men's javelina cooked with beans.

James didn't sleep well, for coyotes came down out of the mountains to dine on the cadavers that Chulo and Vincente had dragged only as far as the edge of the yard. The carrion eaters loosed a haunting cacophony as they fought, snarling and growling, over flesh and bone. When the dissonant symphony finally died, James slept for a time before, deep in a chaotic dream in which he and Willie were running from snarling wolves toward where Crosseye waited for them at his cabin's open door, a near sound woke him.

He opened his eyes. The windows were streaked with the pale light of early dawn. Someone moved nearby, and he turned his head to see Vienna rising slowly from her bedroll and saddle in front of the now-dead fire in the fieldstone hearth. She was entirely dressed except for her boots, and now she picked up each one in turn and stepped quietly into it.

Around the cabin, which was only two rooms separated by a half-ruined adobe wall flanking the hearth, the other men snored softly against their own saddles. Crosseye snored the loudest. The party hadn't posted a watch because they weren't in Apache country yet, and few *bandidos* besides the Mandino gang haunted this neck of southern Sonora. All the men were sound asleep, Apache Jack curled on his side between James and Crosseye, lips moving as he muttered incoherently.

Vienna walked quietly around the crude eating table, the only piece of furniture in the room besides two dilapidated wicker chairs. She opened the door slowly, looked around cautiously, then moved on outside. James felt a protective urge—there could be a wildcat or a wolf nearby, drawn by the carrion. But Vienna had a pistol with which she could hold off most beasts until James got to her.

He closed his eyes, intending to get another forty winks before rising. But then another sound rose, and he looked toward where Chulo and Vincente were sleeping against the front wall, Chulo with his head in the corner between the front wall and the side wall, Vincente with his feet near the door. Chulo was rising. James recognized his bearlike bulk as the big Yaqui tossed his covers aside and, grunting and breathing raspily, gained his feet and stepped into his boots. When he raked his eyes furtively around the room, James closed his own eyes but continued to watch through slitted lids.

Chulo swept his long, tangled hair back behind his shoulders, donned his black sombrero, and headed for the door. He glanced around the room once more stealthily, watching to see if James or any of the others was stirring, then opened the door, ducked his head and heavy shoulders, and went out, leaving the door partway open behind him.

James tossed his own blankets aside, stepped into his boots, wrapped his gun belt and holsters around his waist, and followed Chulo out into the yard. He stopped as he pulled the door closed and looked around. The wagon sat where they'd left it in front of the cabin. Beyond, James could see a couple of scurrying shadows. Straggling coyotes, probably pups that had been forbidden the main meal. The rancid odor touched the cool, dawn breeze.

There was no sign of Vienna or Chulo anywhere in the front yard, so James walked around the corner of the cabin and stared toward the rear. Chulo was a dozen yards out from the back of the cabin and moving toward the brush corral beyond it, where the horses stood still as dark statues. Chulo walked in his heavy, ambling fashion, neither slowly nor quickly but with a slightly halting, secretive gait.

James pulled one of his Griswolds from its holster, checked the loads, then, holding the pistol straight down in his right hand, strode down the side of the cabin and out behind it, gradually closing the distance between him and the big Yaqui. James's low-heeled boots made no sound.

He walked around behind the corral and a small, crumbling stone stable and stopped. There was a line of willows and ironwood shrubs following the bank of an arroyo. Chulo stood with his back to James, using one hand to hold aside a branch so he could stare into the arroyo beyond him.

James walked up behind the big man, who was a good four inches taller than James's six-one, and pressed his Griswold's barrel snug against the Yaqui's head, just behind his right ear. He clicked the hammer back.

Chulo tensed slightly, froze.

He turned his head slowly toward James, who kept his pistol pressed hard against Chulo's head. Those dark eyes regarded James with dull menace. James smiled with only his mouth. His own eyes remained hard, threatening, as they held the flat gaze of the big, lusty voyeur.

Chulo let the branch fall back into place in front of him. James depressed his Griswold's hammer, pulled the gun slightly back from the Yaqui's head. Chulo gave a low snort and then, continuing to hold James's gaze, he brushed past him and turned his head forward and began walking leisurely back toward the cabin.

James followed him from a distance, leaving Vienna to tend her business in peace. Crosseye stood bleary-eyed, holding his Lefaucheux, off the rear corner of the cabin, regarding Chulo suspiciously. As the big man moved on past him, Crosseye looked at James.

"What's goin' on, Jimmy?"

James stopped near Crosseye and watched Chulo disappear around the front corner of the cabin. "Just had a little heart-to-heart with Chulo." James holstered his .36. "Should be all right now, but I'm startin' to see it Jack's way."

"See what Jack's way?"

"Before this is over, hoss, we're gonna have to kill ole Chulo. Till then, let's watch each other's backs extra close."

Chapter 26

The party ate a quick breakfast of grub left over from the night before and moved out before the sun had yet fully risen. As they had done the night before, Chulo drove the wagon while Jack rode beside him on the wooden seat, the red bandanna over his head and the white bandage around his eyes brightening as the light grew. He took frequent sips from a bottle to assuage the pain of the Apache torture that had taken his sight, and rolled one quirley after another.

They came to a village just before noon and took on trail supplies, including feed for the horses. They loaded the supplies in the back of the wagon with the Gatling gun while Apache Jack and Vienna paid out gold coins to the mercantiler's short, chubby wife who wore a red rebozo, with a small child sleeping soundly in a burlap sling hanging down her chest. They filled their canteens and extra water jugs at a community well and rode off into a vast, rugged, rocky desert in which very little but small cactus plants grew.

"We'll be in Apache country soon," Jack said, "so keep your eyes skinned, though it won't do much

good. 'Paches hit before you even know they're near."
He muttered a curse, grinding his teeth, and took
another pull from his bottle.

As the wagon rattled along the old cart trail they
were following across the vast flat ringed with rocky
mountains foreshortening against all horizons, James
rode up alongside Jack. He'd bought a handful of cigars
from the mercantiler's wife, and he bit the end off one
now and touched flame to it. "Tell me about the curse
on them bells, Jack. Where'd they come from and why
are they said to be the Bells of the Devil?"

Jack pulled on his bottle and stared straight ahead,
dust from the mules' hooves wafting around him.
"Franciscan priests established a church around here
over three hundred years ago and brought religion to
the Apaches. They were way out here"—he swept his
bottle around to indicate the lunarlike landscape
around them, shadows slanting around every rock
and cactus—"on this canker on the devil's ass. Backside of nowhere. A small party of 'em alone. Used the
Injuns as slaves in their gold mine. All the gold was
used to decorate the church they built with slave labor,
dedicated to the glory of God!"

Jack snorted, pulled on the bottle. "Well, there was a
drought and them priests' crops wouldn't grow, and a
war broke out amongst the tribes. Anyways, it's said
these priests went crazy from all the strife and blood-
shed, not to mention loneliness and lack of food aside
from rattlesnake, and adequate water, and they turned
to the devil. Yessir, they started worshipping ole
Scratch." Jack chuckled, shook his head. "They turned
their church over to El Diablo, and they turned their

parishioners to him, as well, and they started takin'
Apache girls as wives."

Jack turned to James and grinned knowingly. "More
than just one, ya understand. Ha!" He shook his head
and turned forward once more. "And the drought
ended, as did the war between the tribes, and all was
just nice as fiddle music for many years in that isolated
corner of the desert.

"Then there was an earthquake that wiped out the
whole town in which the padres had built their church,
and the padres and many of their Injun worshippers
were killed, the church ruined. All but the bells. They
tumbled out of the belfry intact. The Injuns saw this as
punishment from the God the priests had first turned
them to; they figured the bells were left as a reminder
of what would happen if they ever turned to the God
of Darkness again. So an Apache leader got a shaman
to put a hex on them bells, and they took them up into
their own sacred mountains and hid them away in a
canyon, where they couldn't do no more harm. At least,
not as long as no one bothered 'em . . . tried to use the
gold in 'em for gain. They were the devil's bells, you
see. And anyone who laid eyes on 'em would be met
with the worst misfortune imaginable, to die a very
painful death indeed."

"Right," James said, "and that was only the beginning of their misery."

"There you have it."

"You believe any of that stuff, Jack?" This from
Vienna riding behind James.

"Why?" Jack said. "Because of my eyes?" He faced
ahead, mashing his lips together pensively, his frail

body jouncing with the bouncing of the wagon. "Nah. I got careless. Had all that gold on my mind, and I couldn't leave it alone, and I wasn't watchin' close enough for 'paches." He sighed. "That's all," he added uncertainly, lifting the bottle high once again.

He smacked his lips and turned to James. "Say, there, young man from Tennessee, been meanin' to ask you . . ."

James turned the chestnut around a nasty-looking nest of cholla cactus, as he'd learned one brush against those poisonous spines could ruin a horse quicker than a rattlesnake bite. "What's that?"

"You're a strappin' young buck, with no injuries far as I can tell—so's why aren't you back East helpin' our Confederate forces whip them evil hordes of Yankees?"

James felt a tightening between his shoulders. He glanced at Crosseye riding on the other side of the wagon. Crosseye scowled, brushed his sleeve across his mouth, and looked ahead. James had to admit it was a good question. A reasonable question. The implication was obvious: was he a coward?

He often wondered that himself, but before he could formulate a response, Vienna rode past him on his right and said, holding the reins of her trotting grullo up high against her chest, "If he hadn't come West, he wouldn't be here to help us get the bells to the Confederacy, would he, Jack?"

As she continued on past the wagon and rode up to where young Pablo was leading the way, James glanced at Jack. The old desert rat was still looking at him, unsatisfied by the response but not pressing the matter. James felt the bunched muscles in his shoulders loosen slightly when Jack turned his head forward again and took another drink from his bottle.

The question remained, however. And he doubted he'd ever have an answer for it—at least, not one that would satisfy his own conscience. Truth was there was still a war going on; the enemy was invading his homeland. And he'd tucked his tail between his legs and run away from it.

Was killing his own brother a good enough reason?

He didn't have to think about it long. Less than a minute later, Crosseye, riding on the other side of Chulo, said, "Jimmy."

James looked at him. Crosseye lifted his chin to indicate their southern flank. James cast his gaze in the direction his old partner had indicated. Slightly behind them a good half mile away, dust rose in a tan smear. James could make out a couple of horses and riders, but from this distance he couldn't see anything to distinguish them.

Then, all at once, as though they were merely a heat mirage, they disappeared.

"What is it?" Jack said, turning his head this way and that, listening for trouble.

James turned to him. "Riders to the south and slightly behind. About half a mile away."

"Can you tell if they're Apaches?"

"Can't tell."

"See any smoke signals?"

James scanned the broad bowl they were traversing, seeing nothing but the bald, sawtooth mountains in all directions. The only movement was a raptor of some kind hovering high above, wings flashing in the brassy sunlight. "Nothing. What do you think, Jack? Should me and Crosseye ride out for a look?"

"Not yet. If they're 'paches, they might be tryin' to lure us into a trap. Best if we go on pushin', keep our eyes skinned and make sure all our guns are loaded." Jack snorted. "Sure am glad we got that Gatling gun. Should be all right," he said but then repeated the sentence in a slightly more uncertain tone: "Should be all right. . . ."

Jack nudged Chulo with his elbow, said something in Spanish. The big Yaqui nodded, glanced to the south, then shook the reins over the mules' backs, stepping up the speed. A low jog of hills humped a couple of miles ahead, stretching for what appeared to be a mile or so across their trail. Apparently, Jack wanted to reach those as quickly as possible.

"This ain't where the band of Lipans that call this neck of Sonora home usually stomps," the old desert rat muttered, perplexed. "Their territory's another day, day and a half ahead . . . miserable sons o' bitches." He tipped his bottle back and cackled to himself and James wondered again if they were out here for no good reason.

When they reached the hills half an hour later, Chulo pulled the wagon up and over the crest. As he continued hazing the mules down the other side, James told Apache Jack that he and Crosseye would scout their back trail in hopes of getting an idea of who was behind them. Jack merely cursed darkly and popped the cork on a fresh bottle.

Vienna, riding out ahead of the wagon with Pablo, hipped around in her saddle to give James a concerned look beneath the brim of her straw sombrero. He waved, trying to put her at ease, and then he and

Crosseye galloped at an angle down the slope away from the wagon. When they reached the bottom of the line of hills, they kept moving south, riding in and out of arroyos and swerving around boulders of all sizes and thickets of wiry brush and cacti.

James turned to angle a glance behind them. The wagon was a thumb-sized blotch of green now about a quarter mile away, continuing east, with Vienna and Pablo riding point, Vincente following several yards behind on his rugged mule.

"This oughta be far enough south," James told Crosseye, and checked down the chestnut.

He stepped out of his saddle, rummaged around in his saddlebags for his field glasses, and slid his Henry repeater from its saddle boot. Crosseye grabbed his Spencer, and they scrambled up the bank, Crosseye moving every bit as quickly and surefootedly as James, though the older man's breathing was raspy, and he grunted and muttered curses at his age.

"Don't ever get old, Jimmy," he said as they dropped to the side of the hill about four feet from the top.

Then they continued to crab slowly up the side of the slope, doffing their hats.

James said, "What's the alternative, hoss?"

"Good point."

James edged a cautious glance over the top of the sandy hill, his keen eyes taking in the terrain they'd just crossed. An arroyo angled across the rocky, sandy ground. A couple of coyotes were sauntering along its bottom, close enough that James could see the sunlight in their dun-and-gray coats, tongues hanging over their lower jaws. They jerked their heads around, investigating every nook and cranny of the wash for prey. The one following the first cast frequent glances behind it, and James stretched his own glance back in the direction the brush wolf was peering.

James picked movement out of the desert—a ragged line of riders moving toward him. Dust rose in the still, warm air. Occasionally, the clang of a shod hoof off rocks reached James's ears, and the occasional murmur of male conversation.

James lifted the field glasses to his eyes, adjusted the focus until the party of horseback riders swam as clearly into his view as possible from their distance of at least five hundred yards away. They formed a ragged line of roughly twelve men and horses, with a couple of packhorses being trailed by the last two men in the group.

James couldn't make out much about their clothing except that it was the attire of white men, not Indians.

James gave the glasses to Crosseye, who adjusted the focus and stared out across the desert for a time, showing his teeth and slowly sliding the glasses from right to left as he tracked the riders.

"Well, at least we shouldn't be in danger of losin' our topknot," he said finally, handing the glasses back to James.

"Apache don't take scalps, anyway," James said, recalling a recent Apache tutorial bestowed upon him by Apache Jack when they'd stopped to water their horses and mules at a rare desert rock tank. "That's a Plains Indian tradition. Whenever the Apaches do it, it's only because it's been done to them."

Crosseye was squinting out toward where the riders

disappeared by ones and twos behind a broad, towering stone escarpment. "You think they're followin' us?"

"Well, we're headin' in the same direction."

"Best assume so, then."

"Banditos, maybe," James said.

"Yeah, well, we got the Gatling gun. If they're followin' us, they've no doubt scouted us and know about the bullet belcher."

"Maybe it's the gun they're after."

Crosseye looked at James. "Or the girl. In case you hadn't noticed, there ain't many o' them to be had out here on this backside of nowhere."

James's lips quirked in a jeering grin. "You'd know that better than anybody."

"Yeah," Crosseye said, nodding and adding darkly, "Me an' Chulo."

James gave a sour grunt. The mention of the big Yaqui reminded him that he'd left Vienna without protection should Chulo and Vincente decide to move on her. He crawled a few feet back down the hill, doffed his hat, stood, and jogged the rest of the way down to where his and Crosseye's horses waited. Crosseye was behind him, groaning and cursing his age again.

They swung into their saddles and started back in the direction of the wagon.

They hadn't gone ten yards before they heard the wicked belching of the Gatling gun. James cursed and ground his heels into the chestnut's flanks, tearing off at a ground-eating gallop.

Chapter 27

Another spurt of Gatling fire rose above the hammering of the chestnut's hooves. James cocked the Henry repeater one-handed, set the barrel across his saddle bow, and stared straight ahead over the gelding's laid-back ears. The wagon was two hundred yards away, angled so that the mules were faced southeast while the back of the wagon and the gun pointed northwest.

Chulo's bulky frame was hunkered behind the gun, and he was jerking the barrel around, aiming at a jumble of rocks and brush about fifty yards away from him. Vincente was on one knee behind a rock near the rear of the wagon, slightly closer to the escarpment. He had two pistols in his hands, and both smoked now at the same time.

The hollow cracks reached James's ears, and their echo was drowned by another spat of fire from the Gatling gun, though James couldn't see what either man was shooting at.

Apache Jack, Vienna, and Pablo were all hunkered down behind the wagon's right front wheel, Vienna with her pistol out though Apache Jack kept throwing an arm out and yelling at her to keep her head down. "These are Apaches, girl, and this ain't no sewin' lesson!" James heard him screech as he brought the chestnut to a skidding stop well back of the wagon.

He leaped from the saddle, smashed the butt of his rifle against the horse's left hip, sending it galloping off and out of the line of fire, then went running ahead to drop down behind a low hump of ground about ten yards from the wagon, on the escarpment side of the trail.

"How many?" he called to Jack as Crosseye threw himself down to his right.

"Don't ask a blind man foolish questions!" Jack spat out. "All I know is Vincente went out to shake the dew from his lily and he ended up with one ear to go with his clubfoot!"

James saw a brown-skinned, black-haired figure in deerskin leggings and a flannel headband lying twisted on the other side of some spindly willow about ten yards off the trail. Both Vincente and Pablo were looking around wildly but holding their fire. The Gatling gun squawked on its dry swivel. Chulo was grunting as he stared toward the scarp.

"Where there's one 'pache, there's more," Jack said darkly. "The dead one there's probably part of a small band. They run in little packs around these sierras, as there's not enough water to supply many of 'em at once. I've never seen a band larger than, say, ten or twelve. Often smaller than that. They're nasty devils, though. One o' them is equal to six gun-handy white men." Jack spat and growled, muttering to himself, probably remembering again the hot knife that had blinded him.

They waited. The breeze scratched the branches of the piñon pines together. A hawk screeched, and a rabbit gave its short-lived squeal.

"Well, we could wait out here all day," James said finally to Crosseye. "Let's check it out."

Crosseye glanced from Vincente to Chulo. "What about them?"

James turned to Jack. "Jack, have your boys hold your fire while me and Crosseye scout the rocks."

Jack nodded and yelled in Spanish. Chulo glanced toward James and Crosseye, his eyes dark, but kept his hands on the Gatling's crank. Vincente stared toward the escarpment but lowered his pistol slightly. Blood from where his right ear used to be had puddled atop the rock beside him and dribbled down the rock to the copper-colored gravel. The grisly wound made James's own ear ache, but Vincente himself ignored it.

James glanced at Crosseye. "Hope they mind Jack," the oldster said.

"I'm gonna run around to the left."

"All right. I'll cover you and then I'll head for that little notch in the rocks over on the right."

James rose to his knees, looked around carefully, then sprinted out around to the left of Vincente. He dropped to a knee again to study the escarpment. When nothing moved, he continued running until he was wide of the first hump of rocks and could see into a hollow behind it.

Nothing.

He ran into the hollow and then through a notch in the low wall of boulders behind it, found himself in a corridor and then in a low tunnel amongst the rocks that angled over and around him. He had to crouch and sort of shuffle forward, pricking his ears for movement around him. His boots clacked softly on the stone floor. It was a cavelike place, rich with the powdery smell of rock and sand and the faint aroma of pine on the breeze.

A shrill rattling rose on his right, and he turned to see a rattlesnake coiled in a deep pigeonhole amongst the slab-sided rocks, flicking its forked tongue, striated button tail raised as it shook. Other snakes slithered out from the rocks around the first, wriggling toward James and jutting their menacing, ribbonlike tongues.

The smell of ripe cucumbers emanated from the nest, and James made a face. Just when the first snake pulled its head back as though cocking itself for a strike, James shuffled forward, and the nasty rattling dwindled behind him.

He shuddered, chicken flesh rising along his spine. That was only the third or fourth Western rattler he'd seen—these fit the description of the Mojave green rattler, with striped tails—but he'd seen the others from a distance. He didn't want to see another one that close again.

He continued to investigate the knotted escarpment with all its nooks and crannies. At one point, he saw a figure down a wash to the east of him, and he whipped his rifle around only to jerk the barrel up. Crosseye grinned, pinched the brim of his gray sombrero, and disappeared amongst the rocks.

James traversed another narrow corridor threading the escarpment. He stopped suddenly.

Something lay on the ground just ahead of him. He

aimed the Henry at it, moved forward, stopped again and stared down at a dead Apache—a boy of no more than thirteen or fourteen. Blood welled from the gaping hole in his belly, just beneath his breastbone, and from the deep gash across his throat. He held a crude, wooden-handled knife in his open right fist. The blade was coated in rich, dark blood. The kid's half-open, dark brown eyes owned a feral quality, and his white teeth were gritted.

James stared at the gash in the kid's throat, amazed at the young warrior's grit. Rather than die slow from the bullet in his belly, he'd cut his own throat.

James stepped over the brave and out of the corridor he was in, and stopped. Something hard pressed up against the side of his head, just behind his right ear. He turned to see Chulo standing beside him, holding a cocked Patterson revolver in his massive right fist. His dark animal eyes bored into James, the Yaqui's lack of expression more disconcerting than any evil leer would have been.

Chulo pressed the gun harder against James's head. James saw the big finger curled through the Colt's trigger guard tighten, and he narrowed one eye, bracing himself for the shot he likely wouldn't hear.

Another click sounded.

Chulo's eyes flicked to one side. Then he turned his head. Crosseye stood behind him, just over the big Yaqui's right shoulder, smiling as he pressed the Lefaucheux pin-fire revolver against the side of Chulo's head. The fancy piece's hammer was angled back, ready to slap forward. It almost looked as if it were eager to do so.

Chulo must have thought it looked that way, too. He pulled his Colt away from James's head, depressed the hammer. Crosseye pulled the Lefaucheux back from Chulo's scalp but kept it aimed at the Yaqui's head. He turned to James. "Believe them redskins done pulled out, Jimmy. If you two are done powwowin' over here, we'd best head back to the wagon."

"Right." James looked at Chulo, who let his pistol drop to his side but continued to give James that eerily expressionless stare. "Till later, amigo."

James stepped around Chulo and followed Crosseye back through the network of stony corridors to the wagon, where Apache Jack was smoking a cigarette near the tailgate while Vincente sat behind the Gatling gun, a bandage covering his ruined ear. Pablo stood a ways from Jack, looking nervous. Vienna stood behind the boy, her hands on his shoulders. She looked relieved as James and Crosseye walked up to her.

"They've pulled out, Jack," James said, giving the boy's sombrero a teasing pull. "Like you said, it must've been a small band."

"Yeah, well, there's more small packs where that one came from." Apache Jack turned and felt his way along the side of the wagon to the front, nervously puffing on his quirley. "Let's find us a spot to hole up in. From now on, we'd best only travel after dark. We still got a good two-, three-day ride ahead of us."

Near the base of the Las Montanas de la Sombras, the Lipan Apaches' sacred range that appeared just as its name suggested—a hulking black shadow angling off the southeastern edge of the greater massive sierra of the Mother of Mountains itself, the Sierra Madre.

It was dusk of the party's third long day of travel.

Coyotes yammered madly in the quiet, high-desert air, snarling. James could hear them fighting over something, hear their padded feet kicking up dirt and gravel, hear the indignant yip of one getting bit. He walked slowly toward the edge of a gravelly wash, peered down over the low bank. The day had gone, leaving only a lilac wash in the far western sky between toothy black ridges, but there was enough light that James could see the fire in the lobos' eyes as they fought, thrashing, over a dead javelina. Or rather what was left of the mottled black beast with its scrunched-up pig's face and deadly tusks now painted with its own frothy blood.

The coyotes were so involved in their fight that none of the five—nor one other, smaller coyote standing back from the others and merely yipping and lifting its long, pointed snout toward the dimly kindling stars— managed to wind or see the tall, dark watcher in twill trousers, buckskin vest, and gray kepi, a red neckerchief knotted around his neck. James stepped back from the edge of the wash, not wanting to disturb the creatures, though they'd awakened him from his sleep in a wash where he and his traveling companions had sought refuge from the sun and wandering bands of Apaches and the occasional passing pack of banditos.

He'd leave the coyotes to their meal. He'd been in Mexico long enough to know that sustenance didn't come easily to man or beast. The coyotes here were spindly and ragged; they deserved to have their bellies padded.

Far back from the brow of the wash, he tipped his hat back off his forehead and surveyed the Shadow Range that loomed ahead of him like a giant dark brown wall, its rim touched with the dying copper and saffron rays of the setting sun. From here it looked like one solid wall rising straight up out of the desert, but Apache Jack had assured him there were fissures and gaps and winding canyons that gave entrance to the forbidden range, and sometime tomorrow they'd reach the canyon in which the bells had been housed for the past three centuries.

James turned and walked up a rocky slope to where Crosseye sat on a flat rock, well below the crest of the hill, running his bowie knife deftly over a hunk of ironwood he'd picked up along their trail. Somehow with the big knife he'd managed to carve the plumed head and tail of a desert quail, though he was now working on one of the feet, holding the piece up close to his face and wincing with the effort. Wood shavings curled down from the bird to his thigh before dropping onto the black rock beneath him.

He held up the bird, grinning proudly. "Not bad for a cross-eyed duffer, eh?"

"You never cease to amaze."

"When it's done, I'm gonna give it to Vienna so when she gets back home she can set it on her mantel to remind her of her adventure in Old Mexico."

James sat down beside the oldster. "You best go back down to the wash, squeeze in another hour of sleep before we pull out. Good dark soon."

Crosseye said, "How come you don't like to talk

about her, Jimmy? She's a good woman, and it's clear by how she looks at you, you shine for her."

James glanced at him, squinting one eye. "You see anything wrong in it—her and me?"

"What could be wrong in folks feelin' good about each other? As long as it don't hurt no one else." The older man studied James for a time, his steady eye boring into James's. "Hell, you can't hurt Willie."

"I reckon I already did that."

"The war did that. You quit mopin' about it. You got you a good woman, and you think to the future, not to the past, or you'll be a miserable wretch for the rest of your days, and you'll make her miserable, too. Vienna's been through enough."

James ground a heel in the dirt. "She'll probably head back home, like you said. That's where she belongs."

"Then you belong there, too. Tell your old man to go diddle himself. He's all swallowed up in the war, so he can't see what's clear—the South is a goner, and he has to make peace with his own, 'cause that's all he has left, or shut the hell up about it." Crosseye sheathed the knife and heaved himself to his feet. "There, I said it. I was out of line, talkin' about old Alexander Dunn that way, but I figure I'm far enough away I can say what I want about anyone I feel like sayin' it about!"

He chuffed, amused at himself, and shouldered his rifle. "Christ, I'm gettin' crazier than Apache Jack. Must be this high, thin air and all that sunshine." He went hopping down the hill in his bandy-legged stride, and James was alone with the calls of the night birds and the scuffs of the nearby coyotes that, judging by the dwindling sounds they made, were now feasting more than fighting.

James leaned his rifle against a rock beside him, dug out his makings sack, and rolled a cigarette. He'd just finished the cigarette when feet crunched gravel down in the darkness at the base of the slope. Vienna called his name quietly. Her voice warmed him, soothed him.

"Here," he said, not having to raise his voice, as the coyote had fallen silent now, and all was quiet.

He heard her boots in the gravel. Then he heard her breathing, saw her shadow move against the fading sky. She sat down beside him, wrapped her hands around his left arm, and snuggled up tight against him, rubbing her cheek against his shoulder. "Done sleepin'?" James said.

He felt her nod her head against him. "Can't sleep well during the day. I'll be glad to get the bells and hightail it out of here."

"Me, too."

"James? I've been meaning to tell you . . ." Continuing to squeeze his arm, she glanced up at him. "What Jack said about you . . . leaving the war."

"About being a coward?"

"He didn't mean it. He doesn't know what happened."

"He doesn't need to know."

"No. No one needs to know. But you need to know that I don't fault you for what happened. And I'm sure Willie, wherever he is, doesn't fault you for it, either."

James placed his hand against the back of her neck, feeling her silky hair beneath his palm, and pressed his lips against her forehead.

"I just want you to know," she said, looking up at him again, her eyes glinting in the starlight, "that I love you, James. And I've buried what happened."

James felt a frown cut into the skin above the bridge of his nose. It was a question that he'd wanted to ask many times but had never found the words. "Vienna, don't you grieve him? I mean, you and Willie . . ."

She gave a little groan, then stood and, crossing her arms on her chest, walked a little ways down the slope. She turned back to him, and her voice was low and firm. "James, frankly, I'm a little tired of hearing about Willie."

"Vienna, Christ . . . !"

"Yes, I loved Willie," she said, extending her arms impatiently. "And Willie loved me. When we were children." She walked back up the slope toward James. "That was a long time ago. Longer ago than what can be counted on a calendar. So *much* has *happened!*"

Vienna paused, looked straight out from the hill for a time at the thickening night cloaked in twinkling stars, and shook her head slowly. She knelt down beside James once more. "I'm a different person now. I'm a woman now. And I know that Willie would understand if we'd found each other . . . and fallen in love. He'd want us to be happy."

She placed a hand on James's thigh. He could feel its warm caress through his trousers, the fingers digging in. She scuttled closer, wrapped her other arm around his neck, and closed her mouth over his.

Her lips were soft and pliant. She groaned, kissing him harder. He wrapped his arms around her, felt her body writhing against his, her breasts swelling behind her shirt and poncho, stirring a fire in his loins.

Pulling away from him, she drew a hard breath, running her tongue along her lower lip. She sandwiched his face in her hands and stared at him from beneath her brows—a bewitching, seductive look that almost made him quiver with a raw, physical need for her.

She smiled, reading his thoughts. "After we get the bells, James, we'll have all the time for that in the world."

She kissed him once more hungrily, pressing her breasts against his chest, then peeled out of his tightening grip with a husky chuckle, playfully fighting his arms away. He grabbed her again, kissed her quickly, and let her go.

A second chance, he thought, his heart quickening at the prospect. She was his second chance. . . .

She gained her feet, her direct gaze holding his. A little breathless, she brushed off the seat of her black denims and threw her thick hair back behind her shoulders. She laughed, a gentle sound in the silence, and reached out to brush the tips of her fingers across the buckle of his cartridge belt.

"All the time in the world, my love. . . ."

She turned and walked back down the hill, her slender figure and the red-and-white-striped serape slowly consumed by the darkness. He continued to hear her boots crunch gravel for a time, and then the sounds faded and she was gone.

But he could still feel the lightning fire of his passion and his desire for her jetting in every nerve.

An honest-to-God second chance. . . .

Chapter 28

In the silvery darkness, Pablo checked his mule down to a halt. He turned and threw a waylaying arm out at Chulo driving the wagon behind him.

The boy slipped easily down from the beast's back, dropped the reins, and scampered up a slope on the right side of the draw they'd been following. James reined the chestnut to a stop to the right of Apache Jack, who sat in the wagon, silent in the quiet night, turning his head this way and that, listening.

The boy's soft, running footfalls had dwindled to silence but quickly resumed, growing louder. James could hear the boy breathing hard with excitement as he appeared once more at the lip of the shallow bank. Pablo rattled off some whispered, ebullient Spanish and grinned.

Jack punched his open palm. "I'll be damned!" He said something else that to James, beginning to pick up some Spanish, sounded like, "You found it, boy!"

As the shaver leaped onto the mule's back, James regarded the sandstone wall looming over them and over the wash. It was a precipitous ridge, jutting straight up to the star-washed sky, its crest a good two thousand feet from the ground. The wall had looked smooth from a distance, but now James could see some flues and fingers and pinnacles of rock jutting separately from the main mass, and gravelly ledges from which spindly brush and shrubs grew.

But he could not imagine that there was any way *into* the mountain from here.

A few minutes later, following the boy and the wagon, he saw that he'd been wrong. As the party traveled along the side of the cliff, they turned into a right branch of the wash. The wall peeled back to James's right, like a massive door opening, and beyond—into the gaping hole—the wash continued, pale with flood-washed and polished gravel.

The canyon at its mouth was wide enough for two wagons to enter it abreast, but it narrowed considerably a hundred feet in, and just when James thought they were going to have to stop and leave the wagon behind, the walls fell back once more. The wagon passed freely, Chulo holding the mules to a slow pace, for the shod wheels and the wagon's rough planks lifted a nasty clatter that could be heard by any near Apaches.

The floor of the wash climbed gradually, and the mules as well as the horses started to strain, but then Pablo stopped his mule at another black gap in the wall on his left. The gap was the mouth of a narrow, offshooting canyon. As Chulo stopped the wagon, Pablo tied the mule to a shrub standing to the right of the gap and whispered to Apache Jack, who nodded and returned several phrases in Spanish, his spindly shoulders fairly shuddering with excitement.

James looked around. The canyon was dark, but a moon was rising. It wasn't yet above the ridge, but enough light angled into the chasm that he could make out the rocks and shrubs and the crenellated walls of the cliffs on either side of him.

High above, an owl hooted. Aside from a rodent scratching in the brush, and the stomping and blowing of the tired horses and the squawking of tack, that was the only sound.

"Up that little canyon there?" Crosseye shouldered his rifle and looked at Jack dubiously. "How far?"

"Hell, we're so close I can smell that gold from here!" Jack covered his mouth as he laughed, and, looping the handles of two lanterns over his right arm, he felt his way around the mules and moved carefully, one step at a time, toward the mouth of the cleft.

"Pretty dark," James said. "Maybe we should wait till morning."

"Jack said we shouldn't be out here during the day." Vienna took one of Jack's lanterns. "Besides, we have these." She stood beside James, her shoulders rising and falling as she breathed, obviously excited, staring into the dark cleft. Crosseye had presented her with the quail he'd carved, and it hung down her red-and-white-striped serape by a rawhide thong.

"That's right. You're a good girl. You remember what Jack says. Wish at least one of my wives would have been like you—then, maybe I'd have kept her." Jack spat and reached out to grab Pablo's arm, the handle of his lantern squawking from where it dangled from his wrist. "We're gonna have to walk from here. Lots of rocks, so be careful. Won't light the lamps yet—don't want any Apaches seein' the light."

"You'd best wait with the wagons, Jack," Crosseye said.

"No, sir. I'm gonna go in and help fetch them three purty ladies out of there. They're heavy. Two of you boys can carry one, but without block and tackle, it's prob'ly gonna take every one of us to hoist 'em over rocks an' such." Jack spoke to Vincente and Chulo in Spanish, and they nodded, Chulo running his sleeve across his mouth hungrily.

James felt the pull of the gold himself. He still wasn't convinced it was gold they'd be hauling out of the cavern, but he'd heard enough about it from Apache Jack for the fever to be catching. Jack didn't know how much they were worth, but he'd said each bell probably weighed a hundred pounds. That was a hell of a lot of gold. Even if none of it would be his, he wanted to see it, touch it.

Chulo and Vincente hurried into the cavern behind Pablo, rocks grinding beneath their boots. Jack took James's arm, tugged on his sleeve. "Remember what I said about Chulo? As soon as we get the gold out here to the wagon, you're gonna have to shoot him."

Vienna started into the cleft behind Chulo and Vincente, and stopped. Running her fingers pensively over the quail, she waited until the two Yaqui were out of hearing, then whispered back over her shoulder, "What if he doesn't try anything, Jack?"

"He will. Somewhere along the trail, he will. Him or

Vincente or both." Jack slapped James's back and jerked on Vienna's wrist. "Come on—what you waitin' for, girl? Have bells cast of solid gold started growin' from the dogwoods in Tennessee?"

As Vienna led Jack into the gap behind Pablo and the two Yaquis, James brought up the rear, sharing a dark glance with Crosseye. He wasn't about to execute Chulo just in case he might try to double-cross him and the others. But he saw no point in Jack knowing that just yet. First, they'd get the gold out, and then he and Crosseye would keep a close eye on the two Yaquis.

The corridor into the cliff wall was narrow and littered with rocks of all shapes and sizes. At one point they had to climb over stone slabs that had torn away from the walls, blocking the trail. James and Crosseye had to take their time, helping the frail Apache Jack. Vienna scrambled over the rocks like the nimble little forest sprite she'd once been back home, when she and James and Willie had explored caves together in the hills around Seven Oaks.

Pablo led the way up a short thumb of rock on the cleft's right side and into a ragged-edged cave opening. The floor was uneven. From somewhere inside came the faint tinkling of dripping water and the creepy sound of unseen, fluttering wings. James recognized the reek of bat guano. The ceiling was just low enough that the men had to crouch, holding their hats.

Jack muttered something to Vienna, and they lifted the lantern cowls and lit the wicks, adjusting the flames until the glow of the lanterns slid the shadows back against the cracked and chipped stone walls.

"That's better," Vienna said, lifting her lantern high.

"For you, maybe," Jack quipped dryly, giving his own lantern to Pablo, who led him forward. "Come on, honey," Jack wheezed lustily at Vienna. "Last one to the treasure's a rotten egg!"

James counted his steps as they moved behind Pablo into the cave, and they stopped when he'd reached twenty-three. Against the back of the cave was a wide stone shelf, and on the shelf were three hunched shapes. Slowly, the lantern light washed like liquid brass over the shapes, revealing them.

"*Sí*," Pablo said through a long, gleeful sigh.

James stared in awe at the three small suns shining in the wan light of the lanterns. He moved forward, all his compatriots forming a semicircle around the bells. Vienna, standing next to James, gave a slow, quiet gasp as she crouched before them, her low jaw dropping.

Apache Jack cackled as though even he could see the three bells sitting on the stone slab before them—all roughly the same size, each about half as tall as a rain barrel, and nearly as broad. Obviously, Jack had been here recently to tend to his three precious ladies. He'd scraped off the grime and bird and bat shit of the past three centuries, and the foul and dirty rags lay around the bells like the soiled robes of saints.

The bells were solid gold. Loops had been cast in their tops through which a wooden beam had likely held them secure in the belfry of a long-vanished church. On the front of each a praying saint had been etched as well as the year in which each had been fashioned from the gold the Franciscans had mined with the help of their Apache slaves: 1567.

James stared at the gold, hearing the quiet rush of the centuries emanating from the three bells before him.

"The Bells of the Devil," Crosseye said, breaking James's reverie. The old frontiersman's voice was pitched with portent.

James felt a twinge of fear strike him from out of nowhere. Annoyance pushed it aside. He'd come too far to be spooked by some old Indian legend.

"Don't think we need to worry about that, pard," he said.

"You don't think so?"

"I think we need to worry about getting them out of here and finding cover before daylight," Vienna put in. "We don't want to get trapped in here."

"Come on, you young bucks," said Apache Jack. "I didn't bring you along so's you could stand here feasting your eyes and givin' each other the fantods. Grab a hold, and let's start haulin' 'em back to the wagon. We'll get two on the first trip, make a second trip for the third."

James crouched over the bell on the far right, tipped it back, and got the fingers of one hand under the bottom. He tipped it back the other way and got the fingers of his other hand under the bottom, as well. He lifted, testing, and discovered that he could lift it with effort, but with a knot of pain growing in his lower back. Two would be able to lift it and carry it more easily, albeit awkwardly, in the close, shadowy confines.

While Chulo and Vincente got a hold of the bell on the far left, Crosseye got his own hands under James's bell, and, grunting, the two Tennesseans began shuffling back toward the cave entrance. Vienna guided them, lighting the way with her lantern, while Pablo held his own lamp for Chulo and Vincente. James and Crosseye had a rough time carrying the bell down from the cave to the narrow floor of the corridor, each man falling to his knees at least once and nearly dropping the bell at least twice.

They grunted and cursed, groaning and sweating, Apache Jack cajoling and offering advice. James felt as though his spine would rip out from his lower back before they finally managed to set the bell on the chasm's floor, and he stepped back, hands on his hips, breathing hard. Crosseye dropped to one knee, doffing his hat and running a hand through his curly, thin, sweat-damp hair. Veins bulged in his freckled forehead flushed from exertion.

"How in the hell did you stumble on these bells, anyway, Jack?" James asked between breaths.

"Same way all great treasures is discovered," Jack said, standing to one side of the cave mouth with Pablo, while Chulo and Vincente carried their bell up from the depths of the cave behind him. "By accident. I was on the run from 'paches, and I came in here to hide one late evenin' without benefit of a lantern. I woke in the morning to see these three beauties glowing at me like celestial virgins."

When Chulo and Vincente, struggling under their own burden, had joined them on the floor of the corridor, James and Crosseye hefted their bell once more and started back along the chasm toward the wagon.

It took them nearly half an hour, with the help of Chulo and Vincente, to get the bell over all the obstacles, but, sweating and weary, they finally set the bell in the back of the wagon, atop a horse blanket laid out for the cargo. They took little time to rest, as dawn was near. They headed back into the chasm to help Chulo and Vincente get their bell over the several stone slabs in the path.

When they'd set the second bell in the wagon, they each took a pull from Apache Jack's offered bottle. Jack suggested that he and Vienna stay with the wagons and keep watch for trouble. It wasn't yet dawn, but the morning birds were beginning to chirp.

"Give a yell if he starts pawin' you," James told Vienna, winking at her, as he and Crosseye and Chulo and Vincente headed back down the corridor to retrieve the other bell.

"I'm armed." Vienna patted her pistol and returned the wink.

Another half an hour later, with Pablo holding the lantern, James, Crosseye, Chulo, and Vincente wrestled the bell over the last rock slab angling over the corridor and set it on the chasm's floor. James had just stepped back against the wall when he saw Vincente lunge toward Crosseye. A blade flashed in the club-footed Yaqui's fist a quarter second before he buried it in the old frontiersman's belly.

Chapter 29

"Look out, Jimmy!" Crosseye bellowed as he fell, Vincente crouching and grunting over him.

James jerked his gaze toward Chulo, who had a long-barreled Remington in his fist, the barrel aimed at Crosseye. The cow eyes held flatly on James, though the big Yaqui's broad mouth quirked in a mocking grin.

Pablo screamed and lurched backward, falling. The lantern clattered to the ground and blinked out. At the same time, Chulo's pistol flashed and thundered. James barely registered a sting across his left forearm as he clawed both his Griswold .36s from their holsters.

The Confederate pistols leaped and thundered, the flashes revealing Chulo's hulking figure against the far wall. Chulo's own pistol flashed and roared. James fired two more times, and in the light of the lapping flames he saw Chulo jerk backward. The man's pistol thudded on the chasm floor.

There was a yowl to James's right. Vincente's thick, short figure bent forward, knees buckling, while Crosseye's silhouette pulled its arm back from the clubfoot's gut. "There you go, you son of a bitch!" Crosseye said in a pinched voice.

James glanced at Chulo's unmoving figure, then ran to Crosseye, his heart thudding dreadfully. He dropped to a knee, holstered one of the Griswolds, and put a hand on the stout man's shoulder. "How bad he stick you, hoss?"

"Ah, hell," Crosseye said, chuckling and getting a knee under him. He placed a forearm on his knee and heaved himself to his feet. "He stabbed one of the shell belts. Poked me a little through the leather, but I been bit worse by skeeters."

James squeezed the oldster's neck with affection. "I thought he'd gutted you clean."

"So did he." Crosseye stared down at Vincente, who was hunkered over his knees, quivering his life out on the chasm floor. Crosseye slipped his Leech & Rigdon from the holster strapped to his right hip, clicked the hammer back, and aimed it down at the dying Yaqui.

James nudged his partner's gun hand down. "No."

He walked over to where Pablo sat on the ground near one of the slanting stone beams. Even in the darkness, James could see that the boy's eyes were wide as saucers as he stared at the two dead men. James extended a hand toward Pablo.

A gun thundered, echoing from the main canyon. Apache Jack's muffled voice was high with anguish. "Oh, you dirty devil . . . !"

James wheeled from Pablo, clicked his Griswold's hammer back, and ran down the chasm as fast as he could without risking tripping over a rock. The corridor's mouth shone like a purple vertical rectangle in front of him, slowly growing as James approached it. He could hear Crosseye's ragged breaths as the older man chugged along behind him.

Vienna screamed, moaned. James dashed out the chasm mouth into the canyon, crouching and extending both his .36s, expecting to see Apaches dashing around in front of him. He stopped, dropped to a knee, and aimed across the canyon toward where Vienna stood with a tall, long-haired man wearing a sombrero behind her, holding a gun to her head. The second lantern was held aloft by one of the other men in the pack standing around the first man and Vienna.

Apache Jack lay on the far side of the wagon, on his back. He was thrashing and groaning, clutching his belly.

All the other dozen or so men and Vienna stood in bizarre silhouette though a faint wash of lilac shone in the sky above the canyon.

"One more step, amigos, and I blow a hole in the princess's beautiful, double-crossing head." It was the voice of a gringo, vaguely familiar, but James couldn't place it.

Double-crossing? Then he remembered: Red Mangham.

"Kill her," said a tall man standing near the Denver City outlaw leader. His voice, too, was familiar. "Kill her and let's get out of here. We've only got about an hour before sunrise."

"Shut up, Stenck!" Mangham barked. "Now that we have the gold, I'm liable to shoot you!"

"You promised to honor our agreement!" Stenck barked back, jutting an angry finger.

Hot bile washed through James. The last time he'd seen Richard Stenck, the tall, yellow-haired Confederate had been riding hell-for-leather, naked, out of Tucson. Somehow, he must have joined forces with Mangham, who'd been after Vienna. Stenck must have told Mangham about the gold she was after . . . and here they all were. . . .

Mangham yelled, "I told you two fellas to throw down your weapons. Your rifles and every goddamn pistol and knife. Do not tarry, understand?" He ground his pistol into Vienna's cheek, making her cry out.

James glanced at Crosseye. He nodded. What else could they do?

He set the Henry down against the cliff wall flanking him. He tossed his pistols down, and then he drew his knife from the sheath behind his right hip and tossed that down, as well. Crosseye threw down his own small arsenal. James stared across the canyon, hopelessness closing heavily around him, weighing him down. They were all going to die—him, Crosseye, and Vienna.

Mangham chuckled and lowered his pistol from Vienna's head, depressing the hammer. Vienna turned to him, wrapped her arms around his neck, and kissed him, moving her body lustily against his.

For a moment, James thought someone had come up behind him and clubbed him over the head. His knees turned to putty. He stared aghast across the canyon. Beside him, Crosseye gave a throaty grunt of exclamation.

"Well, I'll be," the old frontiersman said half under his breath.

Vienna pulled away from Mangham but kept her arms around his neck. "It can all be ours, Red. You an' me."

Stenck said, "Kill her, Mangham. We had a deal. Just you, me, and your men. Come on—*think!* She stole from you, ran out on you!"

Mangham clutched the back of her neck. Vienna tensed. "What about that? What you got to say about that, Mary?"

"I didn't betray you, Red," Vienna, aka Mustang Mary, said in a wheedling little girl's voice. "I just ran away. That's all. Of course I needed money, so I took a few coins from your strongbox. Let bygones be bygones. You've come all this way. Well, now you not only have the gold, you have me, too." She kissed him again, and James clenched his fists at his sides. "You know how you feel about me, Red. You'll never get me out of your blood. What good's the gold without a good woman to share it with?"

Mangham lowered his hand from the back of her neck. "Yeah, you know how I feel. I reckon I can't deny that, Mary."

"Mangham, don't be a fool!" Stenck warned.

Mangham lifted his pistol, turned it butt out toward Vienna. "If you really love me, Mary, go finish that blind old desert rat. I'm tired of the old fool's caterwaulin'."

James stood riveted, only half believing what he was seeing, the ground pitching around him, as Vienna took the Colt in her hand. She swung around and walked over to where Apache Jack lay on the far side of the wagon from James and Crosseye.

"Don't do it, Vienna." James did not shout it. Even to

his own ears, it sounded like a desperate plea. He took two strides out away from the chasm mouth, heard the metallic scrape of half a dozen gun hammers as Mangham's ten or so men aimed pistols or rifles at him while holding the reins of their fidgeting mounts.

Vienna took the pistol in both hands, aimed it down at Apache Jack kicking his legs in agony and rolling from side to side. Suddenly, the blind man stopped moving and stared up at her. He was breathing hard, holding his guts in, but he laughed madly. Quieting down, he turned his head toward James and Crosseye. "The gold was cursed, after all." He chuckled. "It turned this purty little thing into a witch. *Just look at her!*"

Vienna's pistol popped. Flames stabbed at Apache Jack. The old man's head bounced off the canyon floor, then sagged back down against it and lay still.

James had started at the shot. He raked his gaze from the faintly twitching form of Apache Jack to the girl. If he'd ever truly loved her, that love was gone. It had turned to a sharp-edged, cold, killing fury. Glaring at her, he clenched his fists so tightly that his fingernails dug into the heels of his hands.

Mangham pointed at him and Crosseye. "Now them!"

Holding the smoking pistol straight down in front of her, Vienna looked at James and Crosseye. Her eyes were opaque, matter-of-fact. Stenck and Mangham's men shifted around on their boot heels, keeping their rifles or pistols aimed at James and Crosseye, who stood about ten feet out from the chasm mouth, their own guns and knives in a ragged pile before them and to the right—too far away to make a play for them, though the urge drew the sinews and muscles in James's arms and hands taut.

Vienna walked over to him, stopped four feet away. She continued to wear that bland expression on her once-beautiful face. Amazing how such attractive features could so quickly turn as ugly as an ogre's—her once-lustrous gray eyes now as dark as coal.

"Why?" James asked quietly.

"Over the past year with Red, on the run from Stenck," she said just as quietly, so Mangham and the others couldn't hear, "I realized how important money was. With money, you can buy anything—a business, men to help run and protect it. Even the law."

"Did you ever intend to bring the gold back to Richmond?"

Vienna loosed a mocking laugh. "Hell, no! Like you said—the South is finished. We each have to survive any way we can. Me? I'm gonna have money . . . and power."

"He told you to shoot 'em," Stenck said, walking toward Vienna, James, and Crosseye, "not talk 'em to death!"

Vienna swung around, raising the pistol. Stenck stopped, eyes widening in horror. "No!" He raised his hands as though to shield his face, but Vienna's slug plunked through his chest. He grunted, stumbled backward, and fell with a hard thud, mewling and jerking.

As Stenck's shrill death screams died, Mangham threw his head back, laughing raucously. Vienna turned back to James, cocking the Colt once more, squinting one eye, and quirking a grin.

"Thanks for the help, James."

"*No!*" a thin voice cried behind Crosseye.

A fist-sized rock flew past James's face and smashed into Vienna's pistol, which roared and sent a saber of red-blue flames angling toward the brightening sky. Vienna screeched and stumbled backward. "You little *savage!*" she screamed.

Pablo's voice yelled, "Here, senor!"

James turned. Pablo crouched against the left side of the chasm's mouth, tossing a pistol he'd taken off Chulo or Vincente. The Remington careened toward James, who snatched it out of the air by its butt and swung back toward the main cave, crouching and firing at the same time the guns of Mangham's men opened up on him and Crosseye. James's slug plunked through the knee of one man while Mangham cursed and fired a pistol in each of his fists.

James returned fire, wincing as hot lead screeched over and around him, *spanging* off the canyon walls. Crosseye dove forward, grabbed his Lefaucheux and .36 Leech & Rigdon off the ground, rolled once to the right as bullets peppered the rocks around him, and returned fire from his belly, loosing a Rebel yell so shrill and haunting that it got James's blood up, and Forrest's Rapscallion began howling like a maniac as his own pistol leaped and roared.

When the hammer clicked on an empty chamber, he shouted, "Get back inside the notch, old-timer—I'll cover ya!" and lunged toward his Henry repeater. Two bullets hammered the rocks around the rifle, and he lurched away from them, dropping to his butt.

As James heaved himself to his feet, the old

frontiersman dashed past him, shouting, "Come on, Jimmy, before we catch lead poisonin'!" and threw his broad bulk into the narrow gap behind Pablo.

"Got a better idea! Cover me, hoss!"

James reached again for the Henry, grabbed the neck of the stock, and fell back on his rump once more, quickly racking a shell and casting a wild gaze out before him. Several of Mangham's men lay still amongst the wafting powder smoke, while the others were scrambling behind a shallow hummock in the center of the canyon, behind a thin screen of bramble.

James triggered the Henry three times from his butt, then lurched to his feet, fired three more times, levering and firing, hearing the shouts of Mangham's men beneath the racketing echo of his shots. Then he dropped the rifle, wheeled left, and dove into the back of the wagon, hearing the angry thuds of three bullets slamming into the wagon behind him. Another slug screeched off the wagon's right rear wheel.

He got behind the Gatling gun and dropped to a knee as he wrapped his hand around the wooden crank handle. In the dimly lit canyon, he could see the flashes of Mangham's men's guns and the ghostly puffs and wafts of their powder smoke. Bullets sang through the air around him, hammering the side of the wagon and the cliff wall.

The mules brayed raucously, prancing and heaving against their collars, jerking the wagon slowly forward as the left front wheel ground against the brake.

Gritting his teeth and cutting loose with another wild yell, James turned the crank. The deadly canister spun, flashing, the loud reports echoing.

Bam-Bam-Bam-Bam-Bam-Bam-Bam-Bam-Bam-Bam-Bam!

James couldn't see what he was hitting on the dim floor of the canyon that the dawn light was just now finding, but he heard several shrill screams and cries. The flashing of return fire dwindled. Crosseye yowled like a coyote as from the chasm mouth to James's right, the old-timer yelled, "Go, Jimmy. Gooooo!"

James had just stopped turning the Gatling's crank, and the gun had fallen silent though its echoes continued to rumble around between the cliff walls, when the wagon sagged slightly to the right, a spring squawking. In the corner of James's eye, a shadow moved.

He heard a female grunt, felt a gun belt smash against the side of his head. The blow threw him sideways, and he reached for the side of the wagon but only grazed it with his fingers as he flew over it. The ground came up to smack his right shoulder and hip.

He heard himself groan as Vienna bellowed, "*Hyaahhhhhh!*"

Blinking to clear his vision, James pushed up on an elbow, gritting his teeth against the pain stabbing through his head. The ground quivered beneath him as the wagon lumbered away from him, Vienna yelling wildly beneath the team's indignant braying.

"Jimmy!" Crosseye knelt beside him, placed a hand on his arm. "Christ Almighty—you all right, boy?"

Pablo scrambled out of the chasm mouth and dropped to a knee on James's other side, a worried look on his little, dark face.

James turned to see Vienna and the wagon roaring

down the center of the canyon, heading away to James's right. A figure just now touched with pearl light was running after her, his stockmen's boots slipping on the rocky ground, shouting and shooting his pistols.

"Double-crossin' bitch!" Mangham bellowed.

Crosseye grabbed James's Henry, fired from his hip. The repeater spoke once, twice, three times before the hammer pinged on an empty chamber.

Mangham screamed. His shadowy figure dropped. The wagon dwindled off down the canyon beyond him.

Crosseye looked at the Henry in his hands. "Damn fine shootin' stick, Jimmy!" He extended it toward James. "Here, you take it. It's yours . . . and it's empty."

James took the gun, climbed to his feet, and stared after the wagon. Its loud clattering was gradually fading. On the canyon floor, there was no movement, no more gunfire.

The burly frontiersman stood beside James, quickly, deftly reloading the Lefaucheux, working the ejector, placing the caps, conical balls, and paper cartridges in the cylinders, snarling as his hands worked automatically.

James placed a hand on the older man's thick left shoulder. "It's done, hoss."

Crosseye jerked a look at him, blood from one of his several bullet burns dribbling down his chin. "*Wha? Huh?*"

He looked out into the canyon.

Quiet had descended, as though it were a product of the milky morning light. Wafting powder smoke was the only movement. All the horses had fled after the shooting had begun.

Mangham lay howling about fifty yards down the main canyon toward where James's party had entered it. He was sobbing, obviously dying, and calling for Mary.

Mustang Mary hammered off down the canyon with the gold.

A clattering rose around the canyon. James felt a vibration in his boots. "What's that?" he said.

"Look there!" Crosseye pointed toward the top of the opposite ridge touched with pink and gold morning light. Rocks were breaking loose from the sides of the cliff and rolling earthward. Large chunks of both cliffs were slanting inward, plunging downward.

"Rock slide!" James turned and grabbed Pablo's hand, pulled the boy to his feet. "Come on, son—we gotta get out of here!"

James grabbed his cartridge belt and pistols and, holding Pablo's hand, sprinted off down the canyon. The ground pitched and lurched around them. Rocks and boulders smashed to the canyon floor with explosions that in comparison made the loudest thunderclap James had ever heard sound little louder than a hiccup.

One such explosion sent a cold wave of wind and dust pushing against the fleeing trio from behind. Pablo stumbled, dropping to his knees, though he didn't make a peep. James stopped, slung the boy over his shoulder, and continued running after Crosseye, the dust so thick he could hardly see the shambling oldster.

Leaping rocks and low shrubs, they tore off down the canyon as though the Four Horsemen of the

Apocalypse were bearing down on them from behind. They bolted out of the mouth of the canyon as both cliffs gave way in earnest. The ground leaped so wildly beneath James's boots that he thought the earth had come loose from its orbit and was tumbling off into space.

They all lost their footing, fell, rolled, heaved themselves to their feet, and continued running until they were well down the wash. When the cacophony had dwindled to a low rushing sound mingled with the clanks and clattering of shifting stones, James stopped, turned.

The cliff was considerably shorter than he remembered. A vast mushroom cloud of dust rose from behind it to spread out in the morning sky, turning the golden morning sunlight a murky tan. Beneath it, the canyon—and the third gold bell—was buried under a million tons of granite, quartz, and sandstone.

"Jimmy?"

James looked over Pablo's dark head toward Crosseye. The old frontiersman looked like a life-sized figure fashioned from clay-colored dust. His broad chest rose and fell heavily.

Between breaths, he said, "Just so's you know—from now on, when it comes to Apache curses, this dog don't hunt!"

Chapter 30

After a long rest, James and Crosseye managed to run down their terrified horses and Pablo's mule, and, keeping a close eye out for Apaches, they followed Vienna's wagon tracks westward along the wash.

They did not find Vienna or the wagon, however. What they did find was a flurry of unshod pony tracks—a good twenty or so riders—intersecting the tracks. Nearby, the twin wheel furrows left the arroyo and cut southward toward a jagged black sierra hulking ominously against the far horizon.

They followed the tracks for a ways, but more unshod horse tracks joined those of the first set and the wagon tracks, and James and Crosseye gave up the hunt. The Apaches badly outnumbered them. Besides, they needed to get Pablo back to his grandmother.

Vienna—or Mustang Mary—and the gold were gone. For her sake, James hoped she was dead.

Two months later, he and Crosseye had followed the currents of time and chance to a little Mexican outpost along the Yellow River near the Sea of Cortez, and found themselves whiling away an afternoon over pulque, tortillas, fried goat liver, and chili peppers in an outdoor cantina under a brush arbor, when James looked up from his plate and scowled.

Crosseye regarded him over the chunk of tortilla and meat he held up close to his mouth. "What is it?"

James's heart thudded. A short, slender figure wearing Vienna's straw sombrero and her red-and-white-striped serape sat with her back to James and Crosseye's table. The stranger sat with three men and a *puta* with blond streaks in her long black hair. The *puta* was talking and laughing huskily with the Mexican on her left.

James's heart thudded again anxiously as he stood, and a strange hybrid of feelings engulfed him as he strode quickly over to the figure he was staring holes through and clamped his right hand over the person's shoulder.

An angular face turned toward him, scowling. A man's Indian-dark face, one eye slightly higher than the other, a thin, wiry black mustache mantling the thin upper lip. A couple of cracked and chipped teeth shone as the little, savage-looking Mexican scowled incredulously up at James, who dropped his eyes to the ironwood carving of a quail hanging around the man's skinny, leathery neck by a braided rawhide thong.

James wrapped his hand around the quail. "Where did you get this?"

"*What the hell do you think you're doing?*" the man in Vienna's hat and serape said, shrilly indignant, rising drunkenly to his feet. By necessity, James had picked up some rudimentary Spanish.

The whore rose, too, thrusting her hands palm out.

"Please, no trouble," she said in heavily accented English. "What is the matter with you, gringo? You enjoy raising hell so far from home?"

James released the quail, let it fall against the striped serape. He glanced at the whore on the other side of the table. "Ask him where he got this. The hat and the serape...."

The whore stared angrily at James, then, keeping her eyes on him, spat out some fast Spanish, gesturing disgustedly, translating the question. The little Mexican curled his lip above rotten gums as he prattled off a caustic-toned reply.

The whore said, "Abel says he got the hat and the serape, and the quail, too, off a dead Apache. He said if you don't mind your manners you'll get your throat cut and your scalp lifted."

Abel picked up one of the several long black Indian scalps he wore from a wide brown belt around the serape and shaped a gap-toothed, menacing grin. James stared at the scalp. He felt sick as he backed away slowly, raising his hands in supplication.

He slacked back down in his chair across from Crosseye, swept his hat from his head, ran both hands through his hair.

"Well, I reckon now we know what happened to her," Crosseye said, sitting back in his own chair, thumbs hooked behind his bandoliers.

He turned to stare out from under the brush arbor toward the dusty street beyond, where a handcart stacked with split mesquite was being wheeled toward a small stone shack. Chickens scattered from the handcart's path. "Wonder what happened to the gold...."

James leaned forward on his elbows, stared down at his plate. He fought Mustang Mary from his mind. He had to let go of her, just as he'd let go of the war and Willie. "Gone, old-timer. All gone."

"Damn. Sure was purty, wasn't it? Too bad it had to be cursed."

"I heard tell about some more." James looked up at the burly frontiersman from beneath his brows. "I heard a couple of gringo traders tell about it last night. Apache gold up Arizona way, in a mountain range called the Superstitions."

"Ah, hell, Jimmy, tell me it ain't cursed."

"I didn't hear nothin' about it bein' cursed."

"'Cause this dog don't hunt around Apache curses."

James smiled. "I remember."

Crosseye's good eye and his crossed eye wobbled around in their sockets as he pondered the prospect. Then he shaped a slow grin. "Well, hell, what're we waitin' for?"

The two ex-Confederates tossed coins on the table and donned their dusty hats. They headed outside to their horses, swung into the leather, and rode hard for the border.

Also available from

Frank Leslie

THE LAST RIDE OF JED STRANGE

Colter Farrow is forced to kill a soldier in self-defense, sending
him to Mexico where he helps the wild Bethel Strange find her
missing father. But there's an outlaw on their trail, and the next
ones to go missing just might be them...

DEAD RIVER KILLER

Bad luck has driven Yakima Henry into the town of Dead River
during a severe mountain winter—where Yakima must weather a
killer who's hell-bent on making the town as dead as its name.

REVENGE AT HATCHET CREEK

Yakima Henry has been ambushed and badly injured. Luckily,
Aubrey Coffin drags him to safety—but as he heals, lawless
desperados circle closer to finish the job...

BULLET FOR A HALF-BREED

Yakima Henry won't tolerate incivility toward a lady, especially
the former widow Beth Holgate. If her new husband won't stop
giving her hell, Yakima may make her a widow all over again.

THE KILLERS OF CIMARRON

After outlaws murder his friend and take a woman hostage,
Colter Farrow is back on the vengeance trail, determined to
bring her back alive—and send the killers straight to hell.

THE GUNS OF SAPINERO

Colter Farrow was just a skinny cow-puncher when the men
came to Sapinero Valley and murdered his best friend. Now,
Colter must strap on his Remington revolver, deliver some
justice, and create a reputation of his own.

**Available wherever books are sold or at
penguin.com**